A Brief History
of Friendship
Stories from Harmon Falls

by Edward S. Louis

© 2024 Edward L. Risden. All rights reserved. No part of this book may be scanned, copied, uploaded or reproduced in any form or by any means, photographically, electronically or mechanically, without written permission from the copyright holder.

This is a work of fiction. All of the characters, names, incidents, organizations, and dialogue in this novel are either the products of the author's imagination or are used fictitiously.

"Little Fotungus" appeared in *The Long Story* in 2017
An earlier version of "Partytime" appeared in *White Shoes* in 2017

Cover and author photos by Kristy Deetz

ISBN: 978-1-958497-27-1 (Hardback)

ISBN: 978-1-958407-28-8 (Soft Cover)

Book design by designpanache

Elm Grove Publishing
San Antonio, Texas, USA
www.elmgrovepublishing.com

Elm Grove Publishing is a legally registered trade name of Panache Communication Arts, Inc.

Contents

A Cause......7

Love, Death, and How to Tell the Difference......30

The Three Muskeeters......44

Little Fotungus......59

Partytime......80

A Child Who Could Sometimes Fly......95

Suggs and The City......119

A Cup of Envy......136

The Time Icky Growler Kissed a Bee......148

Lunch Date......159

Breakfast with Andrea......173

Friends with Chocolate......188

A Cause

"True friends are proven by adversity."
—Aesop

We gathered in the tennis court around Greco, who was telling the story. Dusk was sliding into dark, and we should by then have been going home. But Greco's story–something most of us had never heard before–held us spellbound.

The tall lights that surrounded the bedraggled tennis court and dotted our park had already come on, and past them the western sky shone orange and violet.

Shoemaker was sitting apart, cross-legged, leaning against the fence. "I don't believe it," she barked. Her face held a resilient pout that would have stopped an old soldier—or an old priest—cold.

"Don't matter if you believe it or not," Greco said. "My brother told me. He heard it at Pizza's parents' shop from some guy who knows."

Few of us understood at first what Greco had told us. We were only kids then, but at the time in life when people can really be friends. We all felt the icy, leaden weight of horror–not the thrill that you get from the old scary movies, but the sort that freezes your feet to the ground and your heart to your ribs and dries up your tongue and the romanticism of childhood.

Greco had told us that Curt Cadogan, the biggest used car dealer in town (because he was the only used car dealer in town), had molested his daughter, Cardolyn. Greco had to explain to most of us how he had done it, since many of us didn't even understand sex yet. Lenny blanched, then stumbled through the door and retched in the grass, where there was a baseball field.

"Who?" asked Flip the Cat. "Who told him that, I'd like to know?"

"I don't have to tell you," Greco said petulantly.

"That's right. You don't. Then maybe you made it up. Sick story, man."

If Greco had made up some lesser accusation, something that made sense to a kid's mind, we wouldn't have blamed him. We had all heard rumors that Curt Cadogan had bought the land on which we were standing, our beloved River Park, the place where most of us had met to play and talk—what we used to call "mess around"—since the time we could first walk. The town, Harmon Falls, had sold him our park with barely a question. So we were eager to hate him and to believe anything bad someone had said about him.

We had played in that park just beyond our mothers' obsessive watchfulness since we had been able to play. And right here, we had heard, Cadogan intended to build an enormous new used car lot.

Infamy.

Until we heard the story of Cardolyn Cadogan, the greatest sin we could conceive was that someone wanted to destroy our park. So, then, hearing the new story, we felt urged to hate Curt Cadogan with a double hate, triple, since he had, according to the story, directed an unknown horror against someone we knew. None of us was a friend of the Cadogans—they had far more money than any of us ever dreamed of, and they lived up the hill above town—but because Cardolyn was a kid like us and possibly the victim of our enemy, she became more than a friend. She became part of our first cause, along with the saving of our beloved park from a human monster.

"All right then, smarty," Greco said, more willing to spread additional trouble than lose the attention he'd gained by telling the story. "Mr. Cole told my brother, and he's an adult. He bought his car from Mr. Cadogan, and he used to bowl with him Saturdays."

"Phil Cole don't know a bowling ball from his testicle," Flip the Cat said and laughed, and so did we, all but Greco, who had to keep a straight face to defend his story. "You should have told us first who told you, since I wouldn't believe anything that fool says."

Flip the Cat was the oldest of us, and he could speak with an authority none of the rest of us could assume, sometimes even about adults.

"You shouldn't call him a fool, Flip the Cat," Joli said. "My mama says that's not nice to say, especially about an adult."

"Your mama's right, but I ain't trying to be nice, and that fool Mr. Cole don't deserve your niceness anyway. If anybody's done that to his kid, it was Phil Cole, and not Curt Cadogan. I mean, you ever seen that boy's house? Looks like some kind of monster lives in there, it's so dark and hidden away down by the river, with dark curtains over the windows and no lights and the whole thing dirty and sweaty and run down. Someone would know if Mr. Cadogan had done that: his wife wouldn't let him. Everybody in town knows them, with that big house and that big front window that looks out over the town. He wouldn't get away with it."

"I still don't understand," Bingo said, "what he did. Explain it again."

So Flip the Cat, who was a year older and much wiser in the ways of the world than any of the rest of us, explained it again. That's not the best way for a kid to learn about sex, but it's the way things often happen.

No one noticed that little Jenver had followed Lenny out the gate and lay in the grass crying. Her parents couldn't decide whether to name her "Jenny" or "Denver," but that wasn't why she was crying. Lenny had come back in, his face blanched, fascinated, half wanting to listen, half ready to get sick again at need.

"I heard Mr. Cole say it myself," Pizza said, defending Greco. "I was in the shop waiting for my brother to clean up and take me home. I heard it."

"Why didn't you say so?" Daph with the Laugh asked him.

"I don't know," said Pizza, moving his toe back and forth along a worn baseline.

"That still don't make it so," said Flip the Cat, "but we should try to find out just in case. If it's true, somebody ought to do something about it."

"What can we do about it?" Bingo asked. "We're just kids."

"Doesn't matter," Flip the Cat answered. "We ought to try. Who else is there? Anybody trust the police? (In those days we all said PO-leece.) But there must be somebody who can do something."

He looked at me, and I nodded, though I had no notion whatever of what to do. The thought struck me, and I was about to say it, that we could tell the mayor, but then I remembered that the Cadogans and the mayor were close friends and that the mayor was the one who probably had given Curt Cadogan permission to tear down our park to build his stinking car lot on our hallowed grounds.

"Willie, you had an idea?" Daph with the Laugh asked.

I felt pleased that Daph with the Laugh asked me, and I told them what I thought, and when they realized, too, that telling the mayor wouldn't help at all, we all sighed together. Then Joli noticed that Jenver was lying in the grass crying and ran over to her. We all followed, rapidly asking questions, which only made her cry more.

* * *

Aside from the story and our suddenly mutual cause, that was in some ways a typical summer night in our town, Harmon Falls. We hung out at least until the mosquitoes got so bad that we couldn't stay out any longer or we'd get sucked vampire-dry, at least not so close to the river. After supper most kids would mess around on their own streets for a time, then wander to the park downtown, where people played baseball or softball or walked or talked or, in the worst days, sold drugs or drank from bottles in brown paper bags. For those of us who lived on the poorer side of town, closer to the river, we'd usually weave our way instead to River Park, little more than a stretch of weedy green, an old baseball field good for no more than pick-up games, some heaps of slag and bad coal, a few swings and a broken teeter-totter, the run-down tennis court where we convened to talk, a drinking fountain where the water tasted metallic, and a few rusty picnic tables that no one had ever used. It sat a couple hundred yards from the river, and from there we could see through the trees the low-slung coal and steel barges that floated south past Harmon Falls.

We'd play rules-optional games of baseball or kick-ball, boys and girls together, until somebody's mother or a police officer came after us yelling for us to go home, and then we'd all run off or ride our old, mauled bikes home as fast as we could go, frightened but exhilarated that we had been chased away and that we had to go home in the dark.

White and black kids played together. Since we were all from the poor side of town, from the railroad tracks down to the river, few people made a big deal about color. If anyone ever said anything in those neighborhoods about race--usually it had to be an outsider--everybody else would turn away embarrassed and not speak to that person again. Black or white, we felt offended by it, and in our own minds we simply ignored that the difference might bother anybody.

We were friends, and that was all that mattered to us.

Little neighborhoods, often no more than a street or two, tended to divide up ethnically: Black, Italian, Greek, Polish, Welsh, Irish, German. We had a couple Asians friends, but few Jewish people ever lived in that town, and we had only one Latino family: the father was a physician—he had moved his family from Mexico City to little Harmon Falls because we had a shortage of doctors—and they lived in a nicer part of town. But our neighborhood boundaries remained fluid, and we--the kids, at least--chose our best friends more by the sports we liked best. Adult motivations meant nothing to us then.

Our ancestors had all come to that town when economic promise had been better: people came from all over to work in the mines or the mills or other small factories along the river. If we noticed differences among the people in town, we felt them more toward the wealthier families who lived north and west of the City Park or particularly those who lived up on the hill, doctors and dentists and shop owners with their lordly Victorian mansions and their supercilious view of our gritty town below.

When the Black Power movement began, even the white kids would at first raise their fists in salute, until some of the older kids, white and black both, got mad at us for it--we didn't understand what the salute meant, but we valued the feeling of solidarity with our friends and the power of difference in which we naively wanted to believe we participated. When whispers of social revolution began to circulate even in our little, isolated town, some of the white kids out of ignorance and sympathy said they wished that they had been born black.

Our black friends just shook their heads, not sure whether to feel angry or appreciative, and they usually said something like, "For now be glad you're not. It's harder than you think."

Though we didn't know it at the time, many of our grandparents, those from Catholic as well as black neighborhoods, had childhood memories of burning crosses, memories that wouldn't die until they did. From their founding and for some time later, those neighborhoods had seen some brief ethnic battles, when workers had first been recruited from the wider world to come there in groups for hard laboring work. The men feared competition for their jobs. But that tendency had gradually faded once everybody got accustomed to living together: if the kids played together, the parents eventually came around. Greeks still went to the Orthodox Church, and some Welsh miners had a choir that sang on holidays, and the Italian Club had not yet closed. Relations strained when the factory managers tried to pit one group against another, hoping to keep wages down, but in time the unions put a stop to that, and any enmities cooled again. Eventually, of course, the unions asked for more than the employers were willing to pay, and many of the manufacturing jobs moved elsewhere, leaving the young people nowhere to work. But for that brief time, despite our hardships, we kids made friends and kept the peace among ourselves. We lacked the adult sense to make trouble over differences we barely perceived and tended to admire rather than resent.

In those days the Italian Club met up the hill, blocks above the railroad tracks to make it a more respectable place. The Greek Orthodox Church held a festival with dancing and gyros every summer. The black neighborhoods would make barbecue in huge metal drums, and anyone could buy it cheap and hot and savory. The German neighborhoods held an Octoberfest, though they hid the beer until the kids went to bed. Welsh families would stroll through most of those streets and carol at Christmas time. Our lives flowed by as steadily as the river, except for the occasional flood.

The summers, too, rolled on and took us with them, growing from cool May to hot, humid August that eventually gave way to fall and frosty November. We believed that if we just played hard enough and refused to allow into our thoughts the merest hint of school, we could make the summer last forever, and once or twice we almost did.

* * *

As things turned out, Curt Cadogan hadn't molested his daughter, but you know how rumors can filter through a small town, more quickly than a yellow jacket can grab and sting your finger. What an awful thing for a person to be accused of.

A week after that night in the park, Bingo was riding his bike in the dark to the Dairy Queen and turned the corner onto the street that passed in front of Cadogan's Car Lot. Cadogan happened to be pulling out in his old Caddy and nearly hit Bingo, who took a skid and tumbled, tearing up his bike and his elbow and scraping his knees, but otherwise surviving. Cadogan jumped out of his car and began yelling at Bingo for riding his bike in the front of a car. Bingo, like the rest of us, was already mad at Cadogan, and so he began to shout back at him. That may not sound like much these days, but back then kids didn't yell at adults: for the most part we feared them and respected them, even if we didn't like them.

When Bingo shouted back, Cadogan, expecting nothing but contrition, flew into a rage, drawing a crowd. Just as Bingo thought the man was going to hit him, Bingo screamed out that we all knew what Cadogan had done to his daughter. As the man stood in the street horrified, with customers and neighbors and passersby gawking, Bingo yelled out in his high, clear, young voice that we all knew that Cadogan had "stuck his thing in his own daughter."

You can image what that accomplished. For one thing it stopped Cadogan in his tracks, so Bingo grabbed his damaged bike and, despite the painful elbow, he wobbled off, leaving Cadogan to deal with cold stares from the onlookers. While most of them didn't believe what Bingo had said, some people, believing a kid wouldn't even know about such an act unless it had some truth about it, had their doubts. Some even, believe it or not, later spread the rumor themselves.

Of course Mr. and Mrs. Cadogan paid a visit to Bingo's parents that evening, and learning what his son had said, Bingo's father gave him one of the worst hidings in human history, at least so Bingo told it. The Cadogans went home unsettled but somewhat satisfied in the knowledge of the beating, but Mr. Cadogan ended up building his new used car lot two towns to the south of Harmon Falls, and the family moved there soon after, beyond our knowledge and memory until high school when we started traveling there in busses for sporting and other school events. Before they moved, though, we all collected candles, and in the evening we'd light them and walk back and forth along a street down the hill from where the Cadogans lived, but where, from their broad picture window, anyone looking out could have seen us. We kept our vigil religiously, chanting, too low for anyone to catch the words, evil things about Mr. Cadogan and used cars and hopeful things about Cardolyn, walking in single file as stony-faced as a group of medieval monks. That much we did in protest. We had gone one morning to the City Building and demanded to see the mayor. He ignored us, and when he finally came out to go to Icey's Diner for lunch, we all fled in an ecstasy of fear, terrified that he might actually talk to us.

The mayor, hearing from Cadogan Bingo's story--and perhaps one about some kids with candles--believed that all of us kids shared the blame, and he never forgave us: he worked a deal with another friend of his to flatten our park anyway and build a warehouse there instead. With the Cadogans' move, we first thought we had routed the evil man and saved our park, so you can imagine our near despair when we learned of the new project and its nefarious objective. I still have a sore spot in my heart for that park after all these years and have never forgiven the mayor. But then again he never asked my forgiveness or anyone else's that I know of.

Two great turns of Fortune's Wheel began that summer: one, and the more important, the friendships that we formed at River Park grew indelible as a result of what we learned together, and two, the protest the we made in response to the warehouse, which became our second great cause, made local history.

* * *

Worse than what happened to Bingo was what we'd learned later that night at the playground in City Park, not about Cardolyn Cadogan, but about Denver, Jenver's brother. We'd all gathered to watch a baseball game, and we found Joli sitting with Jenver next to the merry-go-round and trying to comfort her. Joli was holding Little Jenver's head in her lap, and for a long time Jenver just lay there and rocked her body and cried. We formed a circle around them and waited with what, for children, seemed enormous patience to hear what Jenver might say.

And finally, say she did. What we'd feared had happened to Cardolyn Cadogan had actually happened to Denver, the crime done not by their father, but by a cousin who had visited them. We had not seen Denver the previous summer, and that explained why: their parents had sent him away afterwards--we didn't ask where.

He had returned for school in the fall. Denver had never been a friendly boy, but after that he went slowly crazy, and by the time we got to junior high the family had also moved out of town, partly I think to hide him. By then we had all become too good friends to lose one of our own, so we used to walk in a group the four miles along the railroad tracks to their new house south of Harmon Falls to visit Jenver. Denver would never come down from his room to see us, and being children we were partly glad of that, not knowing what to say anyway.

But that night in the park, as Jenver sputtered out her words, we found a new confusion: the difficulty of the Cardolyn Case had nearly baffled us, but the Denver Mystery fled entirely beyond our comprehension. How could such a thing happen? What did it mean? Some of us grew sick at the very idea. Shoemaker began running in circles around the park, waving her arms and screaming so that she didn't have to listen. Lenny kicked at the fence until he loosened part of it, for which we all got in trouble later, even though the contractors were planning to pull it down shortly thereafter. Like Lenny, I felt like heaving. Some of us went home and asked our parents what it meant. Few of us got answers, and some of us got beatings for that.

By the next weekend we had essentially pieced it all together, but that understanding didn't put an end to our deliberations. It started a flood of tales from nearly everyone. By the time we had all told one another our stories, we would have to have either never seen one another again or become friends for life. Every one of us, we found, was damaged goods. Maybe the vague sense of that fact, our own torments, kept us together more than did the sports and messing around. We had, without knowing it, been experiencing what the military came to call rap groups—much different than what that term has come to mean now. Here's some of what we learned.

Greco's father had regularly beaten his mother, and finally he left her. She miscarried and lost her second baby. The two of them, Greco and Mama, lived together with his ancient grandmother on what Mama earned as a secretary at one of the mills.

Shoemaker's eldest brother had gone to the big steel city up river, had got caught in a bad part of town, and was beaten to death by three hoodlums. Two of them went to prison, but they had both got out before any of us entered high school.

Bingo had lost his younger brother to leukemia. He had lost his eldest brother to the battlefields of Vietnam.

Johnny was adopted and was never able to learn anything about his birth parents.

Flip the Cat's father had been a musician, but had lost an arm in a mining accident. He beat his son periodically with the remaining arm. In his better moments he taught Flip the Cat to play the saxophone, which he learned amazingly well despite threats of additional beatings should he fail to get as good at it as his father wanted him to.

Joli's grandmother had seen one of those burning crosses on her own lawn and had never got over it. Who could? Her parents never came to trust white people and didn't like her hanging around with those of us who were white. She played with us anyway, but felt guilty about it until we had all grown up.

Lenny and Lana's father had lost his business to bad money decisions and so had to get whatever work he could: part time in an auto repair shop. Their mother managed a grocery and made ten times what their father made. That may not seem like such a problem to you, but times were different then. Their home, even after their father left, was always quiet and tense, and for a long time both the kids, though nobody ever abused them, walked around with head down and eyes restless, unable to shake off the cloud of tense parental silence.

Pizza's parents had come over from Italy, his father hoping to get a high-paying job in the mills. He didn't. They opened a pizza shop, but everyone knew their pizza wasn't very good, so they struggled constantly to stay in business. All their kids worked at the shop almost every free hour they had. Pizza snuck off from work when he could to hang out with us.

Daph with the Laugh's mother had died bringing her into the world. You can imagine the guilt she felt. Her father raised her alone.

As for me? My father left us before I was three. My mother, wanting to have a father there for me, almost married again, but the guy drank and hated me. She got rid of him after a couple years, and she didn't marry again until after I was in college.

Two other kids joined us for our protests: Hoag and Lindi. They were still okay then and stood silently side by side. Their troubles came later, so that's another story.

As you look through the list, you'll probably say that some of that wasn't too bad: everyone has troubles. That's right. But when we learned the sorrows of our friends, we bonded, and we have remained friends ever since, friends of the sort you wish were family, because they're the people you want to see on evenings and weekends and holidays, the ones who make your heart feel alive.

When I got older another friend—oh yes, I've been blessed with friends—once told me that compassion is the most highly evolved of human qualities, the most refined and humane, because it comes last if at all and is hardest to acquire. When we heard one another's stories in the park, we learned compassion: I believe each of us felt with the other, and not in a sentimental way. Each of us had already learned about suffering, ours or others', so that we didn't sentimentalize it. But we listened and tried to understand. Had we been any younger, none of it would have made any sense to us, and had we been much older, romance and competition may have got in the way. We formed a bond of friendship-love stronger than romantic love could have been, or maybe even can be.

Here is the most extraordinary thing of all, so I don't expect you to believe it: we are all still friends to this day, and most of us are still alive. We still meet sometimes in The City at a coffee shop called the Arabica and talk about old times and new ones.

Compassion requires some intelligence without cynicism. I suppose compassion is like playing the violin or learning a language or discovering one is a math genius: if you learn it at just the right time in your development, it sticks; otherwise, you may never learn it at all. It can make friends even better friends, and that may be its greatest gift.

* * *

Later, once the builders took aim on our park, came the second momentous event of the summer, our protest to save our beloved meeting place. We failed finally in our aim, of course, but our effort must have been something to behold: we learned from the ignominious defeat of our first attempt with the mayor, and by then we had gained the courage that comes with committed numbers and a desire to win enhanced by a lingering defeat.

Since we had already learned marching, we turned in our candles for some homemade "Save our Park" signs and paraded around the City Building chanting. Some of the signs said "Save r Prak" or "Sav are Plagrond," which brought some hoots even from the barely literate among the adults. But we marched with heart as well as feet, and even when the police threatened to call our parents, we didn't quit. We did quit when our parents came and hauled us off. The luckiest of us got our beatings at home rather than right there in front of the smugly simpering mayor or the hooting construction gang.

The parents, even those who sympathized once they knew our reasons, thought we had learned our lesson, but as soon as we could sneak out, we reassembled at our park to plot a new strategy.

"We need to find a way to stop them," said Bingo, still rubbing his sore behind. "Blow up their bulldozers or something."

"How we going to do that? You some kind of secret agent?" Flip the Cat asked.

"Maybe we can talk to our parents," Hoag offered. "Maybe they can get the builders to put their warehouse somewhere else."

"I ain't asking my parents anything," Pizza said: he too had got double beatings for sneaking out of the shop and for causing a ruckus downtown, and he knew he'd probably get another for the meeting at hand.

We all had to sigh our agreement with that point.

"We can get a lawyer to make a protest for us. This is our place: the park is here for us," Daph with the Laugh said.

"You got the money for the lawyer?" Lenny asked.

"Maybe we can hold some kind of concert and make money, get people to donate, you know, and save the park ourselves? Flip the Cat and his friends could play and we all could sing, or we could get a real band, and everybody would come and no one would let them tear it down then!" Joli got louder and louder as she spoke and ended with a painful sniff.

"We ain't good enough for that," Flip the Cat said, "and we don't have time to find a real band, and probably nobody will care enough to help us anyway."

"I got to get home," Shoemaker said.

"We need to meet again tomorrow and find a way," Lana said, and we all agreed.

Word had got around among the parents that we had our meeting again at the park, probably to stir up some new scheme, so the following night we had to risk big trouble to meet again. After dark we slipped through bedroom windows, through cellar doors, past confused dogs and parents sleeping in front of the television, out attic crawl spaces and down drainpipes, through nasty neighbors' yards and gardens and broken-down garages and dark alleys, without bicycles or skateboards or keys or anything that could make noise, and we dashed soundlessly to the park. The night was dark and cloudy, and we assembled away from the lights, in the shadows.

There for a long time, maybe five minutes, nobody said anything: we just stood and thought and wondered who would come up with a perfect idea, but nobody did.

Finally Daph with the Laugh said, "What if when they come to tear it down, we just stand here and refuse to move?"

The simple brilliance of that idea dazzled us, since we figured that even the worst of the adults wouldn't run us over with bulldozers, but then we remembered how our parents had routed us in front of the City Building, betraying us, their blood, to their own kind, the other adults, who found no pleasure, no significant existence in parks like ours.

"We can't go to parents, we can't go to the mayor, and we can't go to the police," Johnny said.

"How about the priest?" Pizza asked, scraping his toe along the grass.

"What can he do?" Johnny asked.

"Hey, that's not a bad idea," Bingo said.

"And I could get the Greek priest," Greco added.

"And I can ask the Methodist minister," Flip the Cat added.

"And the Baptist preacher," Joli added.

"And my dentist," Jenver said, trying to be helpful.

"Dentist? What can he do?" Greco asked.

"I don't know. He's scary."

"What if we get a bunch of the Big Kids to join us?" Shoemaker asked.

"They'd just laugh and beat us up," Lenny said, truly enough.

"We need someone who can scare the mayor and his friends," Pizza said.

"My cousin fought in Vietnam," Flip the Cat mentioned.

That impressed us all, but we weren't sure if that would help. Would he come with a gun or a pocketful of hand grenades, or would he have a steely stare, spit at their feet, and just stand there with such authority that they would be afraid to try to move him or us?

"But he's only one guy," Flip the Cat added, and we all shrugged.

"That's better than no guys," I said. "He has that cool black leather jacket."

"We could ask the Black Panthers!" Bingo shouted.

"Right," Flip the Cat sighed, as the rest of us hung our heads in embarrassment, but with the tinniest twinge of hopefulness until we heard no more about that. Thinking back on it now, I wonder if maybe they would have come.

"Hey," Daph with the Laugh said: "We could get the Grim Reapers!"

The Grim Reapers were a motorcycle gang who late on warm summer nights would roar like a hundred Messerschmitts through our town with a sound that could make you sure the world was ending. Dressed in black leather jackets with sunglasses even at night and long chains hanging from their belts, riding on their brutal Hogs and sleek Choppers they looked with their calm, forbidding faces as if they would spit in the eye of the real Grim Reaper himself. They parked at the Dutch Oven bar and drank rivers of beer and played pool, keeping the joint open for a whole week at a time--who was going to close it while they were there? Rumor said they smoked pot and dropped a rainbow of drugs, but the police gave them a wide berth, knowing themselves outgunned, and the bikers did little actual damage, though they could frighten the skin off your bones.

"That's the dumbest idea I ever heard," Pizza said.

"Do better then, Smarty," Daph with the Laugh laughed.

"They might do it if we bought them beer and weed," Bingo said.

"They might," Flip the Cat said, "but where would we get the money to do that? If we had that much, we could just buy the park and be done with it."

In the end they elected me to ask the bikers for their help. Next to Flip the Cat I was the fastest runner of the kids, and most of the Grim Reapers were white, so they thought I had the best chance of getting away alive. We walked uptown to the Dutch Oven—slowly, without candles, as if we were plodding our last mile on the way to execution. I prayed harder than I ever had or ever have, and I squeezed my legs hard together to keep from peeing my pants. I waited outside the bar for a long time: it smelled of stale beer plus a sweet-sour, overwhelming stench like sweat mixed with burning leaves. Finally the others pushed me forward just as one of the bikers was stumbling out of the bar. He almost tripped over me and cursed.

He wore faded jeans, a sleeveless shirt with a skull and sickle on a patch decorating the front, and huge, black boots. He wore his biker's cap backwards. He wore sunglasses. He wore several days' growth of beard. Even through the sunglasses his eyes bored a hole through my forehead.

"Get out, you little shit," he said. He got on his bike, kicked it on, flung the front wheel past my nose, and roared off over the curb and down the street.

A second biker, dressed much like the other but taller and slim, stood in the doorway, looking at me, also through dark sunglasses. He held a beer bottle in one hand and propped himself against the doorframe with the other. "What do you want here, little man?" he asked and he barked a burp that echoed down the street.

"My friends . . . and me . . ."

"Well, what about you?"

"We want . . . we need . . . "

"What do you want? Beer? Shit, you're too puny for that, and so are your friends. Are you the brave one, so they sent you to ask?"

"No," Flip the Cat said, "but he's probably best at asking things."

"Well, little brother, if he's the best at it, then you're not going to get anything asked any time soon."

Finally I blurted. "We need somebody to help us save our park. River Park. Where we play—I mean meet. I mean, we go there to mess around, hang out. And they're going to tear it down, the mayor and his friends, the builders. And we don't know how to keep them out. Nobody cares about it but us. We thought maybe you. Bikers don't like police. Maybe you could come with us and just stand there, and when the builders come, they'd be afraid and go away. We don't want you to hurt them, just for them to go away and leave our park alone. We need somebody bigger and stronger than we are. You know?" There: I'd finally said it. I was gripping my legs so tightly together that my feet began to numb.

"Well now I see why they sent you. When you get around to asking, you really ask. What makes you think I can do anything, or even that I'd want to?"

I had asked my piece, but answering questions hadn't been part of the deal. I thought all the words I'd stored up for my whole life had just spilled out, so I wasn't sure what to say next. I just stood there squeezing.

"All of you, the bikers," Joli said.

"They can push us around, 'cause we're just kids," I said.

"But not you," Flip the Cat added.

"They'd be afraid you'd kick their ass," Greco said, figuring some tough language might give us credibility.

"Don't that beat shit," the biker said. "Hey, Joe-Bear, come here, and Lonny and Duck, hey!" He looked back into the bar as he spoke.

Two more guys came out, and a couple more heads appeared around the door frame. The first had to be Joe-Bear: he was huge, sun-browned, with a great brown beard and long hair, and an enormous chain hanging from his belt. The second guy was tall and thin with blond hair sticking out every which way from beneath a black soldier's helmet with a spike on the top. One of the heads in the doorway was wearing a green Nazi helmet.

"These little shits causing you trouble, Abe?" Joe-Bear asked. "How about if we cook 'em and eat 'em?"

"Mince 'em for pies, I say," the blond one said.

"Just sit on 'em and squash 'em, begging little bastards," said the green-helmeted face in the doorway before returning inside.

"What do you want, kid?" Joe-Bear bellowed, slapping his hand on his bare, hairy midriff, where his tee shirt had crept up.

I stood there wobbly as the Scarecrow before the Wizard of Oz, and none of my friends had more voice than I, so eventually Abe told him what we'd asked. Joe-Bear stood open-mouthed, staring at me for what seemed, but wasn't quite, long enough for my bladder to overflow all by itself.

"That's right!" I blurted again. "We need to save our park!"

Then Joe-Bear laughed, long and loudly.

"Don't that beat all," he said, slapping his belly so that it shook and echoed like a drum. "Want us to scare off some police and a construction crew, nice church-going boys like us." Then he stared at me again, his eyes growing wide almost to his ears and his beard bristling like a large, round Fuller brush. He grabbed the massive chain at his belt. "Go away, you little beggar, or I'll send Sasquatch out here to sit on you. Don't know whether the weight or the smell would kill you first." He pulled off the chain, gave it a swing, and smashed it down hard on the pavement in front of him, then he took a swig of beer, washed it around in his mouth, and spat it at my feet. The dust from the spot where the chain had struck and the bitter, acrid stench of the beer combined to make a smell that I still associate with death. I stood my ground simply because my legs hadn't the strength to move.

"Brave little bastard, though," Joe-Bear said to Abe. "Didn't move an inch. Gotta give him that. Most kids would have run off to Mama by now or at least peed their pants." He ambled his considerable bulk back in the door. I could hear my friends rustling behind me, probably rising back to their feet. Abe had a broad grin on his face, but I still couldn't see his eyes, locked up behind the sunglasses.

"Bear's not so bad as he seems," Abe said, continuing his inscrutable grin. "Unless he needs to be." By then I could feel that Flip the Cat had advanced, so that he stood almost beside me, and I could just see him out of the corner of my eye. "I'd almost be tempted to help you kids if we didn't have a rally in two days in Pittsburgh," Abe said. "Might be fun to see just what the pigs would do. I'd tell you just to stand up to them yourselves, but the police treat kids a lot worse than we do, whatever people say. Go find somewhere else to play. River Park's a dump anyway."

"You fought in Vietnam, didn't you?" Flip the Cat asked him, and then Abe stopped smiling.

"Yeah. How'd you know."

"My cousin did. There's something about guys who did. That tattoo on your arm. The way you talk."

"Your cousin still alive? Tell him 'hey' from a brother soldier. You kids best get on home. You, little man, Speaker of the House: you better use the can before you bust a gut. There's one in back of the bar. Git, now!" He let out a yell like a rodeo cowboy riding a bronco.

I wouldn't have gone in that bar for anything. My legs were sweating so badly that I thought the urine had burst a hole in each thigh. The others, who had maintained their capacities better than I had, ran off, and I skipped and wobbled and held on into the alley behind the bar, and, taking a chance that no one would see me behind an old building, fumbled with my zipper for nearly too long and finally began the longest, most satisfying leak of my life. I had to keep spreading my feet wider apart so that I didn't soak my shoes. The relief was exquisite.

When I finally zipped up, I heard the sound of giggling behind me, and when I turned around and looked up, I saw a small face, with its mouth covered by a hand, sticking out of a second story window and looking down at my evil deed. I ran off ashamed, but light on my feet and happy to be alive: I had felt sure that either the bikers or an exploding bladder would kill me.

The kids had reassembled behind Pizza's family's shop. No one had money to buy anything, but we resolved to have one more meeting, the following night if we could get out, to plan whatever strategy we could accomplish on our own to save our park.

We did meet at the park the next night, Saturday, flying there on the wings of our Cause, and resolved amidst the humidity, mosquitoes, weeds, and fireflies that we would make our Last Stand together at the tennis court fence. Hoag, who hadn't accompanied us to the Dutch Oven, had learned from his father that the contractors were to arrive at the park on Monday morning to start work. "Then it's agreed," Daph with the Laugh said finally, summing up our decision. "We stand side by side. In complete silence."

On Monday morning we all got up as soon as we could, skipped breakfast by choice or not, and ran, biked, or skateboarded for the park. I wasn't the first of the kids, but by the time I got there a bulldozer and dump truck had already arrived, and three or four guys in hard hats were already poking around or sitting in their vehicles munching the last of their breakfasts. As the kids arrived, one by one, two by two, we formed a semicircle around the tennis court, standing quietly, spaced just far enough apart that we could cover as much distance as possible, not all the way across the park, but close enough that one of us could dive and bite the leg of anyone who tried to walk past us. On one side I stood next to Daph with the Laugh—I had a bit of a crush on her in those days—and on the other side next to Lana, with whom I would fall in love later in life. The hardhats went about their business as if we weren't there until, just after the sun had fully risen, a white sedan pulled up and stopped above the park entrance.

Three men in white short-sleeved shirts and black ties purposefully got out. One donned a hard hat, one already had on sunglasses, and the third wore a scowl that would have cracked January ice. They were talking, but when Sunglasses saw us, he pointed, and the heads of the other two jerked in our direction. Scowl came striding down the hill toward us.

"What do you girls think you're doing?" Some of us were girls, but all of us resented his tone and knew what he meant by it. We said nothing. We just stood there, held our ground, and trembled.

"You!" Scowl shouted at Bingo. "I know your dad. Tell me what you're up to, or I'll go get him right now, and he'll tan your hide good. You!" he yelled at me. "I don't know you, but I'll tan your hide myself. You kids get out of here right now!"

We all wanted to yell back at him or at least tell him what we were doing, but we had agreed that speaking would do us no good whatever. We managed to stand our ground in complete silence.

"All right, then: who's first?" Scowl asked, slipping his belt out of its loops and striking the leather hard into his hand, making the sound of a whip. I noticed that Bingo was really starting to shake. I felt as though I was, too, but tried desperately not to show it.

Hardhat came down next with a couple of the construction workers. "We could start carrying them out, one by one," he said, "but they'd probably sneak back. Maybe we should tie them up and hand them over to the police."

Shoemaker whimpered, and Hardhat looked at her with a wicked smile.

Then Sunglasses came strolling down, puffing hard, his arms swinging beside him.

"I called the police on the walkie-talkie. They'll be here any minute now. You kids: I suggest you get out of here right now, and maybe all you'll get is a beating from your parents. Otherwise you'll be taken to jail." He yelled to the man who sat by the bulldozer playing with his work gloves: "Fritzy, let's get started. Once we start moving some land, they'll move their carcasses."

Then we heard a roar from the street up above.

Three choppers, long and lean and bad looking, roared into view. I could see from a distance that it was Abe with two of his buddies: the blond guy with the spiked hat and a black rider with a huge Natural and a red bandana tied around his forehead. They rolled up alongside the sedan and sat there, revving their engines.

The Grim Reapers, I thought, had come through for us.

Then from the other direction came a police car—that brought a chuckle from Hardhat. The car rolled slowly down the road and pulled up next to the bikers. An officer stepped out and sauntered over to them. I think the adults were watching what happened as closely as we were.

The policeman, absent-mindedly twirling the nightstick at his belt, spoke with the Abe, then with the black biker, then with Abe again.

"I think I know that cop," Flip the Cat said. "I've seen him with my cousin and some other cats downtown."

Then I didn't believe what I saw. I think Abe looked toward us and nodded. Then the bikers revved their engines, turned their bikes around, and rode back in the direction from which they'd come. My heart sank. I had expected more from them than I did from me.

Then the policeman strolled in his leisurely way into the park and down to our circle. He waved Sunglasses over to him. We all held our breath as they spoke together.

Then Sunglasses shook his head, shrugged his shoulders, and motioned for Hardhat to follow him. The policemen winked at Flip the Cat, then addressed all of us. "You kids enjoy your little protest? You did all right, but don't go causing any more trouble now. These guys aren't going to do anything to your park. Can't say I know why you'd care: place doesn't look like much now. You should have seen it in my day. Yo, Flip-Cat, say 'hey' to John Henry for me."

"Will do, man."

The policeman gave us a little salute and turned for his car. He patted Scowl on the back and gave his shoulder a gentle turn toward the road. I could see that as they walked, Scowl continued to express his anger, wagging his head and pointing back at us, and I could hear him growling through his teeth. The police officer remained calm. We watched astonished as all the adults prepared to leave. The bulldozer driver found a baseball in the grass—we had lost it a couple weeks before, because in places the grass had grown high--and tossed it to Pizza. Within minutes they had all gone.

We didn't know what had happened. We stood silently for another minute, then looked at one another in disbelief. Then Joli started to giggle, and Daph with the Laugh laughed loud and long, so hard that she fell to the grass and began rolling back and forth. We all joined her, yelling and cheering our success.

"Yo, Willie," Greco said, "we won!"

"We won, we won, we won!" Shoemaker sang, and we all picked up the little tune that she invented to celebrate our victory.

We learned later that we hadn't actually won, though we did for a time get to keep our park. The company who had intended to build the warehouse had at the last minute pulled the project, having negotiated a better deal just outside the limits of the next town north.

I had a feeling that the mayor blamed us for that, too, though I don't know how we could have had anything to do with it, unless Hoag's parents or someone better off had intervened, directing the builders to a better property. The bikers had shown their support, leaving when they learned we didn't need them. I wonder what they would have done if we had.

Word did get back to our parents about our "protest," so none of us got to the park for a couple days, and only a few of us could sit comfortably for the rest of the week. I halfway worried River Park wouldn't be there when we returned, that the policeman had lied to us, but there it was, as beautiful to us and as ugly in fact as it had ever been. Our police officer friend had even arranged for the city's summer work crew to cut the grass for us. The field shone gold-green in the afternoon sun and silver under a September moon, and whenever we could, we friends met there to play—to hang out, that is—until, despite us, the summer ran its course and gave in to Autumn.

By the following spring railroad cars had begun dumping more coal and slag on the outskirts of the park, and a year later the pollution had infringed on so much of our turf that we could no longer play baseball there. For some time we continued to trickle down to River Park on most evenings, until the city no longer lit the lights, and a junkyard that had sat for years at the south end of the field expanded and took over the playground and tennis court—the world is always acquiring more junk. If you were to go looking for our park these days, you wouldn't find a blade of grass left from it.

Most important, though, our pact, that second great turn of Fortune's

Wheel—our fulfilling our promise to one another—made us friends forever, or at least as close to that as mere people can ever get.

Love, Death, and How to Tell the Difference

"I'm nobody! Who are you?/ Are you—Nobody—too?"
—Emily Dickenson

When I was eight years old and growing up in Harmon Falls, my great-grandmother died. She was more than eighty years old, which seemed impossible to me at the time: ten times my age! When she died, she still had red hair, only mottled with gray. Ironically, we called her Grey-gramma. She died of a stroke, which I knew to be lethal, though I didn't know why. Struck by what? The hand of God? A lightning bolt? A golf club? Some truth too powerful to bear? Fate? Is that what people meant by a stroke of bad luck?

Mother asked if I wanted to go to the funeral. I had been listening to the Beatles' "I Want to Hold Your Hand" on the plastic transistor radio she said my father had sent me—that was well before "Ob-La-Di" and "Let It Be," which would have made more sense for the occasion.

I thought about it for a long time and wondered why she even asked, since I was nobody important. I decided to go, but not because I wanted to. The way she asked the question meant that I ought to go. But I still hadn't made any promises out loud.

I experienced many oughts in those days and still do.

Mother talked a lot about the "right thing to do," because Grey-gramma loved me. She said something about good behavior almost every day. Sometimes I understood, almost. On the occasion of the funeral I could tell especially by the look in her eyes and the sound of her voice that going was the right thing to do, at least in her mind. I thought about what going to a funeral would mean, but mostly I thought about trying to find a way out of it: I had a cold and would sneeze, an upset stomach and would barf, a baseball game, a doubleheader! a sick friend, probably dying, whom I had to visit before it was too late, a really, really bad itch somewhere that I couldn't scratch around people, an itch that might be terminal. But I couldn't think of anything that would convince even me.

So finally I told Mother I'd go. "Brave boy," she said, and that made me feel good for an instant. Then the chill hit me that I really had to go. I must go or have the compliment retracted and replaced, not verbally, but by implication, with "Coward and loveless little fiend." At least so I imagined. When you're eight years old, imagination has just as much power as the truth, if not more.

Love and death were still little more than words to me. I had seen some dead things—mostly insects, some shrubs, a rose that I had accidentally squashed with my basketball—but their demise didn't fully register with me as important.

My father had by that time been gone for several years. One grandfather was dead, and the other immutably silent: retired, he fished, hunted, fixed the neighbors' TVs, lawn mowers, and toilets. He spoke a total of ten words to me in my life: he said, "Get out of the way," twice. My elderly uncle, who lived nearby and visited regularly, would laugh at me if I ever asked questions about anything serious. Then he would talk about how glad he was when the Pirates had beaten the Yankees in the World Series a few years back. I could understand that.

Nobody knew about male bonding in those days.

So with respect to such difficult issues as attending a funeral, I had no adult males to consult, which left me to ask the other boys in the neighborhood—I knew what the adult females would say: they would unhesitatingly agree with my mother. Duty meant a lot to them.

Of course, that sort of thing—one may call it blind ignorance—happens to many boys with respect to sex, too, which is one reason why many of us grow up having no understanding whatever of its impact on any individual person and the entire adult world, especially on women.

What a shock when we learn that! And another when we learn that isn't love.

Same thing with death.

Boys will giggle about sex and death and say stupid things about them. But they will never, ever talk about love. That just isn't done, and we all know it. But boys will talk eagerly about dead things.

"Wow, a dead body!" Jimmy-across-the-street said when I told him. His muddy green eyes were slightly crossed, and his legs flew out to the side when he ran. "I wish I could go. I'd touch it, too!" he said, poking his left index finger hard into my shoulder. "I bet you wouldn't touch it."

I thought about a retort, but he was right: I wouldn't touch the dead body. The thought struck me that Mother might ask me to kiss Grey-gramma good-bye: I'd always had to kiss her on the cheek on holidays. She would kiss me on both cheeks, then grab them firmly with her hands and pull them out of shape while she cooed something in Italian. My face took about a week afterward to return to normal.

I must have blanched at that thought of kissing that cheek, because Jimmy started to laugh.

"Scaredy," he sang, probably thinking about a terrifying touch rather than a deadly kiss. Then he started dancing around in circles, waving his arms and singing, "Scared a' the dead baw-dy, scared a' the dead baw-dy!" until I wanted to hit him. In all my childhood I seldom gave in to the impulse to hit someone, because I had learned early that if you think you can or should hit someone, there's always someone bigger and stronger around who will hit you, too, and he will do more damage than you and will enjoy it more.

Jimmy-across-the-street danced off, singing, his legs flopping side to side, and I felt glad to see him go. If you had asked me in those years, I'd have said he was my friend, but he wasn't. He simply lived across the street, which meant we played together. Contiguity means a lot when you're a kid. I certainly had no love for him, what the Greeks would have called φιλιο, brotherly affection. I found his attitude toward almost everything repellant. One sunny day around midsummer the year before the funeral, I'd gone across the street to see what Jimmy was doing. He was dancing up and down in a fashion somewhat similar to what he would do when he sang, "Scared a' the dead baw-dy," but when I got near enough to ask or see what he was doing, he was grunting and stomping to death a large number of ants who were mindlessly pouring in and out of a small sand-hill they had made in a crack in the sidewalk. I asked him why he was doing that, but he didn't answer. He just kept jumping and grunting "Die! Die!" each time his foot landed with a thud. He wore sandals, and ever since that day I have hated sandals.

It didn't strike me at the time, but what the ants were experiencing, that was death, whether they were aware of it or not. What Jimmy was experiencing was not love, not even love of having power over tiny creatures. It may have had something to do with the ignorance of power.

Seeing Jimmy-across-the-street seemingly having so much fun, I jumped up and down a few times, too, killing some ants of my own. When you're a kid, seeing someone do something with absolute conviction makes it seem as though it must be right; otherwise, why would a person do anything with such repetitive glee, whether it was planting flowers, washing a car, or beating a child? I think adults' voting patterns are sometimes like that.

The small, crushed bodies looked like little more than firecracker ashes, and hundreds of other ants ran about, some madly, some continuing as calmly as before to complete their individually indeterminable tasks. When I paused in my hopping to look, the ant hill as a whole seemed to have life, but the individual ants none. So the killings I committed had little meaning to me at the moment, other than that they left me with a lingering feeling that I had done something stupid and vaguely sickening but dangerously liberating in its innocuous evil.

That was a feeling I often had in those years and that I still occasionally experience now: having done something sickening, but more importantly stupid and cosmically wrong. I've lost the moral numbness of those years, and now every one of those instances hurts more than I can say.

On the day of the funeral I dressed up in my for-church pants, my only white dress shirt, a striped clip-on tie, and my brown sport coat. I put on my dress shoes, but before we left, Mother sent me back to change my socks: I had forgotten and put on white ones, which I always wore with Converse tennis shoes, which I wore nearly every day of every season except for Sunday mornings. Even then I knew one fashion essential: boys don't wear black socks with tennis shoes or white socks with dress shoes, though I often forgot in the actual moment of dressing. She sent me back a second time, too, to return the baseball cap that I had put on my head as mindlessly as I had put the white socks on my feet. Then I crawled into the back seat of the clumsy Chevy behind Mother and my uncle, with two adult cousins and their two little daughters, one my age and one two years younger. The seven of us sat like French fries getting glued by our perspiration to the vinyl car seat—someone must have invented vinyl for just that purpose, and it succeeded brilliantly.

My little cousins said hello to me, and I said hello back without looking in their eyes. At that age I had a vague sense that looking girls in the eyes was a very bad and dangerous thing, though not cosmically wrong. As silly as that seems, now, years later, I'm not sure I was entirely wrong about that.

I remember the first time I looked Lana, who would later be my first real girlfriend and then the love of my life, straight in the eyes. I'd known her for four years by then. We'd gone to the same grade school, and I was about ten and she was about nine. Her eyes were sky-blue, and her hair was golden blond, and she was thin as a willow twig, and so was I, and when I looked her in the eyes I couldn't help but smile: something about the look on her face, the way the corners of her mouth turned up just a bit, the way her eyes shone always did that to me. To anyone passing by we must have looked like fuzzy dandelions waiting for a breeze to blow us away. When I got near her, even then, I felt more alive than I had ever felt doing anything else. Still do.

Well, when I looked into her eyes, first she looked angry, then she dropped her head back, laughed, and ran away. When she ran, her legs didn't flop to the sides like Jimmy's. She looked athletic, like a tiny, stray Olympian. Her laughter fell around me like rain, like cool blue crystals dropping from the sky, even though the sun was shining bright. Her blond hair bounced on her shoulders. I'm not sure that I remember correctly, but I think that was when I felt my penis bob for the first time. Who can trust memories like that? But I think I remember that as I watched her run away, the fellow moved of his own accord, as he would do so often later in life and will occasionally still do even now. A mind of its own, though one subject to senility . . .

At the time, considering what I felt, I'm sure I must have blushed, because I felt confused and embarrassed. But I also felt warm and happy, listening to Lana's laughter, which I knew was not directed at me, but at the strangeness of the universe. That strangeness very, very occasionally adds up to something good, though I never trust that it will.

The laughter said, and I was dreadfully afraid of reading it wrong, that what had passed unrecognized through my mind had also passed through hers. We never spoke of that moment, and for about the next five years she'd blush whenever I looked at her, and I think I must have done the same. Only about six years later did we look each other fully in the eye again, and by then we could smile without blushing. Not say or do anything, just smile . . .

You may say that story was about an awakening to sex.

I think it was about love.

When I was about two years old, and my father was still with us, I remember, and I think this if my very first memory, his leaving for work in the morning with his metal lunch pail in one hand, stuffing a pack of cigarettes into his breast pocket with the other hand. Mother frowned at the cigarettes, but as she looked in his eyes, she blushed, and he bent over and kissed her on the mouth.

They lingered there for just an instant.

That, I'm sure, was love, not death, for as long as it lasted. About a year after that he had gone, and she was alone. The really remarkable thing: only occasionally did I see her look sad. She must have looked sad sometimes, but she never let herself look so to me. Maybe she didn't feel as sad after Father left as she had in the time just before he left: maybe she felt relieved instead. But I know from that kiss that at one time, and for a while, they both felt love. I saw it, knew it before I knew words. I can't remember that I ever heard them say it to each other, and Mother certainly never spoke of it to me, but I know, that once, I saw it.

Madness, maybe. Why do we try so hard not to show our feelings? Men are supposed to do that, according to the received wisdom of our culture, but in my experience women do it, too. Sometimes they insist on personal stoicism just as we do. Maybe they do that because they must, but maybe because they too have an unwritten code of behavior that says, "Never show you're down; never show you're beaten; never give in." Is that kind of thinking madness or simple necessity?

To this day I don't know exactly what happened between my parents. I also know that Freudianism is largely a load of crock. When I saw them kiss, I recognized love, and I felt warm and safe and good, with no need to displace my father or anyone else. It was good, Hemingway might say, and that was the way the world should work. No "Hills Like White Elephants," no "The Sun Also Rises," just two young people in love, with a baby: within a year of that time something would happen that would so devastate their relationship that they would split and my father would leave and never return. Mother would never speak of it, and nothing would go quite smoothly for her afterward.

There had obviously been sex, but once upon a time there had been love between them. Then some kind of death happened, but I don't know what kind.

Later, when I was about ten or eleven, I had my first wet dream. I woke from a dream about kissing Lana, and I was a mess. I got up hurriedly and washed, scraped my pajama bottoms with a wet rag and buried them deep in the clothes hamper. Then it happened several more times, to the point that I was convinced I had some terrible, seeping disease, and finally in a thinly controlled fright I told my mother about it.

She didn't look me in the eye, but told me coolly and clearly that such things happen to all boys, and it's as natural as eating or sleeping. I felt no relief. I realized I wasn't going to die from it, but also that it might go on indefinitely and happen anywhere: I would have to fear every visit to someone else's house and every nap, as if I were a bed-wetter, but somehow this problem seemed worse, insidious, perverse, and it was one of many problems that made me pretty convinced that if God attends to people at all, He (or She) does so sparingly and without paying complete attention to details. Considering the embarrassment associated with the problem, I entertained the idea that God was a girl and used such tricks to laugh at boys. When about a year later I learned about women's menstrual cycles, I abandoned that hypothesis.

Back to the funeral: everyone dressed as for a winter Sunday morning, in dark suits, all the women and many of the men wearing hats. Everyone spoke in a whisper. The Funeral Home (what a silly name, as if anyone actually lived there) smelled like a mix of disease, cleaning fluid, and out-of-season flowers. Most of the men milled around in the lobby, trying to find someone to smile at them. Cousin Rog, who must have been forty at the time, smiled and waved broadly at me when I came in the front door, but I resolutely refused to smile back, thinking it inappropriate for the occasion. I had a strong strain of Puritanism in those days, inherited from my mother. She was slightly pink around the eyes, and her lips were closed tight in something rather the opposite of a kiss, and her brow wrinkled. That face told me that I had better not make a sound, let alone smile or laugh.

When I didn't respond to Rog, he came right up to me, swiped his hand about two inches from my nose, then stuck his thumb between index and middle fingers and held it in the air in front of my face.

"Got yer nose," he said, smiling, red-faced, trying to enjoy himself and get me in my infinite seriousness to lighten up. I wondered if he had taken a shot of Seagram's before coming to the Funeral Home. Mother or Grey-gramma always gave him one (or two) when he visited. They offered whiskey to every man who visited, but not to the women, many of whom looked as though they needed it more. Rog was one of the few actually to take it and claim to enjoy it.

"Stop it, Rog," Mother said. "It's not the right time."

Rog adjusted his tie and his facial expression. When Mother had passed him, moving toward the other room, he waved the hand with its prisoner thumb-nose at me again.

Mother returned, motioned me to sit down in the row of chairs just inside the door. She looked elegant in her long, black dress, walking as erect as a flag-pole. I peeked around the corner after her and spotted the edge of the casket.

The bottom fell out of my courage, and I sat down, my head spinning. Rog greeted the cousins who had come with Mother and me, then winked at me, holding his thumb again for everyone to see. "Yer nose," he mouthed silently to me. "His nose," he mouthed to the others, then adjusted his tie again, Dangerfield-like, and obediently followed my mother directly toward the you-know-what.

Reflexively I adjusted my own tie and checked for my nose, knowing it was still there but wanting to be absolutely sure.

My two little cousins sat next to me, as grim and silent as I was, and the elder cousins followed Mother and Rog into to the room where Grey-gramma "slept."

Slept was the word my mother had used in the car. "You don't have to come to the casket if you don't want," she'd said. If you do, Grey-gramma will look like she's sleeping."

Scared a' the dead bo-dy, scared a' the dead bo-dy.

I sat for what seemed a very long time in absolute silence. All the time I could see out of the corner of my eye my little cousin's left foot swinging rhythmically back and forth, back and forth. I tried not to think about the smell of the funeral home, which had me feeling sick and edgy even more than did the looks on the faces of the people who came through the door, the men trying to smile and the women without fail looking respectfully grim and tearful.

Finally Mother returned again, smiled weakly at my little cousins, and knelt down in front of me. "Do you want to pay your respects?" She asked. "There's my little man."

Not really a question, and distinctly unfair tactics . . .

She reached out her hand. I nodded and got up. She took my hand and led me into the next room and to the very front where the coffin sat on a table.

When I thought of it as a casket, I remembered President Kennedy's funeral on TV: gray, stately, as mournful a public event as I have ever seen.

When I thought of it as a coffin, I had to keep myself from reflexively coughing.

I decided to follow Mother, stand there silent, mouth a prayer, then look to Mother for a signal about when to leave. The thought of Jimmy-across-the-street poking his finger into the shoulder of the dead body crossed my mind. I imagined his eyes wide and staring, his laugher kicking up like his wild legs, and then I imagined him, having actually touched it, vomiting torrents over the body.

Then I made the dreadful mistake of letting my guard down and accidentally looking at the body.

"See how beautiful she looks?" one of the aunts said.

I had a lot of aunts in those days, and few of them made any sense at all, ever. I remembered one of them, having visited Hawaii on a vacation she won in a raffle sponsored by a department store in The City, saying when she returned that, "Hawaii would be great if it wasn't for all them damned Chinese." Even at seven years old I knew that was a stupid thing to say. I'd got seriously disgusted and went to hide in another room.

"So peaceful," another aunt added.

"She's with God now," a third said. "It's His will. He took her, and she's happy now."

That sounded ludicrous to me. I wanted to hit her almost as much as I'd wanted to hit Jimmy-across-the-street. "Aren't adults supposed to have more sense than that?" I thought, and I almost said it, which would have been suicide. I didn't understand then that nobody had anything more to say than I had, and some lacked the good sense not to say it, and I had better try all my life to keep what little good sense I had and keep my mouth shut.

But my thoughts raced right back to Grey-gramma's face.

It was horrible, pink and waxen and drawn, with the hint of a phony smile and pounds of powder. Her hands lay pink and bony, the brown spots rubbed pink, her dress pink and perfectly pressed. After that day I hated the color pink for a long time, and sometimes it still brings on a touch of nausea.

Before I could draw away from the body in utter horror, the thought struck me.

That's death.

No doubt about it.

I don't know if anyone there expressed real love for Grey-gramma. I hope so. But, like me, they knew they were looking at death.

Dead, not like Jimmy's ants: dozens of tiny ashes on the sidewalk. There before me was a former individual, a not-so-long-ago person, a breathing, maybe sometimes thinking creature dead as an iced cod, with chemical retardant failing to cover the odor of decay.

For the first time in my life, I wished I was Catholic. I'd seen my Catholic friends cross themselves, and I felt the need for some kind of calming gesture. Protestants don't have them, which leaves us wanting some idea of what to do, like a child who doesn't know how to shake hands at greeting or to take the kissing and cheek-pinching from the Italian Catholic aunts at Christmas.

The horror of protracted cheek-pinching didn't compare to real mortality.

No, I didn't think, "My God, that could be me in there." I thought something like this, though not quite in words: "My God, what the hell are we doing here? There's no living being in there! This is barbaric! Why are we doing this! Get me out of here!"

I hung my head, closed my eyes tightly, tried to utter some sort of prayer, spun on my heels, and walked away, hoping that Mother felt I had done proper penance and given proper respect. I wobbled quickly back through the lobby and out the front door into the fresh air. As I went out the door, I heard one of the men utter, "He's a good little soldier," but I was trying hard not to barf. I hoped Jimmy-across-the-street wouldn't ask if I'd touched the body, because the very thought made my bowels feel lose, and then I said a real prayer of thanks to God, male or female or neither, that Mother hadn't demanded that I kiss Grey-gramma good-bye.

I had a sense then that there must be a God, if for no other reason than that Someone had spared me from saying something stupid thing like, "My, she looks beautiful lying there."

Outside I gulped air like ice cream. A little while later cousin Rog came out. "There you are: you've worried your mother. She was afraid you'd run out in the street and get hit by a car."

I turned and looked at him, held up my right thumb between my index and middle finger: "Got your nose," I said.

That was the last time for many years that I went to a funeral home, but it wasn't the absolute last time, as I wish it were. Each time I go, I hope it's the last, and that includes my own final journey: I hope my body will never land in such a place. If you go to a funeral and pay attention, you may get a sense of what death is and why the people there are trying to fool themselves about it. I was eager to fool myself about it or at least to try to forget it for a time.

Imagine the poor people in Palestine and Israel, in Iraq and Sudan, in September 2001 Manhattan, in the coal-mining towns of West Virginia after a collapse, on the streets of 2016 Paris, in Las Vegas: they know what death is. They've seen not just the dead body, but the live body becoming a dead body. They've seen that happen by unnatural acts unworthy of our skittish potential for human kindness.

I went back inside with cousin Rog and sat down again next to my little cousins. The older one smiled weakly and nodded. I looked obliquely at her eyes. She too had visited the coffin, and from the look on her face, I guessed she had managed it a good deal better than I had. The smaller cousin, though, was crying softly and wouldn't look up. A long curl had fallen over her eyes, and she made no move to return it to its place. I had no notion of what to say to her. Her sister just sat there holding her hand and letting her cry. The little girl started to sob audibly, and her father came over, lifted her in his arms, and carried her outside, cooing gently to her and brushing her hair back from her eyes. Her sister took a magazine from the rack next to her chair and began leafing through it. I could see that she wasn't reading, just leafing. Her gestures as she flipped the pages reminded me of her mother's: odd the things we pick up.

When we got home, I turned on my radio: "Twist and Shout" was playing.

A number of years later I kissed Lana for the first time. That happened before we graduated from high school. Once, during junior high, we somehow got in a game of spin-the-bottle at a party. I don't know if our parents knew about it or not. I kept thanking God that, no matter which girl spun the bottle, it never pointed at me, and no matter which boy spun, it never pointed at Lana. When my turn came to spin, I tried to get up and leave, but the other boys grabbed me and pushed me back into my place in the circle. I wanted to pick up the bottle and smash it against a wall, because I both desperately wanted to spin it so that it pointed at Lana and feared that it would do exactly that.

When I spun the bottle, I gave it a dramatic, dicey twist, then glanced at Lana out of the corner of my eye. I believe she was blushing, and I think she was laughing. "I know where he wants it to point!" yelled Johnny Moore, another soon-to-be ex-friend of mine, and everyone laughed uproariously as he pointed accusingly at Lana. As the bottle spun, so did my head, and my heart pounded like Muhammed Ali jabbing poor George Foreman silly. When it stopped, the bottle pointed between Lana and a cute little round-faced girl named Lucy.

"Lucy, Lucy, Lucy!" the kids began to chant. Poor Lana looked somewhere between relieved and horrified, and then I'm absolutely sure she blushed when little Lucy calmly and kindly said, "It's Lana, not me," then sniffed dismissively in a way that would have made anyone's Victorian aunt happy.

"No, it's definitely Lucy," Lana said, sticking her tongue out at Johnny Moore, who had let out a loud whoop. But she stood up, apparently ready for me to come over and kiss her.

I had forced myself to kiss the cheek of the obligatory living Christmas aunt, but I had no notion whatever of how to kiss a real live girl of my own age.

"I'm not going to kiss anyone," I blurted out, to my horror, and to Lana's as well. She looked offended beyond reprieve, and I don't think she has forgiven me for it to this very day.

"Well, shake her hand, then!" urged Sally Jovicic, a very smart girl, and I stoically got up, walked across the small circle, and without looking Lana in the face extended my hand.

She took it firmly, gave it two good pumps, released her hand, and plopped herself back down in the circle for someone else to kiss.

"Oooh," was the general sound that rose like a cloud of cigarette smoke to choke the room, or at least me. I was mortified at myself, not for the last time. I had wanted to kiss Lana so badly that my heart was ready to burst, but uncertainty and embarrassment and terror had turned me from a good little soldier to a trembling mass of pubescent goo. I sat sulking for the rest of the evening and gradually shifted my rear end out of the circle and over toward a wall with an open window. I have no idea if Lana kissed someone else that night. I never asked and don't want to know.

I think that what I felt was a mixture of budding love for her, typical adolescent self-loathing, and a Joycian sense of general cosmic futility, along with a vague and terrifying hope that the universe, perverse though it be, had given me a sign that it owed me a chance to kiss Lana, that it had punched my ticket, and that in some time to come I might get to cash in my claim. I have a strong notion that what I felt, whether or not it was love yet, was better than death.

I do remember the touch of her skin, the palm soft and cool, like butter set out on a countertop. While she looked away from me and I from her, she grasped my hand, for just that instant, firmly. That grasp, to me, to a person with very little optimism, meant at least something.

When Lana and I kissed—no, I'm not telling about that. When we did, it wasn't death. Grey-gramma was far, far from my mind. I do believe that, in my own immature way, when I kissed Lana, I did so with love—it was already love. I think by then I knew the difference. I certainly do now.

The Three Muskeeters

"The truth is, everyone is going to hurt you. You just got to find the ones worth suffering for."
—Bob Marley

Uncle Stash loved to tell stories. He had lots of friends and had stories about every one of them. You might call him a gossip. You might call him a raconteur—though no one in Harmon Falls, not even the French teacher at the high school, would know what you meant by that. You might call him a storyteller, or you might just call him a bullshitter. But the man could talk, and we liked to listen.

I don't know why he was Uncle Stash: our family is Italian. You'd think we'd have had an Uncle Lorenzo or an Uncle Enrico. In fact, we had both, but they didn't tell stories. Like my father they ate a lot and laughed a lot, so they made good company generally and a good audience for Uncle Stash's stories: maybe friends are the people who laugh at your jokes.

On holidays, Saturday mornings, or summer evenings Uncle Stash would come by to visit, almost always when other family had already come over. He didn't come at mealtimes, like most of the family, because then Mother wouldn't have let him talk: she had a particular rule about not talking too much during meals. That didn't bother most guests, since the meals were always good. When Uncle Stash came, unless it was early in the morning, Mother would get out a bottle of Jack Daniels—the only alcohol we had in the house except for wine that Father put out on Fridays or holidays—and pour him a shot-glass-full. He would knock gently at the back door, which opened to the kitchen where everyone invariably met, call out "Yoo-hoo," and let himself in while Mother got the whisky bottle—she needed a step-stool to reach it out of the top cupboard. Uncle Stash would sit down in his usual chair, pick up that shot glass, swirl it gently, sniff the liquor, and smile at Mother, then put it down on the table without drinking. Occasionally he'd take a sip while he told a story or after he'd finished, but mostly he would just forget it was there: the whisky was more of a hospitality ritual than for actual drinking. Uncle Stash's storytelling was pretty much a ritual, too. If the kitchen radio were on, or the black-and-white TV in the living room, someone would turn it off, and a family that often had nearly everyone talking at once would draw up chairs in the kitchen and fall silent in anticipation.

"Did I ever tell you about the Three Musketeers?" he asked one Saturday. He grabbed the tall, red stool that sat under the wall phone, scraped it across the floor, and perched himself atop it. He had by then directed his gaze at me particularly, though we were sitting around the kitchen with seven or eight guests that morning. Everyone but Uncle Stash had eaten breakfast with us, fruit and cinnamon rolls and coffee that Mother had prepared—milk for me and my sister. Sometimes she made polenta, which looked like a thick yellow log on a plate. Mother hadn't got out the Jack Daniels, but she did insist her brother take a cup of coffee—the rich, earthy smell covered the room like a warm blanket. Uncle Stash took his coffee black, in long slurps, following each with an "ahhhhh," and then he winked at me over the edge of his cup and through the cloud of steam that rose from it.

"You mean Three Musketeers," Mother said.

"No, I don't. I mean muskeeters." That was the way Uncle Stash said mosquitoes. "Have I told you that story?" He continued to look right at me as he rolled the coffee cup between his hands.

"I don't think so," I said quietly.

"I've heard that one a hundred times at least," Grandma said, turning her mouth up at the left corner.

"Well, you can hear it once more, or you can have another cinnamon roll and not listen—they smell really good, Angie. No, Mom, I want to tell this one for the young fella there."

"Well, you're going to tell him whether I like it or not," Grandma said grumpily.

"I hear you've been playing baseball every day, and that you listen to the games on radio at night and cheer for your heroes." He stared right at me with a serious look on his face, a deep crevice settling in between his eyebrows.

I don't know why that should have embarrassed me, but it did—maybe just the fact of being singled out for the story. There's nothing bad about liking baseball or even loving it, as I did and do. Uncle Stash's stories often had morals—at least he said they did. I could seldom figure out what they were, and I'm not sure he knew, either. I wondered why he would say something bad about baseball or my love for it.

I must have blushed, because I suddenly felt hot, like a ray of sun had just shone in through the back door right on my face. I looked intently at the pattern on the linoleum and nodded my head.

"Don't worry, kid. This is the perfect story for someone who wants to be a baseball player," he said, and this is the story he told. It actually has three stories in one. I don't know if I felt happier that day for getting three stories just for me or more confused trying to figure out three of them rather than just one.

"They tell me you're a pretty good little ballplayer. Well, I've seen some real good ballplayers. You want to hear this story, don't you, kid?"

"Yes!" I said.

Aunt Annie said something like "Oh, my gosh," and pulled herself up to get another cinnamon roll, and Grandma followed her.

"Playing sports is good, and they can make you feel really good when you win. But they can also make you feel really bad when you lose. Remember that." As well as I can remember, these are the stories he told as nearly as I can remember them.

***

Back in the late '40s and early '50s, just after the soldiers had got home from the war, the high school had for a time a really successful football team. For Harmon Falls, that usually meant simply winning more games than they lost—barely. But that one year in the '50s just the right group of players came along with speed and strength and grit, and they were willing to practice and work hard together. And for just that year they looked like they might not only win more games, but maybe even get to the state championship.

That would have changed everything for the people of Harmon Falls. In all of its history the town has had only two state champions, one boy and one girl, back in the late '70s, in Cross Country. Everybody liked sports, but around there football was and still is king. A championship football team would have charged up the whole town, would have made the people of the town look at themselves differently. Good runners were fine, but trophy cases that lined the walls of the high school were filled with pictures of favorite football players from the '20s and '30s—and very few actual trophies, and those mostly for wrestlers who had won local tournaments or linebackers who had made all-star teams.

A number of the boys from the late-'40s/early '50s teams went on to play football at small colleges, but the pride of the team and the town in the '50s was Paulie Papadakis. He was a hard-running halfback, and he sometimes played linebacker on crucial third-down plays, and he returned punts. When he ambled down the high-school hallway, smiling, on his way to classes, the other kids murmured that he was headed for the pros someday. Today everybody talks about promising toddlers that way, but back then, before pro football became big TV as it is now, that was unusual. Paulie wasn't really tall, but he had thick legs and broad shoulders and a square jaw, and people got out of his way when he came walking by. Not that he was a bad kid—actually everyone liked him then—but he had something in the way he moved that made people notice and give way. Everyone assumed that he would get a football scholarship to some good college, and that would be the start of a famous career.

Well, in each of the first three games of Paulie's senior year, Harmon Falls had won by more than twenty points, and they hadn't played any slouch teams. But next to Homecoming, the fourth game was the most important of the year, the one against Belmont, Harmon Falls' chief rival. That team had beaten ours in every year except one since high school football had begun back at the dawn of time. Belmont always sent players on to college and even two to the pros: one to New York and one to Philadelphia, places that seemed so far away from us that they might have been in Europe, if people had played our football there.

But that was the year, Paulie's year, that everyone believed our team could win. And, oh, how badly our town wanted that win. Imagine the first week of December and how a kid aches for Christmas to come. Multiply that by one hundred—a hundred kids and a hundred times each. Cube the total. Add the distance from the earth to the sun. Mix in how badly Attila the Hun wanted to bring down Rome. Add the relief that everyone felt at the end of the War. Multiply that by the taste of Graeter's Oregan Blackberry ice cream, and you'll still come up short of how much the people of Harmon Falls wanted to win that game. No one talked about anything else for the whole month of September, and everyone has cried about that particular game ever since.

That September saw unusual amounts of rain and warm temperatures. The game finally came at the end of the month on a sticky, muddy Friday evening at our home field. Our little stadium was packed, with all the fences lined three-deep and fans sitting on the brick walls behind them and standing all the way up the concrete stairway that descended from town down to the field. The field sat only a couple hundred yards up from the river: you could smell dead fish from there. The air was full of swarms of mosquitoes (muskeeters, Uncle Stash said), and all sorts of nefarious insects tumbled menacingly around the lights and the patrons. Everyone from Harmon Falls was there, and nearly everyone from Belmont was, too. The only ones who weren't couldn't find parking places close enough to walk to the stadium, and so they stayed in their cars and listened on the radio. Belmont had all their games broadcast statewide, even though their town wasn't much bigger than ours. They loved football even more than we did, and they had an attitude about their team. The two marching bands competed as much as the football teams: they played and marched and stomped and screamed so that you've had thought the world was either beginning or ending.

At the end of the first quarter, the Belmont fans were beginning to worry: Harmon Falls had an 8-7 lead: Paulie Papadakis had run for a touchdown and caught a pass for the two-point conversion. By the end of the half, the score was

15-10 Harmon Falls. You'd have thought our people were going mad for joy, and our cheers rang through the town such that you'd believe VE day had come again. Harmon Falls snuggles down among tall hills like the bottom of a bowl full of warm popcorn, and I'll bet that all along the hills people twenty miles away could have heard the rumble of those shouts that night.

In the third quarter Paulie intercepted a pass, and Harmon Falls scored again, but Belmont had another touchdown and field goal—they had an especially good kicker that year—so the score had narrowed again to 22-20. Neither team could get anywhere in the fourth quarter: the pounding, the pressure, and unseasonably warm, wet weather had worn both teams to the aching bones, and they fought on bravely but with no energy left to make headway. With only a couple minutes to go, Belmont had a fourth-and-ten at their thirty and had to punt and hope for a Harmon Falls error. Paulie and Larry Ray dropped back to receive the kick, and the fans were jumping all over one another with joy. Some wanted Paulie to return it for a touchdown to rub in the victory, while others screamed for a fair catch or just for him to let the ball fall and roll where it would—anything but a fumble to give Belmont another chance to score. The air had begun to mist with a light rain, adding a touch of film noir to the athletic drama.

Belmont's punter made a very nice kick, and Paulie, ever the smart as well as brave player, raised his hand for a fair catch as Larry got ready to block. The ball hung in the air forever before it finally dropped from its melting arc.

Paulie was waiting at about the thirty yard-line, calm and assured, as the Belmont players stormed toward him. The crowd screamed for joy and clasped their hands in prayer.

At the last instant, Paulie's head jerked rapidly aside, and he tried to jump away, but the ball just ticked his shoulder pad, and it landed and began bouncing end-over-end toward our goal line.

The Belmont players pursued, and one of them dived on it at our twenty-one yard line.

Paulie, unbelieving and still on his knees, hung his head, then stood up and flung his helmet into the third row of the stands.

The Belmont fans screamed with joy. The unbelieving Harmon Falls fans heaved a collective, horrified sigh that sifted down to the river and sat there like a fog for the next three days.

The Harmon Falls defense made a brave stand, but Paulie stood on the sidelines with his head bent down and his face in his hands. Belmont made seven yards in three plays, then kicked their third field goal to win.

Some bad things happened later that night. Several fights broke out, and three boys and two older men went to the hospital with broken bones. Belmont fans damaged some cars parked on the Harmon Falls streets on their way out of town, and some local fans showed up at the Papadakis house during the night and shouted curses and threw eggs at the front porch.

That year the team went 6-3. Paulie still played halfback and sometimes linebacker, and he played very well. Belmont finally lost in the state championship game. Paulie didn't get a football scholarship to college.

Here's what Larry Ray said happened on that night in September. He was standing just in front of Paulie during the ill-fated play and heard it despite the noise from the crowd.

As the punt was just about to drop into Paulie's hands, a mosquito ("musketeer") buzzed right into the ear-hole in Paulie's helmet and kept flying all the way up into Paulie's ear.

Some people confirmed that they had seen Paulie clawing at the side of his face just before he heaved his helmet up into the third row.

Paulie never used that mosquito as an excuse. He felt so bad about that loss that he would only hang his head and stand there silent if anyone was mean enough to talk about that game in his presence, and some were.

Larry never blamed Paulie for that loss, but almost everyone else did, though he played a splendid game on offense and on defense. He rushed for over a hundred yards and helped us nearly beat the best team around.

After that season Paulie never played another game of football, and I've heard people say that he never watched one, either. He moved away a week after graduation and never returned to Harmon Falls.

At Homecoming celebrations someone would always mention that game.

Someone would always bad-mouth Paulie, and someone else would insist that he was the best football player Harmon Falls had ever produced, and that Belmont would have won that game by two touchdowns without him.

Here is what happened to Paulie: he became a Greek Orthodox priest and moved to North Carolina, where he built one of the largest and most successful Orthodox communities in the South. As I understand it, he still lives there, retired near Winston-Salem, and the people of his community love him. They know nothing of his high-school-football days, though I suspect they've had their own experiences with mosquitoes.

***

Around 1960, well before the time when Willie White Shoes almost led the baseball team to the state championship, Harmon Falls produced its best baseball player ever: Arty Portalis. Arty played shortstop and sometimes left field, and he would sometimes come in to pitch in relief in the last innings of close games. He was tall and strong and fast, and he hit home runs that people remember to this day. The team was never as good as in Willie's senior year, but that didn't bother anyone: people who liked baseball would go just to see Arty play, win or lose.

Baseball wasn't as popular as football—nothing was—so it didn't draw many fans beyond family and some old-timers who still believed baseball was America's pastime and the best game ever. But those who loved the game and knew it said that Arty had the size and skill to make the Big Leagues—that judgment seems always to have been the death-knell for Harmon Falls' athletes' careers.

High school baseball seasons normally run twenty-five to thirty games. They go from early March to June, but suffer from spring rains and poorly-drained baseball fields. In Arty's freshman year, the team played .500 ball: they hadn't done that well in thirty years. In his sophomore year they had their first winning season, 17-10. In his junior year they went 20-5 and lost by a run in the Regional final on a fluke call by an umpire. In his senior year, despite an unusually wet spring, Arty hit almost .500 with nine home runs, and he led the team to the state finals. They hadn't as good a record that year, only 14-8 in the regular season, but they got hot when the tournament began and started winning every game. Think about this: in those days the baseballs weren't so good, so a high-schooler hitting nine home runs in twenty-two games, often in bad weather, was like Babe Ruth hitting a hundred of them.

In that final game, on a misty June evening, Arty had driven in runs in the first and third innings with doubles, and by the seventh inning (the last inning in high school games at that time), the score was tied 4-4. Playing against a team from Monmouth, just outside The City, Harmon Falls wasn't expected to compete, not even with Arty playing at his best. He had played the first six innings at shortstop, but in the bottom of the seventh the coach moved him to leftfield: the opponent had two right-handed power hitters coming up, and Coach wanted Arty out there to catch anything that could be caught.

Monmouth's first player slipped a single into center field, and the next batter sacrificed him to second base. The third, the first of Monmouth's two great power hitters, hit a hard line drive down the leftfield line, and Arty caught it with an amazing sliding backhand grab and then nearly threw out the runner, who had to scramble back to second base. Coach had the next hitter walked, and then we pitched to a lefthander who sliced a high fly ball into left-center field. Arty scrambled back and was just easing under it, so everyone assumed the game was going to extra innings.

But then something unbelievable happened: Arty's head wrenched down and to the side, and the ball fell to the ground beside him.

The baserunner, stunned by what had happened, gathered himself and darted for third and then rounded for home. Before Jimmy Pensky, the centerfielder, could get there to help, Arty had recovered himself and fired the ball home. The ball got there just late, and Monmouth won the game.

Arty was crushed. He had carried that team on his shoulders for four years. And he felt that, when they had needed him most, and when he most needed to succeed, he had let them down. Not until Willie White Shoes' senior season did the Harmon Falls team have such a chance again, and they haven't had one since.

Most of the good high school players, after they graduated, would play in the summer Miners' leagues: all the coal mines had had teams since the turn of the twentieth century, but most of the mines didn't employ enough good baseball players to field teams without taking on a few of the local grads for the summer.

Arty Portalis went to every one of those teams, and not one of them had a spot for him.

At least that's what they said.

Arty got drafted in the twelfth round by the Cincinnati Reds, but he decided not to try to play pro ball. He went to college somewhere out West, then went on to medical school and became a doctor. Uncle Stash knew Arty's uncle and said that Arty had taken up private practice in a small, poor town out there somewhere where the people really needed a family doctor.

That semifinal was Arty's last game of baseball. "He could have been somebody," Uncle Stash said, forgetting entirely about Arty's medical practice.

***

By the mid-1960s summer basketball leagues had gotten popular all through the state, and Harmon Falls had one of the best around, at least among the small towns. By the early' 70s players came from all over to play in those evening leagues at Memorial Park (right in the center of town), which had two courts that sat right under the hill next to the Little League Baseball field and beyond the World War I and World War II monuments.

When the Little League games ended, everyone would go over to watch the basketball, and they played often until nearly midnight, when local law required that the park close. Gradually the basketball games began to draw more fans than the baseball, because the quality of play got better and better.

If you had known them both, seeing Ernie Peroni would have brought Paulie Papadakis back to mind. Ernie was just middle-height, but had a thick, muscular body and a smooth, easy, natural way of moving. Ernie didn't talk much, but he seemed always to be smiling: just a happy person—every now and then you meet someone like that. And he had the softest, prettiest jump shot you'll ever see.

Not to mention free throws: in high school Ernie had streaks of twenty-nine, twenty-seven, and twenty-six straight free throws without a miss, and no one could remember that he ever missed two in a row.

The high school basketball team had seldom been very good or very bad. Most years they hovered around .500. Most of the students and parents went to the games, but they never drew people who were just basketball fans without a school or family connection. The summer leagues were different: since as the league grew the players came from many other towns, so did fans, and real fans enjoy good basketball, so they got loud about it. By the '70s the teams even had statisticians to keep scorecards the way they did at baseball and football games, though in those days the league champions didn't go anywhere else for state tournaments or national competitions. It was all local. But it was serious business to anyone involved.

Though no one had ever talked about his going pro, Ernie was a fine high school player, so when he graduated, he got on a summer-league team right away. The former high-school football coach, Harvey Sampson, whom everyone in town loved like a saint, had drafted Ernie for his basketball team. Ernie didn't start, but he played as sixth or seventh man, so in the summer-evening heat he got lots of minutes and plenty of points, and his team did well. Whatever Uncle Stash may tell you, I have actually seen Ernie play, and I can tell you that he was smooth and accurate as a shooter and that he played really hard on defense—he just wasn't quite big enough or fast enough to compete with the very best of the players, many of whom had been high school all-stars or even successful small-college players.

Over his years of coaching in the summer leagues, Coach Sampson had finally gotten to ninety-nine wins for his career. He aimed to get his 100th in the league championship game in the summer of '73, and he had told everyone he was going to retire after that game: his wife was worried about his health and wanted him to stay home and help watch the grandkids rather than stay out so late all summer long. Ernie was aiming at a personal best that night, too: he had made his last twenty-eight free throws in a row. The newspaper sent reporters to cover both the coach and the player.

About two hundred football fans came to that game just to see Coach

Sampson reach his basketball milestone. Coach said it was only summer league, so totals like that one didn't really matter. But to those fans their beloved Coach's wins always mattered.

The temperature on that August night hit ninety-two degrees, and the air was so thick with humidity that everyone felt twenty pounds heavier.

Ernie played only sparingly in that game, and by the fourth quarter he had only four points, but his team was leading by five. Then one of his teammates, a forward, fouled out, and in the next two minutes his replacement did, too. Well, Ernie was a guard and not very tall, but Coach put him in anyway. He got another basket, but he wasn't tall enough to stop his man on defense, and the opponents caught up to Ernie's team and then got a two-point lead with fifteen seconds to go.

Coach Sampson called a timeout and worked out a play where the center, a small-college player, would get the ball and everyone else would clear off to the periphery so he could work for a shot. Ernie wasn't even in the play: he just ran to the left baseline to try to distract his man and make as much space as possible for his team's best player to get the ball to the basket.

The other team knew, of course, that they would try that, and though the center got the ball, he was soon double and triple-teamed. He got off a shot from just past the foul line, but it careened off to the side, headed for the out-of-bounds line.

Ernie slid over and got it, but his defender, who was quicker than Ernie, caught him before he could get off a jump shot. Ernie made a fake and then drove for the basket. He pump-faked again, got his man in the air, and spun for a finger-roll.

He missed the off-balance shot, but his defender fell right on top of him and knocked Ernie to the ground.

The referee blew his whistle for the foul, and Ernie stepped to line with three seconds left and his team still two points behind.

Those were his first and only free throws for the whole game.

Though some people thought Ernie was fixated on his own free-throw record, he said later that all he could think about at the time was Coach's 100th win, and I believe him.

As Ernie prepared for the first shot, he had so much sweat welling around his eyes that he could barely see. Nerves got to him, and he fired a line-drive shot that looked nothing like his usual smooth, athletic motion.

The shot clanked against the back of the rim, flew upward, and descended straight down into the basket—ugly, but one point closer to a tie.

The crowd roared its approval. Even some of the other team's fans wouldn't have minded seeing Coach get his 100th win.

Ernie got the ball from the referee for his second shot. The ref whispered something to him, but Ernie would never tell anyone what it was.

He bounced the ball and caught it, dribbled it a few times, held on tight, and peered at the rim. He bounced it again, then dribbled a few more times, and peered for a long time at the rim.

The crowd was just beginning to get surly.

Insects wheeled around the lights like dervishes.

Ernie was just about to let the shot go, when a mosquito flew into his ear and jerked him out of his routine. The ball left his hands before he could stop it.

He got the rhythm wrong, and the ball slid from his sweating palms. It hit on the front of the rim, looked like it wanted to fall forward into the basket, then spun itself out and back and fell toward the ground.

The players wrestled wildly for the ball, but the time clock hit zero before anyone could even pick it up, and the game was over.

The winners celebrated their championship, the losers clasped their heads in horror, and Ernie, one shot short, fell to the ground as though in a faint.

Nearly everyone applauded—it had been a great game—but a number of the football fans promised that they were going to beat poor Ernie Peroni to a pulp for missing that shot.

Coach Sampson, who had lost his game by a single point, addressed the crowd, with the newspaper reporter furiously copying down every word. Coach thanked the players and fans for a great season, assured them that the loss was no one's fault, and said he felt honored just to get to coach in such a great game. He promised that he'd have the football team ready for the fall season, and he said that he might just change his mind and come back again the following summer for one more season to get that 100th win and a bunch more.

The crowd cheered him, and everyone eventually filtered home without any violence.

Poor Ernie didn't know what to do. He spent the whole night walking down the darkest streets and alleys in town hoping that no one would see him, and he finally went home to bed at about six in the morning, just before the garbage trucks began collecting.

Around the end of September, with the football team having begun their season 3-0, Coach Sampson died of a heart attack on a Sunday afternoon while playing with his grandkids in the back yard of his house.

Ernie graduated and moved to The City, where he went to college. He took a job as a grade-school teacher, and before long he earned a master's degree through night school and became his school's principal. He began education reform to make poor or disadvantaged children feel more welcome and find more success at school. He didn't return to Harmon Falls for summer basketball and didn't play anymore once he got to The City, where the competition even to get on such a team was particularly fierce, especially for an Outsider. I've heard one of Ernie's close friends say he never picked up a basketball again.

***

"That was just the right story to tell, Stash," Mother said. "Thank you! He needs to know that sports aren't everything, that people do live real lives beyond all that sports stuff, and they do important things instead of wasting their time with kids' games. You finally told a story with a good moral."

"That's not it at all!" Uncle Stash exclaimed. "You got it wrong, Angie! Look, kid," he said, turning to me again, "the point of the story has nothing to do with all that shi- . . . with all that fancy moral stuff. The moral of the story is, when you're playing ball, watch out for muskeeters! They can fly right in your ear, or in your eye, or they can buzz around and get you all out of whack. Watch out! You gotta be at your best when your team needs you, and you don't want to miss a ball or a shot because of some stupid bug. You may never get to play again! The truth is that those three boys should have been three of the best friends this town ever had, and it just didn't work out. The muskeeters ruined 'em!"

"Oh, Stash," Mother said, "what are we supposed to do with you?" She sounded really disappointed.

"Pour me some more coffee, Angie," my uncle answered, smiling contentedly. "And do you mind if I cut another piece of cake?"

Little Fotungus

"I'm going out to fetch the little calf....You come too."
—Robert Frost

Uffington was the closest person Harmon Falls had to a "man about town." He was also the sort of person for whom someone invented the terms blowhard and stuffed shirt. How he got elected repeatedly to the town council no one seemed to know—I never met anyone who claimed to have voted for him. He ran a repair shop for TVs and vacuum cleaners and other appliances where he overcharged people who went to him because they were trying to save a little money. He was an inveterate, immoderate gambler, a self-styled impresario, and perhaps an invertebrate as well. But mostly he was a talker. He could talk for hours on end or even days. He would talk about any subject, whether he knew anything about it or not, and he could talk anyone else into sullen silence—into a grave, if they were willing to listen for long enough. I don't know for sure, but I believe his first name was Clarence. I never heard anyone use it—everyone, even his wife, just called him Uffington, and that was how he referred to himself.

Most folks treated him like some kind of swell, mostly I think because he intimidated them by talking about the great things he had done. He claimed, for instance, to have met the Beatles in Liverpool and to have suggested to them that they come to the United States. And he claimed he had been the one to suggest to Eisenhower that he run for President. He was tall and broad across the middle and used to walk around town swinging a cane and singing this song to himself, but loud enough that anyone who came close enough could hear it:

Uffington, Uffington,

you don't go bluffing Uffington.

Try to bluff, things get rough,

and that's all right with me!

He sang only the one verse, and that repeatedly, and he would usually end a singing session with a loud laugh. Since he was a fairly large man with a deep voice, and the citizens of Harmon Falls had and still have a general penchant for credulity, everyone thought he must be a pretty tough character. He played poker in the back rooms of several of the local bars and always won more than he lost—that he remained alive is in itself a kind of miracle, since he reportedly talked non-stop through nearly every game. He claimed that his family had been royalty or at least nobility in Britain and that they had a castle where he could go and stay any time he wanted. No other citizens of Harmon Falls, not even the Harmons themselves, could claim a castle in their heritage. Seldom would anyone cross Uffington, until he ran afoul of his opposite, one of Harmon Falls' tiniest citizens, Little Fotungus.

To look at him, you wouldn't think Little Fotungus could do much harm, especially to a man like Uffington. And, for the most part, he didn't. He was just a boy then, not a very big one at that, and he had a fairly sunny character, though he was self-absorbed, as most boys are. He didn't have a theme song like Uffington, but he would walk about at a rapid pace whistling all sorts of silly tunes—you could hear his whistle two blocks away, and, unlike most songbirds (except Mr. Browning's wise thrush), he seldom whistled the same tune twice. He had a special fondness for dogs, but his family would never let him have one. He had tried more than once to bring home some poor stray, but his family would always insist that once he had it he wouldn't take care of it. So every time he turned up with a dog, he had to give up the sad animal. He wasn't forgetful, and he was attentive to whatever he did, so a dog would probably have been just the thing for him, and he for the dog. In most ways, including that one, he was, as I mentioned, Uffington's opposite. Uffington had a dog for which he cared very little if at all. But the two humans, Little Fotungus and Uffington, shared a hard-headedness that made oak trees a little fearful of them as they walked by. That sort of commonality can make two persons friends or deadly enemies.

I don't know Little Fotungus' first name, either, though I think it may have been Arthur. Even his parents called him Little Fotungus. I think I heard his sister grit her teeth and spit out "Arthur!" once when she was mad at him for fixing her new shoes in the fresh cement when they had their sidewalk re-paved. He said that he was doing an experiment, and he would have used his own shoes, but he happened to be barefoot at the time—she, however, did not accept that argument.[1] His father was George Fotungus, who was six-feet four inches tall. His mother was Admirabila Fotungus (née Cesare, a local Italian family from the Piedmont region), and she was nearly six-feet tall. They named their daughter Talia: she was tall from birth and only got taller as time went by. No one could understand how the Fotunguses had a short son, but sometimes the world works that way: it just won't always do what you expect. Little Fotungus never seemed to let his height bother him, though his parents seemed perturbed by it—not so much embarrassed as confused—until they too simply accepted it as an oddity of nature. Little Fotungus was, in his own way, a phenomenon—I suppose one may say that of many people.

Like so many boys at that time, Little Fotungus liked to walk in the woods, mostly alone. I don't think parents let their children do that so much anymore: everyone fears dark places and lurking strangers. He spent most non-school days wandering around among the trees and looking at things: rocks, plants, flowers, insects, birds, cesspools—whatever lay in his path interested him. He treated creatures kindly, whether cats or birds or toads or butterflies. He even tried not to step on ant-hills on sidewalks: I've seen little boys jumping up and down on them trying to kill as many as they can for no reason at all. He would walk up to an adult on the street and say something like, "Do you know why buckeye trees have compound leaves?" The adult, thinking he was probably telling a joke, would reply something like, "No, why?" And Little Fotungus would

---

[1] Little Fotungus later claimed that he had intended that she step into the shoes so he might see at what stage of the cement's setting she could no longer pull her feet, still shod, free from it. She would, he added, have been able to step out of it anytime simply by drawing her feet out of the shoes. He would of course have been there to help her out.

say, "I don't know! That's why I'm asking you!" He didn't mean it as a joke, and he wasn't intending to be disrespectful; he just wanted to know. And normally both the boy and the adult would walk away from the encounter confused.

As soon as he got big enough, from about eight years of age, Little Fotungus spent lots of time in the town library. The Harmon Falls branch wasn't a very big library, and it still isn't, but he would look up anything and everything he could find there about plants and animals and rocks and streams and rivers. He habitually pored over maps and travel books and field guides, and he was reportedly Harmon Falls' first citizen to make use of interlibrary loan. That may not seem like much to you, but to us it was something.

In fact Little Fotungus spent so many hours in the library, sitting in the same chair at the same table in the front near the windows, that one of the library assistants put up a small, specially printed plaque that read "Reserved for Little Fotungus" by that chair. She meant it as a joke, but everyone, even the adults, respected it, and it remains there to this day, just in case he should come in and want that seat again. His best friend, Icky Growler, would sometimes go there with him. Icky didn't care for maps, but he sat and read about frogs and insects and fishing, and the two of them never made a sound, thereby keeping the librarians happy. The library folk thought the two boys a good advertisement for their collection: if two little boys who could be playing baseball out in the sunshine were instead sitting quietly in the library reading, why wouldn't anyone else want to?

Uffington, on the other hand, had little interest in reading or in anything but himself and card-playing. He went to the library only to check the stock reports in the newspaper from The City: he was too cheap to subscribe for himself. He got to the local week-day newspaper and reportedly made notes on the Obituaries, but no one had ever seen him reading a book, either at the library or elsewhere. He had a wife, people knew, but no one knew her very well, and she didn't go outside their house or yard very often. If someone saw her either on their porch or in their yard and said hello, she would grimace, shake her head as though with disgust, and say "hello" as if it were a curse word, and then she would quickly go back inside. Uffington had more than once claimed to have a son, but no one knew anything about him or had ever seen him—perhaps he was back in Britain in the castle. Uffington claimed his son was an important man traveling on international business, which was why he checked the stock reports. When Uffington saw dogs on the street, he would swing his stick at them and shout "Faaahhh!" I don't think he ever hit one, which is probably why no one ever said anything about it or tried to stop him. But the treatment of a dog was exactly where Uffington and Little Fotungus ran afoul.

As I mentioned—what a strange world we live in!—Uffington actually had a dog. And, just as you might expect that Little Fotungus would be the first person you know to get a dog, Uffington would be the last. It may have been his wife's dog, but no one had seen her caring for it, either. Uffington didn't even name the poor creature; he just referred to it as "that daaahhhg." He kept it chained in his back yard, even in winter—a big, black dog, a huge dog, a horse of a dog: looked to be part Rottweiler and part Beagle and part very skinny Grizzly bear—and he didn't even build a house for it. During rain or snow, the dog had just enough chain to scrunch in against the house behind the bushes and beneath the gutters. No one knew what the dog lived on, since no one had ever seen anyone feed it. Passers-by were too afraid to try since everyone who walked by had been growled at by it or by Uffington or by both.

Now, you could trust Little Fotungus to find out about things like that. He wasn't nosy, but he paid attention to things, especially creatures in distress. As small as he was, no one and nothing intimidated him—not even Uffington or his dog. Uffington's house wasn't far below the woods at the base of the hill on the west end of town, and one day Little Fotungus came wandering absent-mindedly out of the woods, twirling a plant of some sort in his fingers, and before he knew it, he stood face to face with Uffington's dog. The chain-link fence stood between them, but that was one rickety fence—Uffington was too cheap to repair it properly since it faced the woods rather than the street and so almost no one saw it. The dog, not the fence, kept folks out of his yard.

That daaahhhg had a history of barking up storm clouds out of a blue sky whenever anyone came around. But that particular day it just sat there and stared at Little Fotungus. The boy went up to the fence and sat down and dropped his head so he didn't meet the dog eye to eye. The dog looked as though it was going to howl, but instead, after a short time, it just whined, the kind of sound that can turn anyone with a heart into instant butter. It tried to inch closer to the little boy who sat silently outside the fence, but it had run out of chain. Only then did Little Fotungus look that daaahhhhg in the eye.

Little Fotungus began searching in his pocket, and he pulled out a half-eaten chicken sandwich. He took out the chicken and, stretching, handed it to the dog through a chink in the fence.

The dog looked at the chicken for a moment. Then a large tongue came out of his mouth and slobbered copiously. Then he surrounded and swallowed the chicken. A sigh of pleasure came from that daaahhhg such as has seldom been heard from a creature on this earth.

Little Fotungus ate the rest of the bread and lettuce and tomato himself.

Uffington must have heard either the whine or the sigh, and he came swinging out the back door and shaking his cane.

"What are you doing to that daaahhhhg, you filthy little—thing!" he said.

"Feeding him some chicken."

"Don't ever do that again! You'll ruin him," Uffington thundered. "I have him perfectly trained, and I don't need the likes of you spoiling him. So you just get out, or I'll sic him on you. Scat, you—now! Or that daaaaahhg"—Uffington drew out the vowel—"will eat you for lunch!" Uffington was fairly fuming. Little Fotungus later reported that a black cloud emerged from Uffington's bald spot and ascended into the sky, covering the sun for nearly an hour.

"Sic him on me," Little Fotungus said.

"What? You little nothing, you puny toad, you miniscule beetle turd, you less than senseless thing! Are you defying me? Why, I will sic that daaahhhhg on you, and I'll do it now, you wad of discharged chewing gum."

The odd thing about that speech is that it shows either that Uffington had once read Shakespeare or that one of the greatest linguistic accidents in the history of English occurred that day in Harmon Falls.

"Do it now," Little Fotungus answered. "Sic him on me. I'll walk around front to make it easier and so your neighbors can see. And then I'll feed him some more chicken. Poor dog."

Little Fotungus's reply of course sent Uffington into a storm of curses and threats. He was bluffing about the chicken, since he hadn't any more, and that bluff must have inflamed Uffington, who so hated bluffs, even further.

"I'm calling the police. Right now. And they'll have you in jail for trying to poison my watch dog. Just now I'll have them after you, you, you, you..."

"Little Fotungus."

"Yes, that's it: you little fotungus, you! And I'll come back and beat you with my stick."

Uffington didn't realize that was the boy's name. He must have thought it a better insult than he had yet attempted, and so he repeated it and stomped inside and called the police.

Little Fotungus put his hand through the fence, patted the dog gently on the nose, and went home in his usual round-about fashion.

About an hour later a police officer turned up at the Fotungus's front door and politely told the parents that they should keep their son away from Uffington's dog, and they answered that, yes, of course they would, Officer.

And equally of course, they couldn't keep him away—not once Little Fotungus had set his mind on helping that poor dog, who had found a devoted friend forever.

Anytime Mrs. Fotungus would make her son a chicken sandwich, which was nearly every day whether school was in session or not, he would make a point of going past Uffington's back yard and giving some of the chicken to that daaahhhg. The animal would rush right over to him, panting and trying desperately to lick both the sandwich and Little Fotungus. Then Little Fotungus would calmly sit there and pet the dog's nose through the holes in the fence, waiting for Uffington to see him. Uffington would run out, fuming and swinging his cane, and then he would run back in and call the police again. Before long the police, realizing no harm had come to anyone involved, stopped responding.

One day Officer Provezis, who was a very nice man, stopped Little Fotungus when he saw him walking along the street. "Look here, young fella," he said, "will you just leave Mr. Uffington's dog alone?"

"No, sir, I won't," Little Fotungus replied, fixing his mouth in a resolved scowl.

The officer kneeled down so he could address Little Fotungus eye to eye. "It's Mr. Uffington's dog and Mr. Uffington's yard, so he has a right to do as he pleases. So just stay out of trouble, okay?"

"That poor dog's hungry and lonely and wet and sad, and I'll give him a chicken sandwich whenever I get one, to make him feel better." Little Fotungus held firm, and the police officer could see he had a case of a hardened offender before him.

"We may have to call your parents."

"You already did that."

"We may have to put you in jail."

Little Fotungus held up his wrists. "Put me in jail. Put me in right now. Put me on hard labor. And when I get out, with the money I get from making license plates, I'll go right out and buy a chicken sandwich and give it to that poor dog for lunch."

Officer Provezis took off his hat and shook his head. "What am I going to do with you, kid?"

"Help me build a house for the dog, and get Mr. Uffington to feed him every day."

"Mr. Uffington must feed the dog, or it would be dead by now. But I see your point about the doghouse. Let me talk to the man to see what we can do, all right?"

"Yes, thank you, sir."

That was probably the first time in years that the prefix Mr. had appeared before Uffington's name, or that anyone in our little town had called the officer sir, but both parties were trying hard to be respectful. Little Fotungus smiled and nodded, sensing victory, and the officer patted him on the head and shooed him along.

Officer Provezis did talk with Uffington, but Uffington growled that of course he fed the dog, and whether he kept a house for the dog or not was his own affair, not a matter for police harassment. He said harassment the old way, ha-RASS-ment, and he said it with zeal. The policeman had a look at the dog before he left, and he had to admit that he didn't think he could do anything to help. The dog looked at him very sadly indeed, a look that seemed to say, you don't have a chicken sandwich by any chance, do you?

Little Fotungus didn't take the news well when he got it from Officer Provezis. He had really believed that Uffington must do something. So he resolved to do something, jail or not.

He didn't ask his family about it, but he did consult Icky Growler. Icky didn't say anything, but nodded when he needed to. Except for one instance, which you'll learn about soon, Icky didn't speak his first public words until he was fifteen, when he asked Annabelle Chance to the school dance. Annabelle reportedly fainted, since she and everyone else (except Little Fotungus) believed Icky incapable of speech. Icky took her by surprise, and he took her fainting to mean "no," so he didn't speak again until more than two years later when he asked Annabelle's sister Clara to the Senior Prom. Clara didn't faint and said "yes" just to spite her sister, and did those two ever make a quiet but happy-looking pair at the dance.

With Icky's help Little Fotungus developed a plan. Having motive and means, he needed opportunity, and that came more quickly than anyone could have thought.

Since the last of the Harmon-family mayors—and they went back to the town's founding—only Mayor Alderman had held the town' highest office. His name had caused confusion at first, but the residents had got over that easily enough, especially once they found that his only competitor for office was Helmut Sportingfarht—you could hardly confuse the two names—who ran a cement-block business in town. When Mayor Alderman decided to step down after four terms, no one immediately came forward to run—accept for, of all people, Uffington. Uffington's campaign for mayor created the quietest uproar you've ever heard, and it lead to one of the greatest confrontations in the town's history. Councilman was one thing, but mayor was entirely another.

At first no one ran against Uffington, because no one had given the office a second thought. Everyone thought that someone else would do it. Uffington quietly filed his candidacy at the City Building, and life went on as usual. Then one day Norma Calabreze, the head librarian, came to the City Building, where all the official town records lay in storage, and checked the ballot and filed paperwork so she could include it in the library archives. That was when she saw Uffington's name and nearly suffered Harmon Falls' first case of spontaneous combustion.

Norma immediately began circulating the word around town, and she made sure that the newspaper got records of the paperwork. The paper ran a story, but the editor, Mort Abrams, included little more than the facts, fearing that otherwise—if he dared editorialize—he would set off a conflagration the small version of which Norma had avoided with a combination of good sense and cold water from a drinking fountain. Having got the essential information out, Norma and Mort stepped back and let the natural, chaotic flow of public recognition take its course. In a column the next day Mort did go so far as to say that at least one other person should run in the name of American democracy. Uffington never forgave him for it: he wanted to run and win unopposed and free of expenses.

Uffington claimed that, given that he was the most nobly descended of all Harmon Fall's citizens, he should be a shoe-in. On hearing that, Little Fotungus remembered his experiments with Talia's shoes. Though he could hardly get a pair of Uffington's shoes, he thought he might find a way to stick his campaign in good, firm cement that even such a blowhard as the old grumbler couldn't get out of them. When a second candidate finally appeared, and the town council decided that the two candidates must have a public debate, Little Fotungus found his opportunity both to square up with Uffington and to do a kindness for his overlooked dog. He had only to complete his plan and have his intuition confirmed. That was when he used the aforementioned interlibrary loan.

Hearing that Norma Calabreze was his only competition for office, Uffington not only readily agreed, but laughed aloud when the other members of the Town Council argued they should hold a one-hour debate a week before the election. They had no precedent for the request, but they didn't know quite what to think of either candidate. No one could imagine either winning: Uffington was a bully, and the town hadn't yet progressed far enough to feel comfortable electing its first woman mayor—believe it or not, that's how things were in those days.

"A libraaaarian!" Uffington spouted. "And a woman. Ha! An Eye-talian woman! Uffington will be ready: make no mistake about that!" And he added, for anyone who would listen, "My people have a castle! Nobility, you know, back in the Old Country, the Uffingtons! Famous, powerful—oh, such a castle as you've never seen. A man with a castle versus a puny small-town librarian!" Nobody liked him any better for saying things like that.

Little Fotungus put in his famous loan request at the library just in time to get the book and take action before the debate.

In the meantime, Icky Growler, whose father worked at the lumber yard, got some cast-off boards and nails, and the two of them collected some slag from down along the railroad tracks. Icky and Little Fotungus got half a gallon of paint and a few shingles from Mr. Little, who had some left over after repairing his garage. The rest of what they needed they collected by going door to door: most folks were accustomed to strange questions from Little Fotungus and an accompanying silence from his friend, so, if they had it, they just gave him what he asked for.

For the next three weeks most of the residents of Harmon Falls were sweating, wondering if some debacle awaited on the day of the debate. They read the ads in the paper advertising the event, and various signs posted around town reminded everyone of their civic duty to attend.

For two weeks Little Fotungus sweated, until his book arrived. Mrs. Calabreze called him at home to let him know it had arrived, and he sprinted from his house to the library to get it. He thanked her breathlessly and opened the book without a second's delay. He began to scan it even as he hustled over to his accustomed chair.

None of the librarians knew why he wanted that particular book so badly, so they all kept a spare eye trained on him as they went about their business. They hadn't long to wait before they got a reaction.

Little Fotungus, poring over the book, suddenly leaped up with a cry of triumph.

'Yes! Better!" he called out. "Even better! The best!" He slammed the book shut and dashed for the door, apologizing on the way out for the noise he had made.

On the day of the debate Uffington went early to the Council Office in the City Building to prepare for his speech and to think of some especially nasty things of which to accuse his opponent. He guessed that the politics of the future would grow even nastier than those of the past, and he wanted to ride into office at the head of the wave of bluster and insults.

Early in the evening everyone began to gather in the park down by the city fountain, the baseball field, and the swimming pool. The Council had set up as many chairs as they could collect, and anyone coming too late would simply have to sit on the ground. By an hour before the scheduled debate, all the chairs had been taken, and people were scattered all over the grass as well. Some had brought picnic baskets. Strawberry Festival queen Carmen Basilica had brought her transistor radio and was playing dance music. Augie Daniels had a hip-flask of Scotch in one jacket pocket and some Fig Newtons in the other, and he was offering to share them. Icky Growler stood unnoticed in back of the crowd, holding a book behind him.

Even Mrs. Uffington was there, out in public for the first time anyone could remember, sitting right up by the dais, smug, silent, and peering about, staring at anyone who looked like a possible opponent to her husband.

As soon as she had left home, Little Fotungus had smuggled a chicken sandwich and a wheel-barrow full of materials up to the Uffington's back fence. He quickly dug a hole under the fence, tossed the sandwich to that daaahhhhg, pulled in his materials one by one, and got to work. The dog offered no resistance whatever.

About half an hour before the debate was to begin, the two candidates arrived at the park to take their places on the dais. They received mild applause, but no one knew what to say: politicking was new to them. Norma Calabreze offered to shake Uffington's hand, but he demurred and offered instead the phoniest flourish of a bow you've ever seen. She just shook her head and sat down to wait. She waved at her husband, a dentist, who was sitting in the front row. Uffington began talking loudly and rapidly at anyone whose face he could pick out of the crowd.

That was when Little Fotungus, with Icky's help, sprung the public part of his plan. Icky opened the mysterious book and handed it to the adult nearest him, Fleena McGee, who was sitting in the back row. He pointed at the open page. Fleena didn't know at first what to make of the book, but when she actually looked at it, she burst out laughing. Icky motioned for her to pass the book to the girl sitting next to her. The book began making its way through the crowd, and a wave of wild laughter and noisy conversation followed as it went. Icky disappeared, and since he hadn't said anything, no one remembered that he had even been there. He headed straight for the Uffingtons' house, and as he got to the street, he saw Little Fotungus, who was on his way to the park: he didn't want to miss whatever was going to happen, and he had finished his preparations. The two of them nodded to each other and slapped palms as they passed.

By the time Little Fotungus reached the park, Earl Fogel, chairman of the City Council, was pounding his gavel on the lectern up on the speakers' dais, trying to quiet the crowd, who had got noisier and noisier as the laughter had grown contagious.

"What's going on?" Earl called out. "What's wrong with you people? We have a serious debate to hold here to help us determine who will become our next mayor!" He did his best, but he got nowhere with the crowd, who were enjoying themselves far more than they'd expected.

Little Fotungus walked right up to the front row and took the book from Joe Calabreze, who had just got a look at it and had a huge smile on his face.

"You do this?" Dr. Calabreze asked.

Little Fotungus smiled.

Earl Fogel saw him standing there.

"Have you done this, Little Fotungus? Are you the troublemaker here?" he bawled.

"Yes," Little Fotungus answered.

"Just what have you got there?"

"A book."

"A book? What sort of book? Surely a book can't cause all this ruckus!"

"A bluff!" screamed Uffington.

"Not bluffing," said Little Fotungus. "See for yourself."

Little Fotungus handed the book up to Mr. Fogel.

For a moment Fogel did nothing. Then his free hand sprung to his mouth, as he tried to squelch the guffaw that threatened to overwhelm him.

"Hold it up!" Fleena McGee shouted from the back. "Hold it up for everyone to see!" She had made no secret of the fact that she intended to vote for Mrs. Calabreze no matter how the debate went.

Earl Fogel held the open book in front of the audience, and everyone, even those who had seen it up close, crowded up to the dais to see it together. They looked from the book to Uffington and back again, and back once again, and they all laughed hilariously.

"What have you got there, you rogue of a Fogel, you pin in a pincushion, you blowfly on a swamp toad?"

Fogel turned over the open book to Uffington.

A sunburn would have looked healthy compared to the color Uffington's face turned just then. He peered. He spluttered. He raged. He stomped. He jumped up and down, shaking the dais beneath him. He gurgled. He whistled. He burst buttons on his shirt. He would have blasphemed had words been willing to come forth from his lips. Then he turned toward Little Fotungus, who in his moment of triumph stood there looking at Uffington with no expression on his face whatsoever.

"You! You've done this, and it's a lie. An untruth! A falsification! A smear! False witness against your neighbor! A prevarication! A perversion! You, you weed, you dung beetle, you ritless wascal (he meant to say witless rascal), you thing-that-has-never-been, you harpy, you, you, you . . ."

Someone called out from the back.

"Little Fotungus!"

"Yes, that's it," Uffington said, "as I've said before, you little fotungus, you!"

I suspect you and I will never again hear such laughter as echoed through the park at that moment.

"That's his name, Mr. Uffington," Carmen Basilica politely corrected.

"And well it ought to be, damned little rumpelstiltskin!"

You can imagine how the Fotungus family were feeling about that. Despite Uffington's girth and tough-guy reputation, George Fotungus was giving serious thought to jumping up on the dais and striking a blow for family pride. He hesitated mostly because he still wasn't sure about Little Fotungus's part in the scene, whether he could strike that blow with pure righteousness or only in defense of his son's provocation.

Through all the clamor and tumult, one person had been slowly making her way to the front of the crowd: the only person at the event smaller than Little Fotungus himself, Lindy Lu Hoobler. She had had to push through adult feet and hips and to duck their elbows until she finally got to where Earl Fogel could see her.

"What's all the holly-bolly?" she asked, trying to say hullabaloo, but not getting it right. "The book," Little Fotungus said. "Did you get to see the picture?"

"No, I didn't," Lindy Lu answered.

"Look," said Little Fotungus as Mr. Fogel handed it down to her.

Suddenly and surprisingly everyone had gone silent. Lindy Lu looked at the book.

"There's nothing there," she said, looking at Little Fotungus in surprise.

"That's right," he said. "Uffington Castle isn't a castle at all."

The book was the Heritage Guide to English Castles, by Guy de Roussillon; the picture had the caption "Uffington Castle"; the picture showed a steep green hill with a stylized white chalk horse carved out on its side, and the top stood completely empty. It had bank and ditch, suggesting that earthworks may, once upon a time, have helped protect a castle. But the top of the hill was empty of any structure whatsoever. The castle everyone had heard so much about was in fact nothing but air.

"The ancient family home," said Mr. Fogel, and then he stifled a laugh that came out sounding something like "Spppllllert!" Another, following the first, came out sounding like "Pffffzzzz!" The third time he couldn't hold his mouth shut, and it came out more like "Bwwwaaaaahhh!"

"I don't get it," Lindy Lu said, but everyone else did, even Uffington.

He raged, he shouted, he stamped, and then he climbed down the steps, took his wife by the elbow, and stomped off home.

"So you found what you wanted in the book you requested?" Mrs. Calabreze asked Little Fotungus.

"Yes, ma'am, I did. And Mr. Uffington will find something else when he gets home, if he takes the trouble to look."

She had no idea what Little Fotungus meant by that, but she motioned to Lindy Lu to bring the book to her. She pointed out to the little girl that the picture showed how, despite the words on the page, no castle stood there.

"So," Lindy Lu said, "there's no Uffington Castle."

"Right," Little Fotungus confirmed, "despite whatever Mr. Uffington may say."

Lindy Lu made a face and tilted her head to one side. Then she began to dance about and sing rhythmically, "No fam-il-y castle, no fam-il-y castle," and she ran off into the dispersing crowd. She did what everyone else felt like doing, but they were just too adult to do it.

"Well, Norma," Earl Fogel said. "Guess there's not much doubt how next week's election will turn out."

Mrs. Calabreze smiled and nodded. She wasn't sure she was going to be glad to be mayor, only that Uffington wouldn't be.

By then Little Fotungus was making his way back to Hill Street, where Uffington lived, to see the upshot of the rest of his plan.

As he turned out of the park, his father was waiting for him.

"What have you done, son?"

"Will you come with me, Dad? I'll show you."

"I meant about the book," Mr. Fotungus said. "You've done something else, too? Are we going to have the police back at our house asking about you again?"

"Yes," said Little Fotungus, unequivocally.

"I guess I'd better go with you then," sighed his father, and they walked up toward Uffington's house. On their way Mr. Fotungus noticed that nearly every street corner they passed had a small sign stuck in the ground with nothing on it but an arrow—after a few blocks he noticed that the arrows pointed the way to Uffington's house. He didn't know that Icky Growler had posted them as part of his son's plan.

"Oh, what have you done, Little Fotungus?"

"Something good, Dad," Little Fotungus assured him.

"We'll see."

When they got to the block where Uffington lived, they could already see a crowd had gathered, mostly at the fence around Uffington's back yard. Since the fence was chain-link, everyone could see through perfectly well.

The two of them squeezed to the front of the crowd so Little Fotungus could show his work.

"That's it!" Little Fotungus said, pointing.

In Uffington's yard stood a neatly built doghouse. That daaahhhg was standing proudly in front of it. Over the entry to the doghouse Little Fotungus had painted the name King Arthur.

"Nice doghouse. Why does it say 'King Arthur' over the door? I've never heard Uffington—Mr. Uffington, that is—call him anything but 'that daaahhhg.'"

"He needed a name, so I named him King Arthur," Little Fotungus explained. The choice of name may have been just an odd coincidence.

"You named him?" his father asked. "He's not your dog to name."

"I asked him about it first, and he didn't object, so I just painted it on there."

"You asked whom?"

"The dog. He didn't seem to mind the name."

"And then you painted the name on?"

The crowd had all along been listening to the father-son discussion, and they had begun to murmur approval.

"Yes. I built the doghouse. Well, Icky and I did, but it was my idea, so I don't want him to get in trouble about it. He helped me because he felt bad for the dog, too. But it's all my fault."

"Well done, boy," murmured more than one voice in the crowd, "and "Nice work" said somebody else, but George Fotungus wasn't so sure. He didn't want Uffington or anyone else angry at his son again.

"Look, son, you don't just go breaking into someone's yard and building a doghouse without asking permission first."

"Yes, I did," Little Fotungus replied candidly. "Don't you like it?"

Before his father, who was trying to conjure up a proper parental response, could think of what to say, Uffington came storming out of his back door swinging his cane and cursing like a demon caught at a church social.

"Who's done this! Who's broken into my sovereign property and assaulted my animal? Why, that daaahhhhg is a pure-bred, trained to take orders and to kill on command!"

The dog sat there impassively with his eyes closed, looking serenely happy and almost noble, even supercilious.

"Someone has destroyed the sanctity of my home, my domicile, my cas— my home, and I want him found and punished!" Uffington scanned the gathering crowd. "Oh, I know who did it: I know who!"

He kept looking around the crowd, waving his cane above his head, and searching for one particular person, one determined, ruthless enemy. And then his eyes settled on that one small figure.

"You! My arch-enemy, that campaign-spy, that parasite on a flatworm, that groundling, that devilish little son of a . . ."

Uffington stopped himself just in time, as he had caught a glimpse of the face of Mr. Fotungus, and that face looked none too happy at that instant. Mr. Fotungus may have been the least violent of men, but he was tall and imposing, and he'd had enough of Uffington's insults.

"That little monster of yours, that ill-behaved, unrestrained, unkempt, trash-picking penny-pinching earwig, that little, that little, that little . . ."

"Little Fotungus!" the crowd said together.

"Yes! Just so! As I've been saying all along. He did it! That little fotungus!"

"I helped, too." The voice came from Icky Growler, and it was the longest sentence, public or private, he had uttered in his life up to that point. Icky had come up to stand right beside his friend.

"I've no doubt of it," Uffington blustered. "To jail with both of them, after they clean my yard of this trash. I hope that daaahhhg bites both of you, bites you to strips and crumbs."

"King Arthur," Little Fotungus said.

"What?"

"He has a name now: King Arthur."

"A name? King Arthur? How absurd. He's a daaahhhg, not a king."

"King Arthur had a castle: Camelot. Now this King Arthur has a castle of his own."

"Officer! Police! Ah, there you are finally. Arrest these hooligans!" Uffington cried.

Officer Provezis had sauntered up and stood beside Icky Growler. He pushed back his hat and wiped his forehead with a handkerchief while Uffington fumed, fretted, and stomped.

"What's wrong, Mr. Uffington. Castle got your tongue?"

"Now, officer," Uffington huffed sheepishly, "do your duty and arrest these boys. They've broken into my yard, probably my house, too, and they've—they've . . ."

"They've built a doghouse," the officer added, concluding Uffington's sentence for him. "And a pretty nice one at that. Looks to me like no harm done. The poor dog needed a house anyway. How about if they just apologize, Mr. Uffington? You boys willing to apologize, to say you're sorrow for what you've done?"

"No," Little Fotungus said, unyielding.

"Hear that!" Uffington screamed. "They're guilty! They admit it!"

By that time Mrs. Uffington had crept up behind her husband and had grasped him by the elbow. He almost fell down when she touched him, but she held on tightly.

"Maybe we can just keep it," she said. "The doghouse. Serve them right."

"No," Uffington thundered, "no, nothing less than jail for the likes of them. Nothing less!"

"Come in, Uffington," she said to him quietly. We'll talk to the officer and straighten all this out. Come along, now."

She guided her husband, wobbly with rage, back into the house.

No one, not even Uffington, had noticed Little Fotungus's final flourish, but folks saw it the next day as they came off the hill. On the back of the doghouse Little Fotungus had painted the word Camelot. If a man's home is his castle, why shouldn't a dog's be, too?

"We should go home, now, son, and talk about this," Mr. Fotungus said. "Officer: is it all right if I take my son home?"

"Of course, George. Don't worry. We'll resolve all this tomorrow. It's getting dark. Got to go around the park and make sure everything's okay."

"Thanks, Icky," Little Fotungus said. "Good night, King Arthur!" he called to the dog.

The dog, still sitting with his head posed proudly, very possibly turned a smidgen toward Little Fotungus and nodded his benign, sovereign approval.

You'll want to know how all this business turned out. The next day the police interviewed Uffington, who assured them that the dog was ruined, that there was nothing more he could do for it with it: it must be destroyed. Fortunately Officer Provezis was there, and he suggested a second solution: that to punish Little Fotungus for breaking into the Uffingtons' yard, they should give him the responsibility of taking care of the ruined dog. He must remove the doghouse to his own family's yard and clean up any damage he'd done at the Uffingtons' (there was none). Mr. and Mrs. Fotungus, confronted with that solution, at first refused: they wanted no dog in their house or yard. But after some cajoling from Officer Provezis, while they still didn't like the idea, they had to admit that they found it just, so they allowed their son to bring both dog and doghouse to their home. Talia was secretly delighted, since she also wanted a dog but would never admit it, and Little Fotungus expressed public delight, saying that the result of the adventure had come out better than he could have hoped.[2]

Despite his parents' fears, Little Fotungus became a devoted and caring companion to his new canine friend, and King Arthur became a beloved mem-

---

[2]Talia, who is blonde, once reported to her parents that she had found a black hair in her favorite hairbrush, but she never did actually see Little Fotungus using it to brush King Arthur.

ber of the Fotungus family, castle and all. He was already an older dog when they got him, and he had never before received good tending, so he didn't live a long life with the Fotunguses, but the years he had found him happy, contented, and for the first time well fed. Even Admirabila Fotungus, famous for her stoicism, cried at King Arthur's passing. A local legend suggests that the Fotunguses interred the dog's bones up the hill in the woods northwest of town, and that at the grave Talia, then a first-year Latin student, inscribed on a nearby stone: *Hic jacet Arturus, canine quondam, rexque futurus*. Eventually Little Fotungus, after many more adventures, often with his friend Icky, grew up, attended college, and moved away.

Norma Calabreze did indeed become Harmon Falls' first woman mayor. She served two successful terms in office, retiring then from politics and soon after from the library to direct Harmon Falls' new branch of the Humane Society. I heard not too long ago from someone who still lives there that in the most recent election Icky Growler was chosen for mayor. His first order of business was to propose to limit City Council meetings to ten minutes' duration and discussion of essential items only. The members, I heard, gave him a standing ovation, to which he said nothing, but only nodded sagely, very much like King Arthur (the dog) might have done.

Uffington, with whom we began our story, somehow got re-elected to a seat in the City Council, but he served only one more term. He continued to win money in backroom-bar poker games, but not nearly as much as before: the other players found that they could both bluff him and beat him if they kept their wits and their nerve. He needed every bit of that poker money, as work at his repair shop steadily diminished. He arranged a couple of midsummer polka-band concerts at the City Park, and that got him some small return to public grace. I'd like to say he became less of a bully and a blowhard, but that wouldn't be true. He never said anything more in that town about nobility or castles, though.

Partytime

"The only way to have a friend is to be one."
—Emerson

When you look back to childhood, do you remember the times when you made good decisions, or when you made bad ones? I can remember plenty of bad ones, but only a few good ones, maybe because the bad ones brought memorably awful consequences, while I don't remember the good ones simply because nothing terrible happened. I just kept being me.

I notice now, with the benefit of distance and memory, that I struggled with friendships, trying to determine who were my friends and who weren't. And yet I had friends, and many of those people remain friends to this day. I've made fewer since. I still believe, though, that friendship is a wonder, an ambiguous and amazing part of this confusing life we lead. I remember when I was a kid thinking about the game of baseball as a special kind of friend in itself, and many of the decisions that come back to mind have something to do with it, with playing or watching or practicing or thinking about baseball.

***

Small, old mill and coal towns like Harmon Falls didn't have much in the way of excitement. In the summer, if we weren't playing baseball, one night a week the park would stay open for a moonlight swim at the pool, where we could go to try to swim with a hundred other kids or just give up and look at girls. In spring the town sponsored Riverfest, but that was mostly just greasy food and beer, so not many kids were there, and when we did go, our parents went along. It only lasted for two days anyway. Around midsummer we had a Strawberry Festival that lasted for about two hours. They had a parade, and people ate strawberries, strawberry pies, and strawberry cakes, and they drank strawberry milkshakes. In early October came the Pumpkin Festival. They had a parade, and people ate pumpkin pies and pumpkin cakes and drank pumpkin milkshakes—you get the idea. In the winter people complained about the weather.

Otherwise, in the summer you could walk in the park if you didn't mind staying away from motorcycle gangs, but that took only a few minutes, unless you'd stop for an extra minute to look at the goldfish in the fountain beneath the World War I memorial or if you saw someone you knew to talk with. On nearly any evening but Sundays you could hang around the donut shop, or get pizza if you had money, or cruise if you had a car, or go to the movies if you had money and wanted to walk four miles to the bigger town across the bridge. Or you could spend the evening throwing baseballs against your garage. I gave that up after a while since it just beat up the balls, and the last time I did it, I knocked a block out of the wall that left a hole I had to try to fix. Ma finally ended up hiring a neighbor to do it. Major league fastball, I'm tellin' you.

If you didn't like any of that, there wasn't much to do. Old people grew flowers or vegetable gardens when they had time off work, or they would go to the tiny downtown to bowl or drink and play softball or listen to radio or watch TV.

You could say the memories come back thick as flies, or maybe those are just real flies. Always seemed that we had lots of those pesky things. Here's a time I remember. Maybe you remember something like it.

***

Sometimes I walk to the top of the hill to the cemetery. I know that sounds morbid, but wait till I tell you about it. The dirt road winds up the hill like a string on a top, past layers of gravestones that get newer as you climb. The place is filled with old willows and uneven stone walls that climb the hill like a drunk with a fresh bottle: stumbling and slow, but tight to the road. The trees bend and sway with the road and make the place seem more alive than it is.

If you go just before sunset you can watch the sky redden over the hills to the west and see the silver light of the rising moon skim off the river like tinsel on a Christmas tree. From the very top of the hill, where there are fewer gravestones yet and few trees to block the view, you can see the river wind for miles, till it cuts and curves and disappears into the hills south gentle as a bad curveball. The birds will chirp loud as a storm till the light dies, and the red from the sky and the green of the grass and the blue of the spruces and the gold of the moon fold one by one into the black of the river till they all close tight as sleep. And layer by layer the houses that stack up along the sides of the hills begin to fade, first into the mist rising from the river, then into the rising night, till you can see only a few that emerge out of the light of street lamps limp as smoke. Then you have to wait for the nighttime coal barges that shoot their lights off the hills as they float south or the one riverboat that still gets this far on its run. Then the blinking lights and the jazz music and the sound of the paddle wheel filter up the hill till they're light as wind chimes on a bare summer breeze.

The top of the hill is cooler than the valley, and when the wind is right, you don't get the smoke from the mill, and you can actually fill your lungs with the real air and think about what it feels like to breathe that.

A dark path cuts off the back of the cemetery over through some trees to the high-school baseball field, and if you're really brave, you can walk past there over the jagged stones to the rock quarry, which glows deep blue under the steadily arcing moon. My friend Lance told me there are copperheads around the woods and the quarry, so I don't go there often, only when town is so quiet that I feel like I'm dead already and I don't care if I meet one or not.

Most nights lots of people go to the center of town, off the park, to the little league baseball field. By dark most of the little league games are done, and men come in for slow-pitch softball games. They have leagues for old men and young men, one now for women, too, but mostly for ex-high school athletes and miners and steel workers and guys who spend their nights drinking at bars, and some pot-bellied local businessmen who think they can make more money by mixing with the working crowd, and guys you've never seen before and you wonder where they come from to a little town like this just to play softball.

There's talk about somebody starting a girls' softball league, too, and I hope they do (but they hadn't done it yet in those days).

Almost everybody comes out then: wives, kids, bikers, bums, third-shift workers on their way to punch the clock, but mostly ex-ballplayers with bad legs and beer on their breath and young guys like me who don't know what else to do and figure that one day we will be here, too, fatter and slower, and everyone in town will finally come to see us play.

This is where the real party is: beneath the lights and the lazy drifting softballs that float up into the night and hang there like stars. People bring beer, even though it's against the law in the park, but the policemen, being polite, don't notice, even though they sometimes stroll by to watch for a few home runs, too. A lot of guys just go for that, the beer, because they know that somebody will have an extra one from a six-pack, or some kid will have snuck a few from home or will have got some old drunk to buy him cans at the store in exchange for sharing a few. And people drink and joke with the players and boo the umpire and ooh and ahh all the home runs that fly gracefully and easily out of a little league park often till as late as midnight. That's what they come for, the home runs. Home runs are something big, even in a little town lost in time. Everyone has a good time but the pitchers and the umpires, which sounds just a little bit like heaven to me.

So tonight I get to the park and it seems half the town is there. It's a hot night, and moths circle endlessly under the park lights. I see Pecks, but he doesn't talk to me; he's the shortstop on our team, so he thinks he's too good to be seen talking to a freshman outfielder, even though pretty soon I'll be a sophomore outfielder. Burger is there with his girlfriend, and Stud with his, but they leave soon. They show up, let everybody know that things are cool, and then go somewhere and do something that freshman outfielders don't know anything about. Probably someone with a car drives them to the movies or to the marina to take a boat ride on the river.

Lowry is there. He'll be a good pitcher—that's right, you heard me say it. Someday, if he grows enough to get some steam on his fastball, he will be a good pitcher. Lance is there, but he lags back in the dark, drinking beer with his buddies. I run into my friend Samula, and we go back behind the backstop to watch balls and strikes, to see how the umpire will call pitches.

Slow-pitch softball is not like baseball, and it's not even like fast-pitch softball. No fastballs, curveballs, bunting, stealing, and the bases are only sixty-five feet apart. No beanballs, few strikeouts: the ball's easy to hit, though I must admit, it's harder than you'd think to hit it well. I once saw this old guy, must be thirty-five or so, Fred Wilson, hit five home runs in a game. Imagine that, five homers, each one high and long as a rainbow, disappearing into the night so you couldn't even see where they landed, somewhere out in the park. Course, the fence is only 200 feet down the line to left, a little farther in center and the power alleys. Still, he hit five straight balls right on the button, I mean cleaned their clock: boom, boom, boom, boom, boom, rising like a rocket and falling into nothing. I bet you he could never hit a curveball, but that's slow-pitch for you. He made the front page of the sports section of the next day's paper. Not his picture, mind you, just his name, but to me five homers was worth a picture, if for no other reason than because he went home with that pitcher's respect, with everyone's who saw the game, and with his own.

This game is between Drift Inn and Beans Foundry. If you'd never in your life seen a game before and you saw this one, you'd think softball was closer to Custer's Last Stand than any sport you can imagine. I mean, this is a bunch of young beer hounds, the Drift Inn team, guys who've played a lot of ball, against foundry workers, guys who look older than Father Time. The Drift Inn guys have beer bellies the size of kegs, but they also have arms the size of basketballs, and they haven't yet lost all of their speed or much of their hair. They have one good player that people around here remember from his high school days, George Jakovich, and a bunch of tall guys named Emil who look like their chins were carved out of the sides of mountains. The Beans boys look like souls that even hell forgot: skinny, whiskery, whiskey-eyed Elmers who've played softball since before their opponents were born. The Beans pitcher is so old he can't even put much arc on the ball: he just can't throw it that high. The slow-pitch is supposed to drop from about twelve feet up straight down on the batter: that's what makes it hard to hit. With this guy, it barely gets above the top of the batter's cap. But he's maybe the only guy they got who can throw it that far and that straight.

If you think this is going to be one of those stories where the underdog comes back against a huge enemy to win an impossible victory, sorry to disappoint you. When the first Emil walks up to the plate for Drift Inn and sees a pitch coming in letter-high from a codger older than his grandfather, his eyes pop big as gum-bubbles, and he's so surprised that he only knocks it off the fence for a double instead of burying it in the fountain in the park out beyond the left-field fence. Now the others from Drift Inn don't hoot and holler like high school players would, but don't go thinking they're gentlemen and will take it easy on the old coots. Each one walks up with a big, silent grin on his face and a big bottle-bat in his hands and a pretty good idea that tomorrow's box score will show some pretty big numbers next to his name.

The second batter, a lefty, looks really disappointed when he only lines one off the right-center field fence instead of hitting it onto the roof of the bowling alley across the street. Beans' centerfielder looks like he could have run once upon a time, but by the time he gets to it, he's too tired to throw it, so he pitches it underhand to the rightfielder. The better part of the rightfielder's arm hangs down below the elbow, so he can only throw submarine-style. He does little better than the centerfielder, which the batter sees as he rounds second base. He shows probably more embarrassment at himself than pity for his aging opponent, so he stops at third with a stand-up triple.

Samula and I look at each other and realize we're not going to see much in the way of balls and strikes, so we head for the street beyond the outfield. We're not bodacious enough to brave the park and Grim Reapers, the local version of Hell's Angels, but maybe we'll catch a few homers that soar over the right field screen.

By the time we get there, Drift Inn already has a 6-0 lead and it's still in the first inning. We find Lance and Ricky Anders out there just as Ricky snags the fourth homer of the inning. Catching the ball knocks a little beer from the can he's holding, so he curses up a storm and wipes his hands on his shirt.

Now, frankly, even though Lance is a ballplayer and all, I don't much like to hang around these guys. Ricky has more than a mean streak, and they've always either got or are talking about getting beer. Now I'm no goody, but I don't like to mess with that stuff. I've got a baseball career to think about, and if I got arrested it would just kill Ma.

Plus, you gotta admit, the stuff just smells bad. Why would anyone drink something that smells that bad?

Not long, though, and they offer beer to me and Samula. Samula takes one. He's a good guy, but he likes to be one of the crowd, not stand out too much, and since everybody else has one, he takes one. He pops open a can, takes a drink, and says "Ah."

Now everybody else has a beer but me. And I'm okay with that.

Pretty soon Ricky comes over and puts his arm around my shoulder. "Come on, my friend Willie, don't be a wuss. Have a beer, man, and you'll feel better."

"I feel fine already."

"Come on, mama's boy, just try it. I'll bet you've never tried beer before." His breath smells like sweat from the beer, and he's not too steady on his feet. His eyes have receded deep in his head, so far that I almost want to reach into his eyeball with my hand to see if I can pull the pupil back out.

"Come on, man," Lance says. "Be a man."

I have tried it, beer, when I was a little kid, at my uncle's house, not knowing what I was tasting. Yuck. It was bitter, sour and warm, sharp and almost vinegary.

Now, before long they're all after me to try one, and pretty soon they're giving Samula a hard time, too, because I won't drink. Ricky threatens to beat up both of us, which of course he couldn't do, since he's nearly drunk, and you can't really fight someone who's drunk, anyway, so we'd just run.

But eventually Samula's after me, too. "It's hot," he says, sweat dripping from his forehead, "and you don't have money to buy anything else to drink. Just have a beer, Willie. Maybe you'll like it. It's really pretty good when you get used to it, and one won't hurt you."

A softball fires down and bounces among us, another Drift Inn homer, knocking Ricky's can from his hand. He curses again, loud and long, and tries uselessly to brush the spill off his shirt.

"Beer doesn't seem to have done those guys any harm," Lance says, pointing to the Inn players, and everybody laughs and gulps. He must not have noticed their round bellies.

"Just give him a break, Lance," Samula says, almost in a whisper. "He'll take some when he's ready."

"All right, it's not me pushing him anyway. It's Ricky. Let him just take care of his damn self."

Another kid has just shown up with a fresh six-pack and starts to pass them around. Nobody says a word to me this time. We all turn to watch as another homer soars way over the centerfield fence, hitting the door of the bowling alley across the street on one bounce.

I glance over at the beer, which is actually starting to look pretty good to me. Must be something in how they design the cans. Samula's right, I'm thinking: it has got hot.

"Last chance," says Samula to me, about to pop open the icy, dripping can.

"All right, let me have one."

"What?" from everybody.

"I'm thirsty. Let me have one, please."

"All right!"

"Good job, Willie."

"We'll make a man outta him yet."

With a sheepish smile, Samula hands me a can of beer.

Now I want you to know: I gave in to thirst, not to these guys and their pushing.

The can feels cold, especially when I place it against my forehead. Words and pictures proclaim the virtues of the regal brew within. The top opens with a crack like the sound from a distance of a bat hitting a fastball. I bend over the can, and then some of the fizz gets in my nose and makes me sneeze. Frankly, the stuff doesn't smell good. I notice the others tilting their heads back. "Chug ya'," says Ricky to Lance, and they both turn bottoms up at once, so I do too.

The liquid tingles, almost burns at first, like soda pop, but the cold feels so good in my throat that I keep swallowing and swallowing. The can is empty before I expect it to be or want it to be. Upon reflection, I find the taste not as bad as I had remembered and much better than the smell. In fact, it went down so fast that I hardly tasted it at all.

I look up, and everyone is looking at me.

"Man. He chugged it, the whole thing."

"On his first try."

"The boy," says Lance, "was born to drink beer."

"Sorry, Willie, that's all we've got," says the kid who brought the last six-pack.

I start to say, "That's okay," but all that comes out is a loud burp. It snuck up on me like a back-door slider. Everybody laughs, except for Ricky, who is howling with glee.

The funny thing is, only a few seconds later, everything starts to blur. I haven't moved. In fact, I don't feel like moving for some time, but nonetheless everybody looks smaller, and the lights look a little dimmer. A softball whops against the fence just in front of us. The aged right fielder, whose beard seems to have grown longer over the past two innings, picks it up and loops the ball submarine-style back toward second.

So now I've had my first real beer.

"You okay?" says Samula. "You look a little funny."

"A little funny yourself," says I.

I don't feel like a man. But not a very stable one. My body feels smaller and loopier. Someone is playing music.

Pretty soon we're all arm in arm, even Ricky, singing Beatles' songs, and I'm wondering if any of these guys knows Sinatra or Tony Bennett. The scoreboard has Drift Inn up about 35-0 after three innings, and they're batting again.

One by one, they step up to the plate, and "pop," the ball arcs high into the night and over the fence. Then another, "pop," and another, "pop." "Pop," "pop," "pop," they sound like beer cans or champagne corks popping, and they fly like Fourth of July rockets. "Pop," "pop," then one makes a sound more like a whip cracking and zips high down the left field line. "Crack," it hits a bulb on the left field line light pole, and the bulb shatters in a thousand pieces, sending sparks that spray round and bright as the best fireworks and fall to the ground in a fiery flower.

"Ooh," the crowd says together. "Aah."

I notice that the fence is starting to imprint my face with a series of squares, and I'm starting to taste metal. I didn't realize I was leaning against it face first.

"Pop."

"Ooh."

Singing: "All the lonely people, where do they all come from?"

I wonder how I came to be leaning face first against the fence. I try to collect myself, and I figure if I run a few laps around the park, maybe my head will clear. Drift Inn in up 52-0 now, and the crowd is starting to thin, so maybe I won't run into anyone. Once around the field, and I look again at the scoreboard: 59-0. Three times around: 65-0. Five times around: 71-0. "Pop."

About now, the cheers have died down considerably, and I have a terrible need to relieve myself. So I finish my next lap and head for behind the concession stand. As I'm about to turn the corner: "Hey, Baseball." There's Norm Jackson, sunglasses and all though it's pitch black out, and on one side of him stands Undo Purdy, a defensive tackle on the football team, and on the other side Steve Presnick.

I ain't lyin' when I tell you I almost peed right there.

I start to move back nice and slow. Norm says, "What's your hurry, Baseball? The game's over anyway. Stick around and maybe Steve will teach you a little boxing lesson." Steve's already got his fists clenched and his mouth foaming, but he's either too mad, too drunk, too rabid, or too stupid to say anything. I keep backing up.

Now I have no idea in the world why Steve would want to hit me, but in those days in that place a guy didn't need a reason. If he felt like hitting you, he did. Steve was the kind of guy who just might take it into his mind to hit anybody, anytime, anywhere. The world's a crazy place.

Then I feel something behind me. I damn near leap away like a frog, but

I'm doing my best to keep my composure, and my legs feel like limp noodles. I turn around and look, and there's Billy Hines and Jim Darrell behind me. I also notice that more people are leaving the park. I thought the game had two innings to go, then I remember the ten-run rule: if one team is up by ten or more after five innings, the game's over. I look at the scoreboard and read 72-0 just as the lights in the whole park go out.

I turn: Steve Presnick's coming at me. I turn again. In the moonlight I can see Jim Darrell's eyes flipping back toward the departing crowd. Is he leaving an opening for me? I turn again just in time to see Steve lunging for me like a fullback about to run over a rookie defensive back.

I step to the side and think about letting go with the nastiest haymaker I can muster. But all I do is duck and swerve aside. Steve trips over my foot and falls flush on his face.

Yep: he's drunk, and now he's really mad.

And I'm drunk, and I'm really wobbly.

He lies there for just a second, gets up, and puts his hand to his face. Then the hand drops, and his eyes are wide and round, and even in the dark I can see blood dripping from his hand and his nose, and he lets out scream like a fire alarm and yells, "I'm gonna kill you, boy!" and he's on me like a bear on a fish and he grabs me in a headlock and he's starting to punch at my face but all he's hitting so far is my hands and the top of my head and the sweat from running has made me slick and slimy and I slip out of his grip like soap outta your hand in the shower and fast as I can I run where Jim pointed with his eyes and I'm not surrounded and now I'm in and out of the last of the fans and Steve Presnick is nearly at my heels and I'm cutting and dodging and he's after me and I come to the bleachers and cut fast to the left and I hear him crack his shin on the concrete and he lets out another yell and he's after me again and cursing like a demon but I've got a lead now and I dodge between some people and head for the backstop where a path cuts between the field and the hill behind it and the path leads back to the park and if I can make it to the park I'll have a lot of directions to choose and a chance to kick in the burners and disappear before I'm dead or the Grim Reapers get me, which would be much the same thing.

As I turn round the fence maybe I've lost him and I glance back and he sees me again and I can hear him yell again, "I'm gonna kill you!" and he's on my trail and I don't have long so I sprint down the path and as I pass the backstop there's a slight turn to the left and the moon shines full on the path ahead of me with the fence on my right and a steep hill on the left, almost too steep to climb, and I see two things. At the end of path ahead of me is a group of bikers, the motorcycle kind, in black leather jackets, chains, and sunglasses. Directly before me on the path at my feet is a stone about the size of a baseball.

Now whether or not these bikers are friends of Steve's, chances are they wouldn't mind watching a kid get beat up, so they just might not let me through. So it looks like I got one chance: Steve can't see me where I'm standing, so I could pick up that rock and wait, and as he turns the corner, I could plug him clean in the face with it. I don't know a lot, but I know how to throw a baseball.

No time to think. I bend over, pick it up, and poise to throw.

But I can't do it.

I don't know if I'm chicken or what, but I can't do it. Not square in his face.

Up to now I haven't really hurt anybody, whether I broke the Law of the Schoolyard or not, but throwing that stone means taking the chance of killing somebody, even if it's only Steve Presnick, who in the right mood might kill anybody.

But I don't want to leave the stone for him either, so with no time to think, I take the only other option: stone in hand, scramble straight up the hill.

Now let me tell you that hill is steep. I'd never seen anyone run up it before. I've seen guys try to climb it on all fours and once or twice make it by grabbing onto roots or stones, but mostly not. They fall back and hurt themselves.

I have no choice if I don't make it all the way up, because in three seconds Steve will be at the bottom waiting for me to fall.

. . . and my feet are spinning and the dirt's slipping beneath me and my hands are clawing above and I'm reaching and straining and one last push and I'm up and up and over the top.

I look down and see Steve charging past me down the path like a freight train, straight toward the bikers, screaming like a steam whistle as he goes.

Damn. I can't believe it.

I don't even pause for breath. I'm on my feet, across the railroad tracks, and sprinting for home with all the energy I've got. I run maybe half a mile before I remember that I have to piss, but I'm too close to town now to find some trees or a place to hide, so now I gotta run the rest of the way home gripping the water in and stumbling and running stiff-legged and feeling the sweat pour down my groin and feeling like the pee is gonna burst out my belly button at any minute.

It might have been easier just to go ahead and get beat up.

Maybe not.

But finally there's my street, and there's my yard, and I jump the fence and I'm in the back yard behind a tree and my fly is stuck oh god I got this far and my fly is stuck and I yank and yank at the zipper and I've finally got it and just in time.

Aaah.

This stuff happens to kids more often than you think. Do adults have these problems?

I take a few deep breaths and compose myself, check for cuts or bruises that might get Ma alarmed, and head for the porch. The moon is round as a turnip and bright as the lights that flash when you get punched in the eye. I feel steady on my feet, not drunk, and I made it home alive. But somewhere under that same moon Steve Presnick is still looking for me.

Ma is lying on the couch in the living room watching TV. "Willie, you're late. You had me worried."

Yeah. Me too: I think that but don't say it.

"You shouldn't be out so late by yourself. You could get into trouble. You could . . . ooh! You smell of sweat. Have you been out running in those clothes? What am I going to do with this boy? Go get a bath right away and put those nasty clothes in the wash. Hurry up now. I'll pour a cold drink for you for when you're done."

Of course, I do just as my mother says.

"What are you watching on TV?" I ask.

"Mutch Humbug."

He's an idiot who has talk shows on radio and TV.

"Why are you watching that idiot?"

"It's nice to know somebody's dumber than I am."

"You're not so dumb."

"Thanks a lot for the compliment. Go get your bath."

"What's Mutch raggin' about tonight?"

"Oh, how the streets aren't safe because of all the young hoodlums and the ACLU and women who work and how we waste too much money on educating hoodlums who don't care and on welfare mothers and sports for children and programs for the disabled. I better not get started if I want to sleep tonight."

"Right, sorry."

She shakes her head, changes the channel and puts on an old movie instead. I know this one: Manchurian Somethingorother. It's the one about this guy who gets brainwashed by Russians to come back home and shoot some important politician. Not much better than Mutch to watch before bed.

As I run water I notice my heart has finally slowed down and I wonder if I'm one of those young hoodlums Mutch likes to complain about and blame the Democrats for. Tonight, I suppose I was, but then I didn't kill Steve Presnick, even though he would have killed me if he'd caught up with me.

My heart's starting to beat fast again.

I brush my teeth, then merge with the water and try to think of something to calm me down so I can sleep. I drank beer tonight. I don't think I'll do that again soon. Better stay on my toes with my life always on the line. For some reason Lana, this girl I know, comes to mind. Gotta get her out of my head; my friend Lenny, her brother, would never forgive me if he thought I was gonna hit on his sister. What made me think of that anyway? I've never thought about hitting on Lana. Not exactly, anyway. Better not think of it exactly or inexactly or any way at all. But Lana's hard not to like. Think about the water. Blend with the water.

Through the window blinds I can see the moon again. I watch a cloud mosey toward it and try to engulf it, but the moon shines right through it, like a lightbulb through newspaper.

***

That happened in the summer after my freshman year in high school. Later I told my mother about the beer part, but not about the rest: would you try to explain that to your mother?

I did run into Steve Presnick again, but not until about three or four years later. He'd got out of high school and the Navy, and something had happened to him. He looked withered and worn out, even though he was still a very young man. I was working in a pizza shop at the time, and he came up to me and shook my hand before I recognized him and had a chance for the fear response to get in the way. "Hey, my friend Willie," he said. I asked him about the Navy, but he didn't want to talk about it. He told me we should have a beer together sometime, and I could tell him what had been going on in the old town. I said "Sure." He picked up a pizza and waved to me when he left, and I had a strong feeling that, though we had never been anything close to friends, I wanted to do something to help him. I just didn't know what that could possibly be.

A Child Who Could Sometimes Fly

"Sometimes being a friend means mastering the art of timing. There is a time for silence."
—Octavia Butler

When I was nine years old, I flew for the first time.

No, not in a plane, and no, I'm not an angel or a mutant superhero or a gymnast, just a normal guy.

When I was about seven, someone, a schoolteacher, I think, asked me what I wanted to do when I grew up. Most kids will say something they've heard about or seen on TV. They may want to be an athlete or a teacher or a fireman or a junk-bond trader. They may say something outrageous, or something funny, or something that one of their parents does. Before taking time to think about the implications of my answer, I blurted out that I wanted to fly.

"Flying is a good profession, Lewis. Do you want to be an airline pilot or a fighter pilot or a transport pilot?"

"No," I said. "I just wish I could fly," and the questioner let it go at that, as adults usually do, assuming I would figure out the sort of plane later.

But I was thinking in that moment that I wanted to fly with my own body, not in a machine or like a bird or like anything else. I wanted to rise off the ground and move around freely in the air. It seemed like a good idea at the time. In retrospect, I'm not so sure.

When you think of all the strange-looking creatures that can fly, though, I didn't know why people don't do it all the time.

You may find it surprising that I've never especially liked heights. Looking down from the edge of a hill or from an upper story of building made me dizzy then, and it still does. Maybe that's why I thought I wanted to fly: I could control how high I'd go, and I could come down softly when I felt ready. When my thoughts began to take me higher and higher, I began to decide I probably didn't want to fly at all, and I felt sorry that I'd wished for it.

But as it turns out, I did fly, sooner than I'd thought I might, though the result wasn't anything you'd call spectacular.

You might not even call it flying; you might say it's more like floating. That's what most people said if they saw it, and it often feels more like that.

The night before my first flight, I had dreamed about flying, which I do now and then. In the dream I was standing outside in front of the house, and my body simply lifted about five feet off the ground. Then, with a little thought, I rose to just about up to the ceiling-level of the front porch. There I assumed the traditional Superman position. At first, though, I wasn't moving forward at all, just lying there in space, so I made a few swimming motions. I tried a butterfly stroke, but got nowhere, except for sinking toward the ground a bit. So I settled into a gentle breaststroke, my arms fanning out horizontally and my feet frog-kicking. That got me going slowly but steadily forward. I flew as far as the end of the house, and then I woke, with the feeling of flying still in my limbs though I was lying flat on my belly in bed.

What I remember most about the dream, even now, is the feeling: I felt almost like I was swimming, except lighter and more relaxed, freer. I couldn't swim then and still can't swim well: from the first time someone dropped me in a pool, I've sunk immediately to the bottom. To this day I can walk across the bottom of a pool by drawing myself forward with my arms and pushing on the bottom with my legs, but I can't float—on water, at least. Now I can swim a little with lots of effort using a vigorous crawl or backstroke. If I lose energy or stop for an instant, I'll sink.

But unlike swimming, in the flying dream I had a feeling of letting go of the earth, releasing myself from gravity, and allowing myself to participate in the air rather than applying my feet firmly to the ground and jumping off. I just let something natural happen by forgetting any prejudices I had about doing it.

Relaxation, more than I have in the pool, seems to me a key component to get up off the ground and stay in the air. The thought strikes me to let go, and I do, and up I float.

So in the morning after my dream—a Saturday—I was playing in the living room in my pajamas. Christmas was only a couple weeks away, so we had put up a tree and many other decorations. The dream came back to mind, and as I thought about flying, my body felt very light, and the feeling in the dream flooded back into my limbs, but mostly in my torso, just below my stomach. I liked the feeling of freedom that the dream had given me, so I waited for it to grow. I stood on tiptoes, reached my right hand up as far as it would go, pointed my finger to a spot in the air above me, and thought, "I want to be right here."

Then with no effort, right there in the middle of the living room, my body seemed to get lighter, and my feet gradually left the ground—I didn't even jump—and I began to drift upward until my body sat in the air right at the spot where I had pointed. Having got into the air, I then floated all the way to the ceiling and began moving around the room. When I reached a wall, I'd push off with my hands and go in a different direction. I remembered that Mother had got upset that the angel on top of the tree wasn't sitting straight, so I floated over and straightened her. I had to admit she looked better that way. Then I dusted the lintels on windows and doors with my sleeve: from above I could see fuzzy grey carpets of dust on them, so I brushed them clean. Through the front window I looked down on the sidewalk and watched a dog going by wagging its tail and breathing with its tongue out. It did look up toward me, and I caught its eye, but it didn't seem to find anything special in what I was doing and just trotted on.

After a bit I wasn't sure what else to do, so I just moseyed over to one of the corners and flattened myself against the ceiling and the walls with my arms spread out, and I waited.

About a minute later my mother came into the living room looking for something. She looked all around and apparently didn't find it. She shook her head and sighed. Then, from above, I caught her eye.

"What are you doing up there? Get down before you break something!

You know how hard everyone worked getting those decorations up! Come down this instant!" She let out a kind of screechy growl, shook her head a couple times almost violently, and stormed back into the kitchen.

"Dennis!" I heard her call to my brother, "Tell your brother to get off the ceiling!"

So I floated down to the floor and sat on the couch. I wasn't sure I wanted my big brother to catch me up there. He might start throwing things at me and bounce a ball or something off a lamp or the mirror or a window and break something. Then I would get the blame for it. That was how things usually happened. May brother always liked to throw things at me, and he still does to this day, which makes me glad that we no longer live in the same town.

As I think back on that morning, I wonder why that was the first day it happened—the flying, that is. I felt as though I could have done it before if I'd concentrated on it. I didn't learn how to fly. I didn't discover how to do it. I didn't even terribly want to do it. I just got this feeling, the feeling of release that I had in the dream, and let the air take me up. And there I went. And there for a little while I stayed, until someone told me to stop. I'm pretty sure it had a lot to do with the dream: the dream gave me what I needed, that feeling, and then I just had to let it happen while I was awake, once I felt ready.

After I'd come down, Dennis bounced into the room and serially pelted me with three whiffle balls. "Mom said you were up on the ceiling! Were you climbing on the tree? If you break it, I'll break your legs, you little twerp. It's almost Christmas, and you'd better not ruin it, or I'll ruin you."

My life was like that a lot in those days.

Mother or Dennis would always yell at me about something. Dad never did, though.

The second time I flew was in the summer following that Christmas. I'd had the flying dream the night before, and again I was standing in the living room. I was watching TV when the feeling returned. Dennis was away at some kind of summer camp, and my parents were in the back yard planting roses, so I felt comfortable just letting myself float upward, and that time I drifted right up to the ceiling. I tried the swimmer's crawl stroke to get going forward, but all I accomplished was scraping my knuckles on the paint. That made me anxious, and I began to sink, so I just kicked a little with my feet and used the breaststroke, and that got me right back to the top again. I was floating, getting a good like at a spider that had crouched in one of the corners, when Mother's voice surprised me—I had been concentrating and hadn't heard her come in.

"There's that boy again!" she shouted. "Didn't I tell you once to get down from there? Do I have to keep telling you? People don't just go floating in the air like plastic balloons. Gilbert, come in here and see what your son is doing!"

I hadn't realized that telling someone not to do something once meant that he shouldn't do it again for ever and always.

When she addressed my father about me, Mother always called me "your son," as though she'd had nothing to do with me. I was more curious than worried about what my father would say. I turned around and faced them both as my father came in from the kitchen.

He stood there and looked at me for a few seconds with his hands on his hips. Then a little smile crossed his face, and he shook his head a couple times.

"Darndest thing," he said, looking at me. "Better come down, Lewis. You don't want to upset your mother. Look, how do you do that, son? No, don't tell me. That might spoil it. Didn't somebody give him a book of magic for Christmas? If you don't have enough to do, Son, you can come outside and help me plant the rest of the roses—I think it's got too hot for your mother out there. I'll get you some ice water, Hon. Do you know where that other clipper went? It used to be in the utility drawer next to the trowel."

Mother tried to stare a hole through me, but when Dad brought her some water, she took a sip, stretched out on the couch, put her hand over her forehead, and closed her eyes with a long, sorrowful sigh. "What are we going to do with this son of yours?"

"You know, I think I saw Grandma do that once," Dad said.

"Don't encourage the boy," Mother said, groaning.

By that time I had drifted back down to the floor, so I followed Dad out back to help with the roses. Later, in the evening, I found him in the living room reading his newspaper, holding it up like a shield.

"I'm sorry I was flying, Dad. It's not so much that I want to do it"—I said that at the time, trying to be penitent. "The feeling to do it just happens." I tell you truly, I was doing my best to feel bad about it, if for no other reason than to please Mother.

He glanced overtop of his paper at me for just an instant, then re-covered his face with the Times. "Don't worry about it, Son. Darndest thing. I'm sure you'll get over it when your hormones kick in." I thought I heard him chuckle.

I had no idea what that meant. To him it must have seemed like one more things boys do to irritate their mothers. When I went off to bed that I night, I overheard Mother saying to Dad, "You'd better have a talk with that boy. We can't have him floating around the house like a ghost." Dad said, "Okay," but Mother spoke loudly enough that I could hear, so Dad knew he didn't really need to say anything more. At that point I, of course, resolved to keep flying, but to try to do it outside or when Mother wasn't around.

About a week later I acquired a friend—they were scarce in those days. We'd never had a pet. Dennis had often asked for a Rottweiler or a Doberman, but both parents had agreed, for once, on "no" to that—but one night I woke up listening to a very strange sound outside my bedroom window. I opened the window and looked out, and in the darkness I could just see a cat sitting on a low roof ledge on the next-door neighbors' house, which was only about three feet from ours—in our neighborhood the builders had stuffed the houses in together almost like books on a bookshelf. The cat was making such a howl that I couldn't believe it hadn't wakened everyone else, too. I slipped outside as quietly as I could and walked to a spot underneath where the cat had perched itself like some sort of night bird. I was going to float up to get it, but before I could, it jumped—I don't think it flew—down into my arms, the skinniest and most bedraggled little fellow I'd ever seen.

Trying to figure out what to do with it, I took it to the back yard, which at least had some shrubs and plants where it might hide, but it had dug its nails into me and wouldn't let go. Seeing that I couldn't detach it, I brought it inside, took it to my room, and made a little bed for it out of my blanket, where it finally let me put it down. I padded back to the kitchen and got a little bowl and put some milk in it, just an ounce or two, and took it to the cat. The poor, skinny little fellow lapped it up, then promptly vomited it on my rug. I cleaned it up with some paper towels and soap and put the cat back in his bed, where he fell asleep. I got back in bed wondering what I'd do with him in the morning.

The first thing I did in the morning was to unstick the cat from my chest, where he had crawled up during the night. The next thing I did was clean up the poop he'd left of the floor. That was harder to do and even stinkier, but I had to do it. I got him a couple pieces of chicken from the cold-cuts drawer in the fridge, and he absorbed them and managed to keep them down.

Mother must have told Dennis about the cat as soon as he got home from camp. The morning after his return, he came into my room and punched me in the arm. "You're such a dork," he said. "You'll never have any real friends, not even a half-dead cat." He hit me once more, hard enough that it made a noticeable sound, and then he walked out. He passed Mother on his way through the kitchen to the back door. I heard her say, "Try not to hit your brother. I know it's hard, but try. And remember: friend is just a word." I have no idea what she meant by that.

I won't go into the details of how the cat finally got permission to stay. I immediately got sentenced to extra chores for the remainder of the summer just for bringing him into the house. Dennis of course assured everyone that the cat was "toast" and would within days meet his doom whether he remained with us or not. Mother refused to do any sort of cleaning or feeding associated with the cat and insisted that she would throw him out bodily if he ever again made the howling sound that had brought about our introduction. Dad finally said, "You take your friends where you find them," shrugged, patted the cat and me on the head, and consumed himself with having his breakfast while he looked through the phone book for a vet. A visit to the vet took care of the howling, a litter box took care of the pooping on the rug, and a family schedule for pet duties took care of who would tend to what: to keep things simple, I was assigned all of them. No one else cared to name the cat. Not because of what Dennis said, but because of the color of his fur, I named him Toasty. Dennis proclaimed that I was a sissy and a dweeb for having a cat and not a dog that could kill people.

Toasty was a good friend indeed. He stayed with me through my high school years, as I learned more and more about what care-giving meant. When I left for college, Dad acquired clean-up duties while I was away. But Toasty pined, and I ended up taking him back to school with me, where we together we navigated lodging that permitted both of us. A year after I graduated from college, Toasty graduated from this life, and I will miss him always. I imagined his little spirit flying off to better climes and better times.

I flew once more that summer, the one when Toasty appeared, on a cool morning with blue skies and bright sun. I had climbed into the maple tree in front of our house and happened to look over the hedge into the yard across the street. Hannah lived over there, a little girl about my age, and at the time I had a crush on her. She had thick, soft, wavy brown hair that fell around her shoulders, and when she smiled, she looked really happy. She was sitting in the grass while two of her friends were playing badminton. One of them had knocked the shuttlecock onto the garage roof, and she was starting to cry.

I got down out of the tree and walked over. When I went through the opening in hedge, Hannah looked at me sadly and pointed at her crying friend, and then she turned and looked at the shuttlecock, which was sitting right on the edge of the roof as if it wanted to fall off, but couldn't quite. She looked back at me as though I should and would know what to do. Her friend was beginning to cry harder.

Well, I didn't know what to do, but before I realized what I was doing, I walked over to the garage and floated right up and got the shuttlecock. I dropped down softly and took it over and held it out to Hannah's crying friend.

Then she really started to cry: buckets and buckets with wails and wails that echoed around the yard like stereophonic sound. She waved her racket in the air a few times and dashed inside the house. The other friend stood there with full-moon eyes and her mouth wide open, and she had begun to tremble. I looked down at Hannah sitting on the grass, and she was smiling.

"Cool," she said, smiling, and that made me feel very happy.

Then Hannah's grandmother stuck her head at the window and scowled at me. "Stop showing off!" she barked at me, and she closed the window with a thud. The grandmother had been a grade-school teacher, I think, and she found boys showing off especially distasteful.

Hannah threaded her arm through mine and walked me back to the hedge. "Thank you," she said. "Better not upset Grandma any more today." Hannah was always a calm person. I wanted to touch her hair, but didn't.

When I got back across the street, I was going to climb the tree again: I'd seen a nifty bird's nest while I was up there. But Mother came storming out of the front door.

"Go play out back," she called, "and stop showing off to the neighbors!" Hannah's grandma must have called right away to complain about me. I tried not to let that bother me. I'd been having a nice day. The curious thing to me at the time was that I couldn't remember having had the flying dream the night before.

Flying outside turned out, usually, to be harder than flying inside. The energy feels more scattered. When I'm inside, I can feel a sense of increasing lightness right in my middle, but outside the energy seems to stray every which way. The next time I got it to work properly, I was walking in the woods: we had a woods just up the hill from where we lived, and by then I was old enough to go walking there by myself—at least Dad thought so. Mother would say something like, "God knows what he'll do up there," but Dad would say something like, "Look, Madge, he's a boy, and boys like to walk in the woods. It's good for them. They learn about things like trees and flowers and insects." Mother was into decorative trees and flowers, but she didn't care at all for insects, so Dad had almost overplayed his hand. "Stay out of trouble!" she shouted at me, and then she screech-growled and turned away. I nodded at Dad, who gave me a little wave of the hand to say "Better get going."

In a small clearing among some oak and buckeye trees: I worked it out there first. Because of the canopy, I think, it didn't feel so different from being in a room in the house, just more full of different energy. Without having open ground where the energy could spread out, I relaxed and focused more easily. Of course that's the wrong way for me to say it, because the whole thing comes from a feeling, not from thinking or focusing. I had been walking around enjoying the place: that woods has a beautiful little stream that comes down off the top of the hill and lots of flowers and different grasses and many of the trees that you can find in this part of the world if you look around. Empty-headed and chewing the stem of a flower, I sauntered right into that clearing, maybe twenty or thirty feet across and shaped almost in a circle. The trees hadn't grown too tall there yet, and sun filtered in comfortably through the branches. I felt the feeling, and without much thought I reached up and with a little lift of my chest drew myself right up off the ground.

That was also the first day I flew with any speed, though even at that it wasn't very much, about an adult's fast walking pace for exercising. But I was also able to change height more easily: I could go well up into the trees or loop down to just about the normal height of my head above the ground. I didn't need to crawl about or swim in the air, just point myself in a direction and off I'd go. Even Mother couldn't have called that floating. The fact that no one else was around helped me a lot, and the birds didn't seem to mind at all. They went about their business, and I didn't bother them. I flew upside-down for a little bit, with my back toward the ground and my belly toward the sky, and that felt really good until I hit my head against a tree branch and fell to the ground. I felt stupid for taking flying for granted, so I ended up just going home. I couldn't get my feet off the ground for the rest of the day

The next incident of any consequence came about a year later, in the fall. I was shooting baskets next door: the neighbors had torn down their garage that used to sit back in the alley, and they had put up a basket for their son, who had since graduated from high school and gone away to college. They didn't mind if other kids played there as long as we didn't stay for too long or make too much noise and as long as we'd quit when they'd ask us to. I was getting a little taller and more athletic, but I still couldn't jump nearly high enough to touch the rim. One of my shots got stuck between the rim and the backboard, and I couldn't get it down. I couldn't jump and knock it out, but before I thought about what I was doing, I floated up and pulled the ball free. While I was up there, I happened to look over on top of our garage, and I spotted my baseball cap, which my brother had thrown up there a couple days before just to torture me. So I pushed off the basket, gave my body a little porpoise-twist in the air just for fun, and grabbed my hat off the roof. I was just floating, looking around, when Dennis came walking up the alley and spotted me.

"What are you doing up there, you little shit? Who do you think you are, Superman? Wo, look at my stupid little brother, floating around like he thinks he's Stupidman. Are you looking into people's windows, or what?"

Just to surprise him I flew down and landed right in front of him, almost on his toes. He fell back on his rear and looked up at me in shock. When I landed, I remembered that I'd had the dream again the night before, and I reached a hand down to help Dennis up.

"Woooo, can you really do that? Can you really . . . fly? I thought it was just some stupid joke."

I probably should have pressed my advantage, but I just can't get myself to do that sort of thing.

"Not always. Only sometimes."

"How do you do it? Can you teach me?"

"I don't know how. Sometimes it just happens. Usually I dream about it first, and the next day I can do it. Other times not at all."

"You're lying, you little wiener. You just don't want to show me. I should punch your lights out. Maybe then you'd just fly away and leave everybody alone."

That thought had never occurred to me, to fly away and leave everyone alone, but I filed it in my memory to think about it later.

"Do it again!" my brother said.

"I can't."

"Do it again," he insisted, and he pushed me hard in the chest so that I almost fell. "Do it again, or Mom and Dad will have to rename you Bloodynose, cause you'll have one for the rest of your life." Dennis pushed me again, and that time I did fall.

"I can't, really. I have to have the right feeling." Anger is definitely the wrong feeling to have if you want to fly.

"Feeling, stupid feeling. Get up and fly, or I'll kick you in the balls."

At that point I didn't fly, but I did get up and run. I could always run faster than Dennis, and I got to the back door well before he did. Mother was in the kitchen making supper. I dashed for my room, and Dennis threw the back door open wide open when he came in after me.

"Stop that, you boys!" Mother yelled. "Lewis, did you do something to make Dennis angry? Came back here and apologize."

"Yeah, come and apologize," Dennis muttered.

But I closed my door tight and put my desk chair up underneath the knob to hold it tight, and I didn't go to the kitchen until Dad got home and called me himself.

Supper started quietly, until about halfway through Dennis said, "Lewis won't teach me how to fly."

From the look on Mother's face, you'd think he'd said "I caught Lewis riding a rhinoceros bareback through the rose beds." Dad just looked perplexed.

Mother took another bite of potato, shook her head several times, and said, "Lewis, teach your brother how to fly if he wants to learn."

"I can't."

"Yes, you can. You think I don't know things, but I've seen you do it when you think no one is looking. When I told you to wash the windows out back, I saw you float right up and scrub bird droppings off the glass way up high." She was right; I'd forgotten about that.

"I mean I can't teach him, because I don't know how to do it. The feeling just comes, and I do it. I've tried to do it by thinking about it, and nothing happens."

"That's because you don't think hard enough and because you don't want to help your brother. Sometimes you're not a very nice boy, Lewis. You're just selfish."

Dennis was glowing with pride, happy enough that he forgot for a little while about not flying and basked in the joy of my getting a scolding. After supper Mother said, "Now, Lewis, you just go to your room and stand in the corner and think about why you're so mean to your brother."

I went back to my room happily enough, but I didn't stand in the corner.

I felt gleeful about not getting kicked in the balls. I thought about my clearing in the woods, and in a little while I floated right up to the top of the room, and I just plastered myself against the wall and the ceiling for a while. Toasty watched me, but didn't say anything. A little later I heard Dad say, "Don't be so hard on the boy, Madge." But she wouldn't have any of that; "He has to learn to be generous, especially with his own brother," she said.

A little while later Dad knocked at my door. He opened it and found me hanging out on the ceiling. "Son, come on down and listen to the baseball game with me on the radio. We'll make some popcorn."

About a month after that, with my brother's urging, I got pressure to demonstrate my unusual skill. Dennis had gone to the Harmon Falls highschool football coach and told him he had a secret that could really help the football team. Dennis's one weakness was football: he loved to play it, to watch it, to talk about it, to pretend that I was a football he could throw and kick. Even Dennis had too much sense to go to the coach and say "I have a brother who can fly, and he can really help the team, but he'll only do it if you let me on the team, too!" which is what I'm sure he wanted to say. But somehow he had got an appointment and told the coach that if he would come to see, his doofus little brother had a special skill that could help the team win more games. The coach had called my father, who said maybe that was true, and he invited the coach to come over one evening to see for himself.

The coach did come over, and he was nice enough—I'm sure he had no expectations, especially after he got a look at me—but his visit was a disaster, because of course I couldn't perform. Dennis assured the man that I could fly. I hadn't had the dream since the night before the incident with Dennis, and the best I could do was a Michael Jackson move, standing there on my toes. I couldn't summon the feeling and couldn't get myself into the air at all. The coach thanked all of us and shook our hands, but said he didn't know what to do with someone who could stand on his toes, since that wouldn't especially help his football team. "Not sure what we could do with a flyer, either, unless he's really fast: too much football field to cover!" He may have been trying to find a way to make me feel better.

That night Dennis gave me the meanest look I have seen in this lifetime, and I think the only reason he didn't kill me is that at bedtime I climbed out the window of my room, eased my way up the side of the house using various footholds and handholds and spent the night huddled on the roof.

Not long after that, though, Dad redeemed my life from Dennis's wrath with a better idea. Without telling me, he told Dennis that they should try again, but the second time with the basketball coach. Dad was almost as dedicated a fan of basketball as Dennis was of football, and they both must have realized that the applications for basketball looked more immediate and obvious. Someone who could float and hover could either block the opponent's way to their basket or stand by his own goal and drop the ball in rather than having to shoot over defenders. Now that could win games. Dad was assuming, too, that if I tried hard enough, I could learn to fly whenever I wanted to. I've never been able to convince anyone who has seen me do it that flying isn't that easy. You'd think they'd understand that.

But I don't blame Dad. He'd seen me once out back dunking a basketball. He thought I'd jumped, and that after the dunk I was hanging on the rim, but then he watched a bit more and saw that I'd just float up, drop the ball in, and then hang out up there for a while longer to look around. Dad did love his basketball—still does.

So one day he asked me to let him know the next time I had the dream. That seemed a reasonable enough request, though I had no idea why he'd want to know. So I did it. The dream happened to come on a Saturday morning, an especially good one (both the morning and the dream), where I stayed in the air for a long time and flew around with some speed and grace, more than I could ever remember doing before. Mostly the dreams went just like the waking experience: I would rise up a bit and then paddle along like I was floating on a slow stream.

At breakfast I told Dad about the dream, and he just said, "Okay, good," but I thought I saw out of the corner of my eye Dennis giving a fist pump. Mother said, "Gilbert, why do you want to encourage those silly dreams?" Mother didn't love basketball or football, or tennis or volleyball or even bowling.

A little bit later I was sitting in my room reading a book, I think it was H. G. Wells' " The First Men in the Moon," when Dad knocked at the door and asked if I wanted to walk down to the park to shoot some hoops. What kid's going to say no to that? "Look, Lewis, let's go to that little park right at the bottom of the hill below the woods. It's got a good basket and backboard and lots of trees around. We'll shoot some baskets, and then we'll go to the Dairy Queen and get a milkshake. Whatayasay?" Again, who would say no, so he got the basketball, and the two of us went to the park, talking about what a nice day it was.

Dad didn't tell me that Dennis had gone to get the basketball coach and that they'd be watching us from a distance.

So Dad and I were having a nice time, and Dad had never objected to my flying, and he never got mad if I missed shots or even if once or twice while we played I'd float up and block his shot, so before long I was lifting off the ground as naturally as could be. I had no idea anyone else was watching, so I felt no anxiety, but I also felt no desire to fly very fast or very far.

At one point Dad said, "Look, Lewis, do you think you can fly from that basket down to the other end of the court?"

I thought I could, so holding the basketball with one hand I gave myself a push of the backboard with the other and began to make a leisurely pace down court.

"Do you think you can dribble as you go, Lewis?"

I thought about it, couldn't imagine how to get the ball to bounce that high, and floated back toward the basket where we'd been playing. Then I heard another voice.

"Look at that, Mr. Phelps! I told you he could do it! I told you!" I heard Dennis shouting as he and the basketball coach approached, and I dropped gently to the ground, not having to try very hard to figure out what was going on. "I wish he'd teach me how to do it. Flying's wasted on that boy."

The coach shook hands with my father, and then the three of them stood there looking at me, Dennis with gleeful hopes of exploitation, the coach with a look of puzzled consideration, and Dad with a perplexed half-smile, not sure if he should feel proud or protective of his peculiar son.

"Well," the coach said, "he has an unusual talent, no mistake about that.

But I'm not sure how we'd use it. Lewis, how long can you stay up there, and can you jump up quickly, or do you always just float, like what we just saw?"

"Not very long," I answered. "Sometimes for a little bit, but sometimes I'll come right back down. I can jump a little bit—I can touch the rim now—but that's different than flying. I sort of float up and around when it feels right, but I can't always do it."

"We met with Coach Sayers, and Lewis wouldn't fly at all for him," Dennis blurted out.

"You wouldn't fly for the football coach?"

"I tried, but I can't always do it. Not when I'm nervous or when the energy isn't right."

"Ah," said the coach. "Well, even if you could fly in front of the fans, we couldn't have you just sit in the air in front of the opponent's basket: the refs would call goal-tending. And if you can't fly any faster than that, you could do better by running up and down the court and jumping. And if you tried to float up like that to shoot the ball or dunk it, the opposition could defend easily enough just by claiming you were traveling. Don't get me wrong, I think this is great stuff. I've certainly never seen anyone do it. But I don't think we can use it on the basketball team. Can you shoot pretty well and play defense?"

"So-so. I try hard."

"Well, when you're ready, if you want to try out for the basketball team, you'll be welcome, but I think we'll have to stick to regular playing and leave out the flying."

At that Dennis let out a string of cursing that, when she heard about, made even Mother angry. Dad blushed, and the basketball coach didn't quite know what to say, so he just nodded good-bye and left Dad to deal with it.

Dennis screamed and came after me—he would have taken me down right there on the basketball court if Dad hadn't grabbed him and held on until Dennis finally cooled off. Eventually Dad let go of him, and he insisted on walking ten feet in front of us all the way home, saying things like, "What a stupid brother I got stuck with," and, "How's a guy supposed to get ahead around here?"

Dad took me to the Dairy Queen anyway and bought me a cool, creamy vanilla shake. That was my favorite at the time, and it made me feel a little better.

I didn't end up going out for the basketball team. I did play baseball, but never flew in or around a game—though a couple times it helped me jump higher to catch a ball that was headed over the outfield fence. For the most part everyone forgot about my flying, except for me. Dennis had given up on me after the basketball incident, and for the next three years he didn't speak to me, which was good, because he mostly stopped beating on me. I would fly a little now and then for recreation, but once I got to high school, a whole new set of anxieties broke in on my life, and I began dreaming about girls instead of flying, so I most stopped thinking about it, too.

During my freshman year of college I flew once accidentally.

I had gone to the college bookstore to get my textbooks, and I overheard a clerk telling her boss she couldn't remember where she'd left a box of class rings, and the boss was getting upset, because those rings are expensive. I happened to be looking around the upper shelves for a text I needed, and I spotted the edge of the box: someone had left it on top of one of the bookcases, and just the edge of it was sticking out. I could have gone over and told them I thought I'd spotted the box, but without thinking, I just floated up and got it. You see, I'd had the dream the night before, and though I hadn't been thinking about it, the feeling came right back to me. Once I'd got the box, I dropped right back down and walked over and handed it to the clerk.

The boss looked at me and screeched, "Where did you get that! Were you trying to steal it? I'll have Campus Security after you!"

Three sorority girls and a large football-player type wearing a letter jacket with fraternity letters on the back had come over to watch the fracas.

"He didn't steal it," the clerk said. "I saw him: he floated up and got it off the top of the bookcase. Now I remember that's where I left it. I went up on the ladder to get an old volume of Sherlock Holmes stories that somebody had left up there: a patron wanted it. And I set the box down there and forgot about it."

"Floated? What do you mean he floated? People don't float, except on water."

"He did. Thanks," the clerk said, and she patted my wrist.

"You," the boss said to the clerk, "get back to work before I fire you. And you," she said to me," "get out of this bookstore, and don't come back unless you want to get arrested! Sneakthief." She turned on her heel and stalked off. She reminded me a little of Mother.

Now that, the namecalling, got me upset, and without realizing it I began floating again, and in an instant I was bouncing around the ceiling like a very, very slow tennis ball. I heard some bubbling sounds from below. The sorority girls, all dressed in the same style jeans and sweatshirts with their three Greek letters across the front, had begun to giggle.

"What do you think you're doing up there, kid?" the football player said. "Watch this, Lisa."

He was quite tall, and he caught me by the ankle and gave me a push across the room. Before I could stop myself, I'd flown into a display of stacked cups, and a number of them fell to the floor and broke with a percussive crash.

The girls and their football player were all laughing, and of course the boss came storming over. "Now you've done it! I'm calling Security right now, and you'll pay for this!"

"Try to stay out of trouble, junior," the football player said, and he waved to the girls and left. One of the girls said to the others, "Did you see that, though: he was flying! Well, not exactly flying, but sort of floating."

"Not possible," the second one said.

"Not possible for a geek like him," the third said.

"He's not very tall," the first one said, flipping her hair to one side.

"Not very handsome, either," the second one said, also flipping her hair.

"Must be some kind of physics experiment," the third one said. Her face scrunched up, and she almost looked me in the eye. "Nerd," she said, turning up her nose and flipping her blonde curls. Then the three of them flounced away.

"I hope they make him pay for the cups," the first one said on their way out the door.

The clerk came up to me. "Sorry you got into all this trouble trying to help me. I'm off shift and I have to go to class now. The floating trick is pretty neat, though." She left, and I never saw her again.

Running away didn't seem to me to make any sense, so I just waited. In a couple minutes two hefty Campus Security guards arrived. The boss screamed about how I'd been causing all sorts of trouble, that I'd probably been stealing, and that I'd certainly broken some expensive college-logo cups that the bookstore would have a hard time replacing.

The guards looked at me as though what they really wanted was to try out their new self-defense skills on me, but they realized I looked pretty downtrodden and harmless.

"Did you try to steal something?" the first one asked.

"No," I said, "I wouldn't do that."

"Did you break these cups?" the second asked.

"Yes," I said reluctantly. I knew I couldn't explain what had happened. "I just came in to get a textbook. It was an accident. I'll pay for them."

"I know you will. Come on to the station: we'll have to write up a report. You'd better borrow that book from a friend, if you have one."

Security did write me up, and then they let me go, but I got into no more trouble for the rest of college, so nothing bad came of it beyond a couple days of not eating because I had to pay for the cups (which weren't really very expensive) and so had no money for food. I didn't fly again, except for a couple times in the summer when I was home and walking in the woods, until my senior year. I was working pretty hard in those days between classes and a couple jobs I got to help with tuition and room, and I had a different sleep cycle than when I was younger, so I seldom had the dream at all, or at least couldn't remember it.

About a week before graduating I was taking final exams. I'd spent most of those last college days studying in the library. I had a favorite table I used as long as no one else was there: it sat right by a high window, and from there you could watch the seasons change. That May afternoon the weather had warmed up, and the grass had turned green, and leaves were gradually filling the trees. I love the clean smell of spring, when the decay of the leftovers from fall and winter has faded, and the sweetness of growth spreads in gentle waves.

So I went out for a walk. By that time I had only one exam remaining, and I'd done about all I could to prepare for it. I let myself drift, not walking to any particular place or in any specific direction—other than opposite to Fraternity and Sorority Row.

A few clouds had gathered, so that the sky alternated between grey-white and bright blue.

As you walk through the south end of campus to where the college's land ends, a number of small streets fan out into rows of old houses that landlords rent to students and laboring people. One heavily tree-lined street leads down a steep hill to a woods with a stream at the bottom. Just before the woods stands an old retreat center, a sturdy, rustic building with a large lounge, a kitchen, and small meeting rooms. Some of the college organizations would still meet there, but usually the building was empty. I liked it because it was made of old wood and had tall windows and unusual angles, and in back it had an enclosed yard with a basketball hoop, a volleyball court, and a tether-ball pole. I found myself headed there, and as I walked downhill my feet began to feel light.

In the back yard of the one of the houses I saw a girl I knew from Asian History class. She was standing by a picnic table with two of her friends, and they were spreading out food across the table top. I waved. She looked a little surprised, almost confused, but tentatively waved back. I thought she recognized me from class, but I didn't imagine that she knew my name. After that I didn't spot anyone along the street the rest of the way down. But the long walk down—the streets move downhill for nearly half a mile—had begun to make me feel the lightness not only in the pit of my stomach, but also in my head, which started to spin. I remember that I hadn't eaten anything since a piece of wheat toast with butter for breakfast.

I turned back behind the retreat center, and as I reached the open part of the yard, a thick cylinder of golden light fell right down on the grass. Before I realized what I was doing, I was rising up into it. I must have gone about ten or twelve feet up, and I lay on my back and began making circles of about eight feet in diameter, floating happy as could be. After a pleasant time, I made a move like a diver doing a straight-bodied back flip into a pool, and I landed gently on my feet, realizing that I was finally beginning to enjoy my flying, maybe even wanted to do it.

"What in the world was that?" I heard a voice say behind me.

I turned, and there was the girl from Asian History class.

"What was what?" I asked.

"That: what you were doing. You were flying! I saw you!"

"Sort of."

"What do you mean sort of? You were flying. I saw it! Do you always do that?"

"No, not very often."

"Did you learn that in a class, some kind of gymnastics or karate?"

"No, it's nothing like that. I can just do it sometimes."

"Do you know other people who can do it? Did someone teach you?"

"No, I didn't really learn it. One day I just did it. Not much anymore."

"That must be so much fun!"

"Yes, I guess so."

"You should teach people to do it. You could make millions of dollars."

I guessed she must be a business major.

"I wouldn't know how to teach it. It's just something I feel sometimes. It's not really good for anything. I can't use it for football or basketball or anything. When I use it to try to help someone or to do something useful, I get into trouble."

"But it's amazing! I've never seen anything like it before."

"Thank you."

"Sorry to interrupt. I saw you walking down the hill and I recognized you from class. I thought you might want to have some lunch with us, me and my friends."

"Thank you. Do you know what time it is?"

She looked at her watch and told me.

"I have an exam in about half an hour, so I'd better not, but thanks for asking."

She walked back up the hill with me as far as her house, chattering away, and I said good-bye and walked back to the library. I didn't really have an exam then, not for another couple hours—I felt sorry about lying, because she had been very nice—but I couldn't see myself sitting there having lunch and trying to explain to strangers how I fly.

I finished my exam, graduated from college, and never saw that girl again.

After I graduated, I got a job back home working for UPS for a few months. Then I got an offer to join a computer start-up in marketing and product development in a suburb of The City. Not that I was all that hot on computers, but the pay looked good, and I liked the town where I'd be living. Dad moved me up, and Mother made us peanut butter and red lettuce on whole wheat sandwiches (still one of my favorites) to eat on the way. Dennis reluctantly helped me pack—he had taken a job at the dairy right there in Harmon Falls and was renting the upstairs of a house a couple blocks from our parents'.

When Dad dropped me off at my new place, a nice-sized apartment in a four-unit building by some woods, he said, "Look, Lewis, you're not that far away if you need something. Call. Don't be a stranger."

That was a while ago. I'm married now. I met a musician who was playing with her alt-band at a bar-restaurant not far from where I work. They performed her compositions, which as far as I could tell came out different every time they played them. She'd mix passages from Classic melodies with jazz riffs, bits of folk music, and all sorts of strange percussion. I heard them play a few times there and at some other places around town, and one evening between sets I went up to talk to her as she was arranging and rearranging drums and rhythm tools that looked an assortment of toadstools, tree stumps, party favors, and art-workshop cast-offs. One of her friends played base, another did baritone sax, and the third used either an electric keyboard or a series of metal triangles.

I asked her how they managed to make the music feel so light and mobile, how they could take a bunch of heavy instruments and make sounds like wind over a mountain or springs of water when they melt at the end of winter or columns of light that pour through the clouds.

She liked the question and talked to me for a while about her ideas and why she loved to make music so much.

I understood and said nothing more, just listened.

The next time I heard her, the band was playing in a little theater downtown in The City. I didn't go there often, to The City, but I went especially to hear her play again, hoping she would talk to me some more about her thoughts and her compositions.

The crowd was a little rough that night, but the music was amazing, dancing around as if the whole building had come alive and was about to rise off the ground and float. I hadn't flown in quite a long time, hadn't got the feeling, but I got it that evening from her music. I had to make a special effort and grab my chair with both hands to stay in my seat and not float straight up to the ceiling.

She must have noticed me while she was playing, because right as they broke after the first set, she came out into the audience and sat next to me and began telling me about a new piece she was composing for clarinet, three bongo drums, a banjo, a potato masher, and a three-foot bamboo flute.

After the show she asked me if I'd help them load the instruments in their van and if she could get a ride home with me—she lived less than a mile from where I did. All the way back she talked about her new song, and she asked me lots of questions about what I thought of the ideas and sound combinations. I couldn't have helped much, because though I like music, I know nothing about it. At one point she said, "When I make music, sometimes I almost feel like I can fly. Does that seem crazy?"

"Not to me."

When I dropped her off, and just as I was thinking that she and I might be friends, she took hold of both my hands and kissed me. It wasn't a quick thank-you kiss. She lingered for a while. I don't know of anything in my life up to that time that felt better than that kiss, warm, moist, fully present—better even than flying, and that feels pretty good.

Her name is Christie.

To this day I don't think that she's ever seen me fly, though she may have. We've never talked about it. I've done it a few times since we first got together, but only at home when I felt sure I was alone or out in the woods far from other people. I almost got caught once when I got a neighbor's cat off her roof. She must have jumped from a nearby tree and couldn't get herself to jump back. So without thinking I just floated up and got the cat, who seemed grateful though she dug her claws tightly into my shoulder as I brought her down. She wasn't like Toasty: she felt firm and healthy. The neighbor, who may have been looking out the window when I left the ground, thanked me when I brought the cat to her door, but either she knew how I got it, she didn't want to ask me how I'd got it, or she didn't care.

Time has flown by, and Christie and I have a daughter, little Beatrice. Now I live with my two best friends. Beatrice is walking well already, and yesterday when we were in the back yard I watched as she was reaching up to try to touch a butterfly. I think that for a moment her feet just barely left the ground, and she hovered there, floating.

Suggs and The City

"There is nothing on this earth to prize beyond friendships."
—Thomas Aquinas

Ezekiel Suggs worked in a little auto shop up in the north end of town with my friend Lenny. Lenny called him Zeke, but nearly everyone else called him Suggs. Suggs was a year or two older than we were, but you couldn't really tell by looking at him. He had a slight build and wasn't very tall. You wouldn't especially notice him in a crowd. He always wore the usual blue work shirt, jeans, black Converse sneakers, and a baseball cap that he placed backwards on his head, the way a catcher would wear it. Lots of kids do that now, but only catchers and working people who wanted to keep the bill out of the way did it then. If you'd see Suggs after work, then his clothes would look dirty. If you'd see him before work, they would look clean. That was the only difference you'd notice in his appearance from day to day.

But I can assure you: with respect to auto repair, he was a genius.

Give him the right-sized tools, or the opportunity to adapt any other tools to fit, and he could repair anything automotive. Anything, even Japanese or German or Italian cars before they became popular enough that many garages would take them and might possibly fix them.

In his senior year of high school, Suggs was voted the Most Likely Never to Move from the House He Grew Up In.

In my senior year I was voted the Most Likely to Be Voted the Most Likely Never to Do Anything in Particular. But that's another story, and since it has nothing to do with Suggs, I won't tell it here.

Not that it was much of a house, the one Suggs lived in: a light-blue frame affair near the bottom of the steep hill where Lenny and Lana lived up closer to the top. The front yard, which mostly looked like an uncombed mop of green hair, had a chain-link fence and a few tires and odd auto parts tossed about, but otherwise it didn't look all that different from most houses in that part of town. Young Suggs himself gave the house a paint job every couple years. It had a concrete porch with no cracks in it and some decorative black railing, and Suggs's mother hung flower baskets along the length of it. The short back yard, abbreviated by the rising of the hill behind, always had at least one auto body up on blocks—you could see it if you were coming up from the south, but not from the front of the house. You can't really blame Suggs or his family for that: his father had to have some way to teach his son the family trade. The Suggs family, male and female, had been repairing cars since the days of the Model-A. They kept a small repair shop in a tumbledown garage at the northwest end of their yard. The garage had "Suggs" painted in white letters over the large door, not even "Suggs Auto." I guess everybody in town knew that anything "Suggs" also meant cars. That sign may be why people called him Suggs rather than Zeke.

Suggs's ancestors had moved to Harmon Falls from one of the deep hollows in the mountains of West Virginia back around the 1900s. I'd heard more than one person say they had cousins involved in running moonshine, but I never saw any reason to believe that. They were a clean and even slightly Puritanical-looking lot. They seldom smiled, but if you walked or drove by and they were sitting on the porch at the time, which almost everyone in Harmon Falls did most evenings if they weren't at the park watching baseball or softball or at the football field, the Suggs family would invariably wave hello. They weren't much for long conversations, but that doesn't make them unfriendly—just shy.

If Suggs hadn't been voted the award he got, about living in the same house, he probably would have won instead the Least Likely Ever to go to The City, Not No Way, Not No How.

But things don't always work out the way you'd expect.

I learned that fact early in life and have re-learned it many times since.

In Harmon Falls people thought of The City with both excitement and trepidation. To them it was a place of possibilities and of horrors, of money and sin, of excitement and terror at the same time. Most people talked about it at one time or another, but few actually went there. In the old days Harmon Falls was a small-town person's small town. In more recent years its economy has taken a deep-water dive, and from that dive it has never emerged.

In those days, when I still lived there, people tended to grow up, live, and die where they were born, not to move to one place to work and then still another to grow old and die. Their town was their town. I'll bet you know places like that, too.

No one would have guessed that Suggs ever thought about The City at all. Like the rest of his family, he wasn't the sort of fellow who ever said very much, except when he was talking about automobile engines. But after he went to The City, I believe no one ever heard him ever again say anything more than "hey," "'bye," "uh-huh," "huh-uh," and "cash only, please."

That's right—you guessed it: of all people, Suggs did go to The City.

Odder yet, he went to The City to visit a college, or, more exactly, a university.

Suggs wouldn't have struck you as a university man—maybe the local Branch campus for automotive tech or that sort of thing. But then by the time he was seventeen, he probably knew more than any two of their instructors together. He could have taught courses rather than taken them.

Well, someone at the Tech University, a big-shot place in The City, had sent him a letter suggesting that he apply, and so he did. He took the whole thing absolutely seriously. No one exactly laughed at him, at least not that I saw, but nearly everyone guessed that the University had made a mistake. Not that Suggs wasn't smart, only that everyone wondered how the Tech University had found out about a car-repair specialist from a small town whose only interest in school was getting through it so he could get back to his shop to work on cars.

Only my friend Lenny believed that the University was at last, for once, showing that they had some smart people: he believed Suggs was among the most brilliant people he had ever known. As I said, Suggs could fix just about any car from anywhere, and if he didn't have the proper tool, he could find it or jerry-rig it, and in many cases Lenny had seen him do it. Suggs could fix a car and get it running when no one else in town would touch it even for scrap.

Here's what I think happened with the University: I believe that Montmorency McGee, or maybe her parents, called them and practically ordered them to send Suggs application materials. She had a big crush on him when we were in high school. To look at the two of them, you'd never guess such a thing would happen. Though her folk had also come up from Appalachia, she had been born with the look of nobility about her: something in the long, even, balanced structures of her face and her upright posture and balletic way of walking required that everyone notice. You can never tell who will end up with traits like that, regardless of parentage.

Montmorency didn't make homecoming queen, but she was chosen as a member of the court, even though her mother had a hairdressing salon and her father was a mill hand. Usually those honors went only to the children of better-off families, those with an important parent, someone my Italian uncle would call a "bigga shotta." She had great hopes for Suggs far beyond anything he hoped for himself, and she believed that with the right motivation—in her mind, that meant her affection and encouragement—he could become a great man: an engineer, a designer of futuristic vehicles rather than a repairman of old, dingy ones. She felt certain he could grow into someone worthy of a girl who had made the Homecoming Court. Montmorency thought she was the one to make a real man of Suggs, a somebody with money and professional status. Well.

One evening I was sitting on the porch at home reading by the last light of the setting sun when Lenny showed up.

"Do you think Zeke should go up to The City to visit the university?" He didn't say hello, just that. Lenny was the only one who called him Zeke, except for me when I was hanging out with Lenny, so I tried to answer in a way he'd consider respectful.

I didn't know what to say, so I thought about it for a minute.

"Zeke? What would he study?" I asked.

"I don't know," Lenny said, leaving his mouth open after he stopped speaking. "Maybe engineering. Don't they teach auto engineering up there?"

"Well, he's worked on just about every sort of car that's been made, customized, or imagined," I said. "I thought he wanted to be a mechanic like his dad. But I don't see why he couldn't go up and study to be an engineer if he wants to. He's a smarter guy than people think."

A big smile crossed Lenny's face.

"Yep," he said, "just what I was thinking. Thanks!" And he took off at a run.

I don't know that I really believed what I'd just said, but it seemed to me the right thing to say at the time. As I worked it over in my mind, The City seemed exactly the wrong place for Suggs, but who was I to say that? I'd only heard about The City—hadn't ever even visited there myself. To me it was a place of myth, legend, and sports teams. I'd been reading Sherlock Holmes when Lenny came up, and I remembered Holmes saying something like, "It's a cardinal mistake to reason without data," and that seemed like a pretty good warning to me. My mother had often said to me, "If you can't say something nice, then don't say anything." I was a kid and didn't always remember that at the time, but I often have since. I hoped that what I said to Lenny, which I intended to be something nice, wouldn't do more harm than good.

Suggs had got hold of a '73 Plymouth Duster at the auto shop—the one with the slant-6 engine and that looked like a sharp-edged, stretched-out Valiant—yes, that one. It looked like the sort of car a poor, small-town boy who wanted but couldn't afford a Mustang might get. An older guy who had got into a drag race outside of town against a Super Bee had run that Duster off the road and banged it up pretty badly, so he had sold it to young Suggs for $350: repairing it would have cost more than the value of the car.

Anyone else in the world could have told the guy in the Duster he had no chance—No Chance—in that race, but guys, young or older, do stupid things. I once ran a race—on foot— against a guy driving a Chevy Vega. It was only a forty-yard sprint, and the driver was a friend who was really proud of his new car. Most of us didn't have a car of any sort. I won the race that day, but I lost a friend: he never forgave me for beating his car. He was proud of that car. Well, Suggs was prouder yet of his Duster.

Suggs worked on that car lovingly, piece by piece, until it really didn't look too bad—for its time, that is. If you'd see one today, you'd laugh at it and wonder why anyone ever made anything that looked like that—or why anyone would buy it. To tell you the truth, I'd have been glad enough to have one back then since, as the joke says, like Moses and Joshua and Jesus, everywhere I went, I walked. Suggs banged out all the dents, rebuilt the engine, buffed the interior until it was immaculate, added a racing steering wheel and a spoiler on the trunk and fresh, whitewall tires, and he painted the whole thing jet black with silver-grey accents and red flame-shapes feathered back along the sides. He came to love that car, and it would turn a fair number of heads when he'd drive it around town, at least until folks realized it was only a Plymouth Duster.

So after I said what I said, Lenny ran right to the Suggs's garage and gave his buddy a long pep-talk. After that, Zeke went inside and had a heart-to-heart with his father around the kitchen table. Lenny later told me that the two of them stayed up talking almost all night. Guessing the content of their conversation doesn't take much intelligence.

I'm thinking about college, Dad, young Suggs must have begun. Why? old Suggs must have asked. Because they had written to him, not he to them, and some other people he trusted thought he should go. Was he sure he wanted to go? No, the son probably replied. But he'd like to do something to make his family proud of him. They were already proud of him: wasn't he the best car repairman in town, and not even out of high school yet? Maybe he could do something better yet, the son would have speculated: design cars that would be faster and safer to drive, that would burn less gas and last longer. Cars like that would cost too much, the father would have said, at least for folks like us to buy. But if I get to be an engineer, I'll make lots of money, and we can buy a better car and get a better house, the son would have countered. We're happy where we live now, Son. Wanting more is just greed, and that's sinful. Okay, Dad, I understand. But, Son, do you really want to go? I know lots of the kids are going now. Only rich kids went when I was your age, and not many from this town: just the doctor and dentist and lawyers, and the undertaker went to tech school, and the teachers went to teachers' college. I don't know what to tell you, Son. I don't know what to do, Dad. I'll help you all I can, Son. I know, Dad.

That, I suspect, was the gist of the conversation, though the Suggs family, being quiet types, must have taken about six hours to get through all that.

Sometime later Suggs told Lenny that his father had called the Tech University and talked with someone there, and they decided Zeke should go up for a visit before he committed to try to go there: an education at the TU cost a lot of money. That seemed to everyone a good idea, except to Zeke's mother, who insisted that The City was a sinful place, and no good Christian child should go there: they should all be happy to stay where God had the good sense to have had them born. Zeke and his father went through the finances together and decided the boy could probably afford two years if he kept busy all summer with repairs and saved his money, and his father would start taking more repair jobs again on the weekends. After that, they'd have to see what they could do. Maybe he'd do well enough to get some scholarships like the rich kids got. So they arranged for the high school to send an official copy of his records and waited for matters to take their course.

You can imagine how proud that made Montmorency, since she felt sure that once Suggs got to the University, he'd realize that every talented person should go there to get an education and become a contender, a somebody, not just a poor auto-jockey from a small-town, family-owned repair shop. Montmorency herself had no interest in studying cosmetology to work at her mother's shop or to learn secretarial skills to work at the mill: she intended to go to the Branch Campus to learn dental hygiene and work in a health profession, something more dignified. She persuaded Zeke to take her to the senior prom in the fall, and though poor Suggs looked as awkward as a warden at an ex-cons' convention, they claimed to have had a good time together.

You'd have thought that Montmorency would have ditched Suggs for some doctor's or lawyer's son if you'd have seen how spiff she looked in her prom dress and how hickish he looked in the five-dollar tux he bought at a yard sale. But she stuck with him, certain that the University and The City would make something out of this small-town genius. At the prom they even danced, holding onto each other and rotating in a small circle to "Knights in White Satin" and "Stairway to Heaven."

About a week after that, Suggs drove up to The City for the first time in his fancy Plymouth Duster to talk with a dean about an education.

He left very early on a Friday morning, proud of his car, taking his first-ever day off from school for his appointment at the University. He was supposed to return on Saturday evening.

He got back Tuesday night on the Greyhound Bus.

What actually happened I have been only partially able to reconstruct after years of bits and pieces of conversations with Lenny and some others who knew him, plus a few odd hints from Suggs himself. I always liked the guy, though I hadn't Lenny's knowledge to understand the depth of Suggs's automotive skills. As far as I can tell, Suggs's visit to The City went something like this.

The drive up went fine—Suggs was a skilled driver, not a motorhead—and he'd left an hour earlier than he thought he needed to so he'd be sure to get there on time. But once he got to The City, he had a hard time finding his way through poorly marked streets. He'd had no chance to get accustomed to city traffic, criss-crossing streets, and lanes that changed directions at certain times of day as traffic patterns reversed. His father had turned up an old City map, not realizing how much the streets and traffic load had changed in recent years. Suggs got lost twice, tried to stop at gas stations to get directions, got bad ones from people who didn't care, began to panic that he would miss his appointment, called the University from a phone both twice, and finally got to his appointment at the dean's office fifteen minutes late.

He parked in a twenty-minute-limit space, the only one he could find near the building where he had to go for his interview, and he had to dash down to put money in the meter twice while he waited for his dean to finish another meeting. The man turned out to be some sort of assistant or associate dean, and while he welcomed Suggs, he told him that his high school grades weren't good enough for acceptance to the Tech University, who kept the highest academic standards. He also said that Suggs would need to learn to get to his appointments on time.

The dean, apparently a learned man in his academic field, showed little sympathy when Suggs had to run outside once more to put money in the meter. Finally he told Suggs that he might try a junior college for a couple years and then apply at the University once he'd shown he could do college-level work and show college-level responsibility. Mechanical Engineering, he explained, required theoretical study well beyond the simplicity of auto repair. He shook Suggs's hand perfunctorily, wished him a safe trip home, and walked him out the door: he had another appointment he needed to get to. More rich kids to see, I'd guess, or an event at the Symphony Hall . . .

On their way out they passed the dean's assigned personal parking space right next to the building, and he waved to Suggs as he slid into his Jaguar. Suggs waited for a moment to find out what the engine would sound like: he'd never encountered a Jag before.

But the engine sounded like nothing, because the car wouldn't start.

The dean got out and looked, embarrassed, at Suggs. Then he asked if Suggs could give his car a jump. Suggs said no problem: he had cables in his trunk. When he got his car, he found a ticket on the windshield: time had run out on the meter. He drove his car over and parked it next to the dean's, partway on the sidewalk so he could apply the cables, and the dean turned his key.

Nothing happened.

The dean cursed a little and complained that he'd have to call a repairman and that he'd be late for his next appointment.

Suggs offered to have a look at the engine.

The dean laughed, saying that one doesn't just repair a Jaguar without experience: it's nothing like experimenting with simple American cars. Besides, the dean said, he had no tools with him.

Suggs had brought a tool box in his trunk—he carried it whenever he drove—and again offered to try.

The dean checked his watch, shrugged, and warned, "Don't mess it up."

Suggs disconnected the cables, got out his tools, and buried himself in that Jaguar engine.

The dean was starting to tap his foot, worried about his appointment, and was about to tell Suggs to give up messing around with his engine, when Suggs emerged, looked him in the eye, and said, simply, "Start 'er up."

The dean, disbelieving, figured he had nothing to lose, so he got in and turned the key.

The Jaguar started as smoothly and quietly as ever, if not a little better.

"I don't know how you did it, Son, but I'm impressed," the dean said.

Suggs explained in technical terms what he'd done, how he did it, and why it worked.

"Son," the dean said, "tomorrow I'm going to have another look at your paperwork. I'm going to find a way to get you admitted to this University."

Suggs was going to show the man the parking ticket, but the dean drove off hurriedly, pausing only to check the crosswalk and wave to Suggs.

Suggs went back up to the office to thank the dean's secretary—she was the one who over the phone had finally given him good directions to get there—and she had also arranged for him to meet some other people before he left. She also told him that he could park in the dean's spot for the rest of the day, since he wasn't returning until Monday—she'd give him a special pass. She said she couldn't help with the parking ticket: he'd have to take care of that at the security office. So Suggs got a brief tour of a library, a dormitory with a dining hall, a gymnasium, and some of the classroom buildings and laboratories where the engineering students took their courses. By the time the tour had ended, the security office had closed. The tour guide ran off to meet his fraternity brothers for dinner and left Suggs outside the dean's building with no idea of where to go from there.

Suggs's father had found him a hotel about a mile from the University: it was the cheapest place he could find, and he didn't understand why anyone would pay a penny more for a night's sleep than he had to. He didn't know that he'd booked a flea-ridden dustbin in a dangerous part of town with no parking lot and no security. Suggs drove around for about an hour trying to find it and finally did, but he had to keep driving to find a parking lot another couple blocks away.

Suggs took his satchel and walked back to the hotel—no more than a storefront in a tangled nest of semi-crumbling buildings. The hallway smelled of dust and mold, and the lobby smelled of worse, but he didn't know what to do other than check into his room. The clerk wore a visor, smoked a cigar, took the room fee in advance, and pointed to the stairs—he said nothing more to Suggs, and Suggs didn't know what else to ask.

The steps were creaky, the room dingy, and the floor was still dirty from previous guests: popcorn spilled on an ancient carpet marked with cigarette burns—it still smelled of smoke and sweat. The bathroom had only a commode, a sink, and an empty pitcher—the communal shower room was down at the end of the hall. He left his car keys in his satchel, left the satchel on a small, rickety nightstand: the satchel held only a change of clothes and a couple paperback books on auto repair that he liked to re-read before bedtime. He thought to lock the door—something he never had to do at home—and left his room to go out to find something to eat.

Down in the lobby the clerk had left his desk, but a tall man wearing a fur coat and a hat with a fancy feather sticking up out of the band was looking out the front window. He turned and addressed Suggs, asking what he was doing there and if he might help Suggs find anything he needed.

Suggs replied that he wanted to find a place to get supper.

The man insisted that he could do much better than that. He asked where Suggs had parked his car and promised to keep an eye on it. He said he would provide a nice dinner companion so Suggs wouldn't have to eat alone. And he would make sure the lobby was safe when he returned.

Suggs didn't like the sound of that last remark, but he had already paid for the room, and no one was around to give him his money back.

Then the man said he would do all that, and even get him a discount on dinner, for only twenty dollars. The man thrust out a beefy palm, and when he did so, his coat fell partly open, exposing a large hunting knife stuck in a sheath strapped around his middle. Suggs thought about running, but he had no clear idea of where he was or where he might run to. "Come on, Son," said the man. "I'm your friend. You'll see."

Suggs handed the man twenty dollars.

"Better service with a tip," the man said.

Suggs handed him another five.

The man was clearly hoping for more, but shrugged and smiled, deposited the money in his pocket, and said "Wait here." He walked down the short first-floor hallway and knocked on a door. Suggs noticed that he knocked three times, pausing briefly after each.

In a moment, the door opened, and a woman came out—or maybe just a girl.

She was slim, blonde—probably bleached—had a long, fake-fur coat thrown over her shoulders, and had very high heels that made her look taller than she was. She wore a very short skirt, and black stockings covered her thin but shapely legs. Her skin looked pale, but she seemed to be blushing. The man nodded his head toward Suggs, and she looked over as if to examine him. She smiled, but the smile looked to Suggs emptier than a midnight sky covered layers-deep with clouds. She looked back at the tall man, who shrugged.

"Hi," she said to Suggs, almost looking at him.

"Take him to Mama's for dinner," the man said in barely above a whisper, "and then come back." He placed his hand on the small of her back and directed her toward Suggs.

"My name is Sterling," she said. "What's yours?" Her voice sounded tired and detached. "Would you like to take me out to dinner?"

When he saw her up close, Suggs noticed the layers of make-up: they seemed to him aimed to cover up ill-health rather than because she wasn't pretty underneath. She might have been seventeen years old, or she might have been thirty. He also noticed a strong and cheaply alluring perfume, more designed to stimulate sexual desire than to suggest warmth and cleanliness. Suggs helped her put her arms through the sleeves of her coat, and they walked outside. Suggs had a strong feeling that he was doing something wrong, but he got so caught up in the mixture of loneliness, fear, loss, and desire for some kind of company and assurance, that he couldn't think through what to do. Sterling slipped her arm around his, and off they went. Having someone close to him felt good in a way, even as it also felt cheap and empty.

On the way to Mama's, the girl, Sterling, talked about her all favorite drinks, and she asked what he liked to drink—a topic designed probably to stimulate a teenage boy's appetite for the forbidden. Suggs replied that he didn't drink, which she claimed to find charming.

About a block away they found Mama's, another storefront operation not so different in feel from the hotel. The waiter, with a blank expression and no apparent interest in serving anyone, took them to a table in the back.

The service was slow, and the food was heavy and unsatisfying. Sterling talked on in a low voice about The City and the places she liked there. She ordered two cocktails, and she got Suggs to try a glass of beer. By the time they'd finished eating, he had drunk two glasses and was feeling tipsy and more than a little sleepy.

"Let's go back, dear," Sterling, nuzzling close and holding Suggs up by the elbow. "Pay the waiter, and we'll go to my room, and Sterling will take good care of you."

Suggs remembered some of what happened after that, but he didn't entirely remember how it happened. Sterling took him back to "her room," not his, helped him off with his clothes, and got him into bed. They must have had two go-rounds, and he was starting to fall asleep, until he heard her crying. She told him what a difficult time she was having in The City, how she had so little money and could hardly get by, and she would be so happy if he could just lend her some until she could get on her feet, and she would love him so much for helping her, and maybe they could have dinner together again. He gave her almost all the money he had left, and then he fell asleep.

Early in the morning, Suggs woke up. Someone had dropped him in the dusty old straight-back chair in the lobby of the hotel. His wallet was still in his pocket, but all his money and his room key and his shoes were gone. In his stocking feet he went to the desk. The clerk was sitting there chewing on his cigar. He handed Suggs his satchel, which had most of his clothes still in it, but his car keys and even his books were gone. He told Suggs that his time for the room had run out, and someone else had already checked in. When the clerk learned that Suggs's room key was missing, he charged him his last two dollars to replace it. Suggs had seventy-five cents left in his pocket.

He tried knocking on the door where the tall man with the fur coat and feathered-hat had knocked the night before, but no one answered, even when he tried the three knocks that had got the door to open before.

He thought about calling the police, but the hotel had no public phone, and then he wondered what he would tell them anyway. He thought about what had happened, what he feared and believed he had done, and he remembered that prostitution is a crime. He had not been able to think about that the night before.

He took his satchel and went outside—he wished they had at least left him his shoes.

He walked to the parking lot where'd he'd left his car, but the car was gone.

After a time he could think of nothing else to do, so he caught a bus that read "University" on the marquee. All the offices were closed for the weekend. He had a quarter left, not even enough to get something to eat. The weather turned cold, and he didn't even have a jacket in his satchel, only a flannel shirt, which he put on over his other shirt. He pulled on a second pair of socks and spent the day walking around campus. He wanted to use his last quarter to call his parents, but he didn't know how he'd explain to them what had happened.

He kept walking through the evening. He found a twenty-four-hour medical clinic with its door unlocked, and he slid in and slept in the lobby until a janitor threw him out just after dawn. Late that night he found a pizza box outside a fraternity house. It still had half a pizza in it, and he ate it feeling like he had reached the lowest point of a very sorry life.

On Monday morning he caught a ride downtown with some University students who were driving that way: one of the boys had a new Mustang. Suggs had asked them how to find the Greyhound station, and they said they could take him there. They were going to the Arcade, which was only a couple blocks away. They asked why he wasn't wearing shoes, and he told them he'd got drunk and lost them. They laughed and said that was pretty cool. They asked why he didn't just call his parents to come and get him. He couldn't explain why he just couldn't get himself to do that.

At the bus station Suggs tried to convince the clerk that, if he could get a ticket, he'd pay them for it when he got home. But the clerk told him he'd call the police if Suggs didn't either buy a ticket or go away. Suggs slept off and on in the lobby, and when a guard threw him out, he spent the rest of the night walking round and round the bus station.

On Tuesday morning, Suggs used his last quarter to make a collect call home. His father would have driven right up to get him, but he had never gone to The City and had no idea how to get around there. Earl Suggs called the police about his son's car. The officer on the phone said they had too many stolen-car reports to pursue all of them and that his son was stupid for parking where he did. If they wanted the car, they could find it themselves. Then Earl went to the bank and had them wire enough money to his son that he could buy breakfast and pay for a bus ticket home.

Father and son said nothing to each other when Zeke got off the bus at the station across the river from Harmon Falls, but Suggs's father was quietly fuming. When they got home, Suggs explained to his mother, who cried and cried at how cruel he'd been to worry them to death, that his car had been stolen, and the thieves had left him downtown with no money and no way to get anywhere.

On Wednesday Suggs went back to school, but he avoided talking with anyone, even Lenny, and Montmorency immediately sensed that something serious was wrong, and she kept her distance.

On Thursday Suggs and his father had another all-night heart to heart, and on Friday Suggs senior took his son to the doctor for an examination and some tests.

Suggs got through the school year, but no one, except for Lenny and me, talked any more about his going to college. I don't even know if he ever got that acceptance letter. He went straight home from school every day and got right to work in his father's shop, repairing anything that came in just deftly and efficiently as he had done before. As far as I know, he and Montmorency never went out again. While no one knew for certain what had happened to Suggs, rumors got around, and by spring Montmorency was dating the son of a music teacher from across the river.

Some of the details of Suggs's story probably come from my own imagination as I try to recreate and not over-embellish his adventures, but I suspect I've got nearly everything pretty close to right. I wish the story had some better moral or a happy ending, but I can't think of one. He and Lenny remained friends and often worked on cars together. Every time I got back to Harmon Falls, I'd stop by the garage-shop in back of the Suggs's house to say hello to Zeke and find out what he'd been working on. He'd show me what they had in the garage and how he was fixing it and explain in as few words as possible any interesting cases they'd had in recent months. Lenny told me that Zeke always gave everyone a price-break on labor for repairs: he charged for parts and enough to make a living and not a penny more.

Over the years I've had two friends who told me about encounters with prostitutes. One was a rich man I met in The City at a benefit for the new theater. He said that he saw them regularly: to him they made more sense than getting married, which from his point of view led to nothing but entanglements. He didn't much care about what they said or how they looked, as long as they took care of his needs at the time. Another, a man from a town across the river from Harmon Falls, told me that he went once, after his wife had left him, and the girl was so young and pretty and kind and vulnerable that he cried the whole time and never went back again.

I've lived in The City for a few years myself, and I've never had anything like that happen to me, though now and then I've heard similar stories. A person has to be wary, and that's another sad thing about The City and about this weary world.

Just this past summer I heard that Zeke Suggs had died—I don't know from what, but he was certainly too young to go. His parents both died a few years ago. Lenny told me that a cousin had taken the house and the garage, so the repair shop is still there. I'm certain they'll never find a better repairman than Zeke.

Montmorency went to school and got her degree in Dental Hygiene. She got a job in the town across the river from us and married that music teacher's son, who also became a successful music teacher, putting on many wonderful shows with his students. They had two children, a daughter who plays oboe and a son who plays bass violin.

Suggs never married or had children. He went to church with his parents for as long as they lived and by himself after they died, and eventually he became a deacon: by then everyone had forgiven or simply forgotten anything they guessed he may have done in The City. I never got the sense that he had many friends—even fewer, if that's possible, after he returned from his one visit to a university. I think that, privately, early on, people made all sorts of guesses about what happened to him, and whatever they thought it was, they didn't want to be tainted by it. Or more probably Zeke felt he had tainted himself and so didn't quite know how to deal with people thereafter. I know that on summer nights he'd sit on his front porch and listen to baseball games on the radio with a stray dog he'd taken in. He'd wave to everyone who passed by, just as his folks always had. But I don't think he had many visitors, though Lenny would stop by to listen to games with him, and I never heard that he took a trip or a vacation to get a break from Harmon Falls. He lived a slow, steady, if not very long, life. Nearly everyone in town knew his surname and associated it with the best auto repairman anyone had ever heard of.

I've heard Lenny swear, though, that he's never known a smarter guy nor had a better friend than Zeke Suggs, and I believe him.

A Cup of Envy

"A true friend never gets in your way unless you happen to be going down."
—Arnold Glasgow

A bunch of friends gathered one evening at the Arabica coffee shop east of downtown, and Lenny read us this story. He had written it for a college creative writing class he was taking at the Branch campus, and he drove all the way up to The City to read it to us—writers do get all excited about their work, you know. Lenny's new to writing stories, so please don't be too tough on him. I won't say if I think the story's any good or not, so please don't ask. He's my friend, and friends listen to one another's stories, so here it is, pretty nearly as he wrote it.

Sam Dayton didn't like his neighbor, and he had reason. One cold December night the guy had left Sam, his car dead as a plucked turkey, standing in front of his condo, freezing and shivering—he refused to give Sam a jump, calling him a "dumb Yank" for leaving his lights on while he went inside. One time the guy had pitched his scrub water out his front door, only for it to run in front of Sam's step, freeze, and cause Sam to take a pratfall, his legs flying, like some kind of clown. And often he would cook things that smelled wonderful, that smelled French and tangy, and never once would he invite Sam over to taste any of it, even when neither one of them had a woman over.

That was another thing he didn't like about Damen Pythian,

who lived in the condo next door: let the limey go back to England instead of dating nice American women who should have been dating American men instead of some fox-chasing cricket-playing tea-drinking four-eyed Brit who didn't even know that a football is oval, not round. And that wimpy gold-lettered plate on his front door that read "Pythian's Proper English Teas": why keep something stupid like that on your front door as if your apartment were some sort of fancy restaurant? Sam had worked for years at his uncle's auto repair shop to save money to open his own little garage, buy his own condo, and start to make something of himself, and this Johnny-Bull-come-lately waltzed right in probably on family money and bought the place next door and then acted like Sam wasn't good enough for the neighborhood and didn't even bring his damn Limey car to Sam's shop when it needed repairs.

Well, Sam had got even. Late at night he would crank his stereo up louder and louder, till his neighbor would bang and bang on the wall for him to stop. But he wouldn't stop till he was damn good and ready. He'd shoot peas at the birds that would come to his neighbor's bird feeder. He'd kick Pythian's evening paper off the step into rain puddles. He'd kickstart his Hog extra loudly and extra early on Sunday morning, especially if his neighbor had had a late date. And that wasn't the best of it.

As you know, the English love their beer, and Sam made just about the best home brew anywhere. His father had taught him, and his father had taught him: a family recipe, dark, rich, nutty and smooth. In August, when beer tastes best, and when his neighbor would leave his door open from the heat, he would call his friends over and conspicuously give them cases of home brew out on the front step, making sure that Pythian could hear the bottles jingling. In the evening he would sit on the step, read his paper, and slowly drink a couple bottles, popping off the bottlecaps with a satisfying snap. He wouldn't even look up when his neighbor came in, let alone offer him a bottle, and Sam could tell that hit him where it hurt.

These things will come to a head, and one day Sam saw the thing that bent him to revenge for good. There it was in the evening paper: his neighbor's engagement announcement. Well, dating is one thing, but marrying another, and that was too much. Worse yet: the girl was Persephone Willis. Sam had had a major thing for her in high school and had even gone out with her once, but you had to stand in line to get a date with Persephone, so he'd never had a second chance. Back at Harmon Falls High School she was small and sweet and quick as a young hunting dog, but lately when Sam had seen her around town he could tell that she had grown into her body and was just waiting for somebody to pick her like a ripe apple.

Somebody had picked her all right. There was her face in the evening paper, smiling seductively in the marriages/engagements section. "Willis-Pythian," it read beneath. "From the notable English tea brokers," wow, "just set up a local distributorship," fantastic, "couple to relocate near Boston," yeah, good news all right: just what Sam needed to read. If the family were so notable, what was the guy doing in little old Harmon Falls? But now Pythian had fired his Limey musket, and Sam was ready to shoot back with a good old American shotgun.

Sam's first thought: steal his woman. That should be an easy job for "Handsome Sam." And what better way to get even? He hadn't talked to Persephone in a while, but she wasn't the only one who had grown up since high school. "Why not just call her?" he said to himself, and turned for the phone. He got her number from the phonebook, then twiddled his thumbs for almost an hour trying to figure out what to say. Finally, "Why not just wing it?" won out, and he dialed.

"Hello?"

It struck him suddenly that he might be there. Sam checked quickly and saw, with relief, Pythian's car parked out front.

"Persephone?"

"Yes."

"This is Sam." Pause. "Sam Dayton?"

"Sam Dayton?"

"Yeah, Sam Dayton. From high school. I was on the football team. We went out. Remember?"

"No."

"I was a linebacker."

"First string?"

Reluctantly: "Second string. Number 54."

"Hmm. Oh, yeah, Sam! We went to see some movie, didn't we? Hi, Sam. What do you want?"

That question didn't turn out to be so easy to answer.

"Well, it's like this, you see, back in school, well, I kinda, that is, we grew up together and all, sorta. So . . . I saw your picture in the paper today and I just wanted to call up and say 'congratulations.'"

"Well, Sam, how nice of you to think of me and to remember me after all this time."

"No problem. Remembering you wasn't so tough."

"Well, gee, Sam, thanks for calling. Didn't I hear that you run some sort of car garage in town?"

"I have a place of my own."

"That's great, Sam. Are you married?"

"No."

"I'm sure someday soon some smart girl will find you and just latch on tight, and you'll be as happy as Damon and I are. Well, I gotta run, Sam. Thanks for calling."

"Yeah, you bet. Bye."

He heard the click. "Fine job, Sam," he said aloud to himself. "You sure got even."

For the next couple days Sam followed Persephone around town, driving a pickup with tinted glass that some guy had left in the shop for repairs. But that wasn't Sam's style, and he didn't really want to hurt Persephone. He wanted to hurt Pythian, and hurt him bad.

One evening Sam had a vague notion that a late model Mazda RX7 had been following him. "Who do I know," Sam wondered, with an RX7?"

Then worse again: the next two times he ran across Pythian, his neighbor did notice him. He didn't say anything, but he gave a particular look, and Sam wasn't sure whether that look meant anger or disdain. Either way, the guy had clearly given him the stink-eye, so Sam had to come up with a plan.

He sat down at his kitchen table and thought some more. As his father had told him, you can do anything if you just think first. It was almost autumn, and he opened the first bottle of a fresh, crisp batch of beer. He fingered the cold bottle, frosty with condensation that shone with the moonlight that poured in his window. He thought and he thought. And then he got it: home brew, a special batch, just for his neighbor, an engagement gift, goodwill and all that rot—but with a twist, one that would make Damon Pythian wish he had never crossed Sam Dayton.

Sam gave the problem a whole Saturday. He didn't go in to the garage at all. He sat and he drank and he thought, and he drank and he thought and he walked, and he rode and he thought and he drank. Now Sam was no dummy, and by mid-evening he'd got an idea, and all he needed to carry it out was a flashlight and a little luck.

He started his Harley and rode out of town into the country, to the little town of Cosmos about twenty miles from town and deep in the country, where his great Uncle Ned had once had a seed mill. Pretty isolated now, the mill hadn't operated for probably twenty years. After Uncle Ned had died, a cousin had taken it over, but since it was only a small operation, and the farms were failing and the city was growing, he had gone out of business in less than a year. He cleared out most of the stock and then just let the old building go to hell.

Sam got there in the dark of the night, his path lit by a sliver of moon and a froth of stars. No houses stood within a mile of the mill, and the scraping of the crickets was nearly enough to drown the sound of his motorcycle entirely. He parked his bike and pushed through some brush to the door. Luck! He wouldn't even have to pick the lock. The door was rickety enough that he could pull it out at the bottom and duck in. As he stretched the door against the lock, the sound of beating wings rose rapidly: swallows flying from the rafters.

He pulled out his flashlight, pointed it ahead, and looked around. The smooth floor, thick with dust, disappeared into the black distance. The shelves, mostly bare, had some bags, some burlap sacks, and a few tubs lying here and there. He stepped quietly. No sound of rats: a good sign . . .

Sam had poked around for maybe fifteen minutes, working his way into the back rooms, when he spotted what he was looking for. In a small bag, back in a corner on the floor against the back outer wall, under some loose boards: rat poison, the old kind that they don't even sell anymore, with arsenic. Arsenic, of course, has a slight, sweet smell of almond—they always mention that in the movies—which would mask perfectly in Sam's rich, nutty home brew: ah, the perfect gift! And the police would easily understand how Pythian could get poison in his system: he always got apples from up north, probably because they were cheap, not knowing that the growers had had problems with arsenic in their produce. And Sam had seen him carrying in bottled water from springs in the western part of the state where the water tended to run high in arsenic naturally. How sweet Nature can be!

Putting on the plastic gloves he had got at the drugstore and pulling out a small paper bag from his jacket pocket, Sam brushed a little of the lethal powder into the bag and returned the bag to his pocket. He made his way out silently as a dead mouse, crept through the front door, started his bike, and headed for home. Mission accomplished, and no one the wiser.

On the way home he nearly trembled with anticipation. He got home without a soul seeing him, parked in back, and went straight to his basement. He had hidden the bag of arsenic, figured he'd burn it later, realizing that after he used what he needed, he had to get rid of the rest, bag and all. Sam turned to a fresh batch of beer he had been brewing and found it nearly ready to pour. Tomorrow would be the day.

Sam got up early to sample the beer. Smooth, creamy, nutty, with a thick, foamy head--he'd made an excellent batch, the kind you want to share with friends. It even had a little sediment drifting near the bottom, enough to mask any arsenic that wouldn't dissolve.

Sam carved the top off an old half-gallon juice carton, washed the carton thoroughly, and poured in some fresh brew. Then he put on a clean pair of plastic gloves, covered his face with a dust mask, uncovered the hidden stash of arsenic, and began carefully, carefully dissolving the poisonous dust in the beer. It didn't take long. He sealed gloves, mask, bag and arsenic remains, leaving just a little in case he dropped a bottle, in a heavy paper bag, which he'd later take out to the country to burn, and he'd bury the ashes. He picked up the carton, swirling the contents: typical, but with a lovely hint of almond that gave this batch a special character. He poured the beer into two bottles, capped them, and prepared to deliver them with a handshake and a smile.

He got as far as the front door when it struck him that he'd never get away with it. He'd seen Quincy and Columbo and Perry Mason on TV. Of course the police would figure out Pythian's murder, tracing it to his neighbor. Motive might be a problem, but then there wasn't exactly a local tea mob making cement shoes for the competition. Proximity and opportunity would stand against him. He'd have to be sure that his neighbor drank all of both bottles, and he'd have to remove the empties, otherwise the murder weapon would be obvious.

And how much arsenic would it take to kill a man anyway? Would he die immediately? After one bottle? Two? Would he die at all? Would he just get sick, know why, and come over with a gun to get even? Not a gun: that was too American. Something devious, like in those English mystery stories. But there'd be no pipe-smoking detective to figure out Sam's murder and get revenge for him. Sam imagined himself dead and decided it wasn't worth that kind of chance just to get even with a man he hardly knew for a few small annoyances and for marrying a girl who didn't love him anyway.

What had he been thinking? Murder? How childish. Sam had things pretty good: a business of his own, a condo, his Harley, women enough, and all the beer he could brew. Why throw his future away on some guy who would soon move away and whom he'd never see again forever after? Funny, Sam thought, what your own brain would almost make you do. Had his neighbor really done anything anyway? Maybe he didn't even think about Sam at all. Maybe the whole thing was in his imagination. Could you kill a guy who didn't even hate you back?

Sam shook his head, turned on his heels, and headed back for his basement. He re-gloved his hands, opened the two bottles, and carefully poured their contents down the floor drain, washing it with water. He broke both bottles and stuffed them deep in the trash-- he'd take the trash himself tomorrow to the city dump. He got rid of the gloves, and then got a feeling that even though he hadn't done anything, he really ought to make amends, for his own sake if not his neighbor's.

So Sam poured two more fresh bottles of beer, capped them, took a deep breath, and waited for his heart to slow down before heading for Pythian's door.

The door opened a few seconds after his knock. The Englishman looked startled. "Yes?" he said.

"I'm your neighbor."

"Yes, I know." He had a pleasant enough voice, Sam thought, though it had a ring of impatience in it. Why had he wanted to kill him?

Sam looked his neighbor up and down: average size, trim and athletic, receding hairline, gold wire-rimmed glasses.

"Well, I know we ain't had a very good start, but I just felt like I should say something."

"What do you want to say?" The guy wasn't making things easy.

"For starters, how about 'congratulations'? I knew your fiancée in high school."

"So she told me." That was odd.

"She told you?"

"She said you called her. I told her that you live next door. It really isn't gentlemanly to follow a young lady."

How did he know about that? Sam looked down the street to see if he could spot a Mazda. He was beginning to get nervous and a little angry.

"Now all she's done for the past few days is talk about you. How remarkable that you remembered, how kind that you called, all that."

Here's a new development, Sam thought.

"But no harm done. We appreciate your good wishes. All's well that ends well. What have you got there?"

"Oh: these are a couple of bottles of my best home brew. Family recipe. Call it an engagement gift or a peace offering, if you like. Why not sit down and try one?"

"Awfully sporting of you. Say why don't you come in for a moment?"

The door opened, and Sam stepped in. He could smell something pleasant, something like tea steaming.

"Sit down, if you'd like," Pythian said, stepping into his kitchen. "As a matter of fact, I was just about to knock on your door. I've brewed up a pot of tea. Also a 'family recipe.'"

Sam sat down lightly in an easy chair away from the window. He opened one of the beer bottles and set it on the coffee table, patted it gently.

Pythian returned to the living room carrying a cup and saucer. "I think you'll like it: special family secret, just a hint of vanilla and almond, you know," he said, placing it on the table.

Sam smiled and pushed the beer across the table toward his neighbor. He took the cup of tea from the saucer. He smelled the almond aroma. He moved the cup toward his lips, paused for a moment in thought, and gently put it back on the saucer on the table.

Lenny had stopped reading. For a moment, no one said anything. I jumped up and went to the bar to get everyone another round of drinks, giving Lenny the thumb's-up sign. Lana just beamed at her brother's work. Flip the Cat was the first to reply.

"I like it," he said. "Just like one of those mystery movies on TV. Well done, Len, my man."

"Where did you get the idea?" Lindi said. "I hope you haven't been brewing any beer lately."

"It's just a story," Lenny said. "I didn't mean anything by it."

"Kind of scary," Daph-with-the-Laugh said. "Maybe Lenny will be the next Mickey Spillane."

"Or Edgar Allen Poe," Lindi said, looking down into her empty coffee cup.

"I don't know," said Stephen, a new friend who'd joined us for our regular meetings at the Arabica. He had grown up in The City, and I think he enjoyed poking fun at a bunch of small-town kids moving up to the big town. "I'm not sure about the point of it. What's it supposed to do? What are we supposed to get from it?"

Lenny didn't seem to know what to say.

"Epiphany, Len," I said, returning with a tray of fresh cups and glasses. "He wants to know about the epiphany, the big charge that comes at the end. Situation, complication, epiphany: that's how short stories usually work." I was trying to cover up that I wasn't sure what to say.

Lana shot me a sharp look as if to say, "Don't push Lenny! Just encourage him and let him enjoy himself!" Lana and I had been married for a while and could read each other's looks pretty exactly.

Lenny looked down and waved off the cup I offered him. "I'm not sure it has one. I wasn't thinking about that."

"I think it does," I added quickly. "These two guys who have made enemies of each other for no good reason may have gone too far, and they think about poisoning each other. And you're not sure if one of them will or not. The irony is that they could have been friends instead: that would have been a lot easier for both of them."

Lenny gave me a look as if he wasn't sure if I was helping. I got the sense he really wanted me to like the story and just say that and no more.

"So it's about not getting self-obsessed and violent, but trying to appreciate what we have in common instead," said Helen, Stephen's girlfriend—she joined us sometimes when she didn't have to work evenings or after work if we stayed long enough.

"I'd say don't quit your day job yet, Lenny," Greco said, ever the realist. "It seems to me a little bit cooked, you know, too artsy, like you're trying too hard. I sure give you kudos for trying, though: I couldn't write anything like that. It's just, maybe, too neat. And it doesn't have an ending. So what do they end up doing? That's what I want to know."

"That's what you're supposed to wonder about," Lenny explained. "You're supposed to guess what they'll do."

"Like a Rorschach test," Daph suggested.

"I'd rather you just told us, Len," Greco followed. "Otherwise, it's like one of those old symbolic stories, ya know, but without the ending. So we never know what really happened."

"Allegory," I said, but no one else cared much about literary terms, so I decided to shut up.

"Could you make it a little rougher?" asked BC—he played drums with Flip's band sometimes and had been coming to the Arabica forever. "You know, edgier: these guys seem too civilized to me."

"That's the point, if you ask me," Lana said, defending her brother. "They should be civilized and be friends instead of thinking about killing each other. That they even think about it is awful, and that's what the story shows."

"I'd rather feel good at the end of stories," Greco said.

"I don't know," BC added. "There's a place for uncertainty, too, like in that old TV show—not Outer Limits, the Rod Serling thing: Twilight Zone, that's it, man."

"That's kinda what I was thinking of," Lenny said.

"Keep at it, Lenny," Daph said, "and come up and read us another one anytime you'd like. Lots better gathering with your friends at a great coffee shop than watching TV."

"Maybe," Lenny said. Lana tousled his hair.

"Raise you glasses, friends," I said. "Here's to our buddy Lenny: live long and prosper." I gave him the Vulcan salute from Star Trek.

"Live long and prosper, Lenny," everybody said, all giving the Vulcan salute, too.

"Man," Lenny said, "you guys do watch too much TV."

The Time Icky Growler Kissed a Bee

"A real friend is the one who walks in when the rest of the world walks out."
—Walter Winchell

"He did it!" screamed little Seala McGee. "I saw him do it! I saw him!"

Seala was one of those human beings who proves once again that we live in an allegorical world. While her mother had red hair and looked about as Irish as a person can, her father had black hair, which Seala inherited, and from him she also got the traits that gave her face the look of a startled seal.

"I don't believe it," said her best friend Marilyn Carrolton. Marilyn stood very tall for her age, and she had the roundest, tallest, most perfect Afro that I've ever seen, making her taller yet. Her eyes, too, had grown as big and round as Seala's when she heard the news.

"It's true!" Seala insisted. "I saw it with my own eyes." That's an odd phrase that one hears sometimes despite its silly redundancy, as if we could see something with our ears or nose or someone else's eyes. If only we could see through another's eyes!

"It flew right up to him," Seala exclaimed, "a great big bee, and he kissed it right on the lips! Ask Slinky: he was standing right there watching. They were playing ball when he did it."

That part at least was true: Icky and Slinky had been pitching a rubber ball back and forth in Icky's back yard. But when the event-in-question supposedly happened, Slinky had just bent down to pick up the ball after he'd missed Icky's toss.

Those were the sorts of things that happened in Harmon Falls in those days, especially in the summer, when kids were out of school and had time to play and didn't spend all day fiddling with cell phones or thumbing away at computer games. Funny what a person will remember after all those years . . . Some stories rebuild themselves over time so that we feel better about what we think happened, and some try to stay the same no matter how much time goes by or how much we tellers change.

"What kind of bee was it?" Marilyn asked.

"One of them great big fuzzy ones that buzzes so loud it sounds like an airplane when it goes by! A bumbletybee!" Seala almost always spoke with an exclamation mark at the end of her sentences, but seeing someone actually kiss a bee in flight was perhaps an event worthy of exclamation.

"Why would he do that?" Marilyn asked.

"Icky doesn't need a reason," Seala said. "He just does things!"

"Let's ask him," Marilyn hinted, thinking that a logical way to proceed.

"He won't say anything: he never says anything! He's so weird!" You might guess kissing a bee is weird thing to do, or you might not, but Seala wasn't very forgiving about anything she observed—or thought she observed—and that she judged out of the ordinary.

"Then we'll ask Slinky," Marilyn suggested.

"He never says much more than Icky does. And he'll probably just lie to protect him!"

Slinky happened to be one of her brother's best friends, so Marilyn wasn't too happy at the insinuation. "Slinky is one of Herbie's best friends, and Herbie doesn't lie, and he wouldn't hang around with someone who does," Marilyn said decisively.

Seala, afraid that she'd hurt her friend's feelings, backed off a little. "Let's ask him, then. He'll tell us the truth. Slinky!" she called out. "Slinky, did Icky Growler just kiss a bee? You were standing right there: you must have seen it!"

Just then little Lindy Lou Hoobler was walking by. Her brother, Ned, was holding her tightly by the hand so she wouldn't run away. Their mother had given him some money to buy her an ice cream cone. The June afternoon was glowing brilliantly, while a light breeze shimmied in the trees. So an ice cream seemed the perfect item to keep Lindy Lou occupied body and soul for at least the time it took for her brother to walk her there and back and for her to eat it. Lindy Lou could take a very long time eating an ice cream cone, taking only the tinniest licks and nibbles, and Ned was willing to take his sister only because he'd get an ice cream, too. Lindy Lou was big enough to eat only one scoop, but Ned could easily handle two large ones. She would get chocolate chip, and he would get butter pecan. They always did.

"What did Icky Growler do?" Lindy Lou asked.

Seala felt only too happy to tell her story again. "You should have seen him! He kissed a bee! I saw him do it! The bee flew right up to him, and he kissed it right on the lips!"

No one seemed to be wondering whether a bee actually has lips.

Lindy Lou's mouth dropped wide open. Then she started to bounce up and down on both little legs at once, and she began chanting: "Icky kissed a bee-eee, Icky kissed a bee-eee!" Ned just shook his head, took the incident as one more trial he had to endure to get his ice cream, and pulled his sister along toward the ice cream shop. Ned couldn't get her to stop until she actually had a cone in her hand and chocolate chip ice cream in her mouth, so by then most of the people around Harmon Falls on that June afternoon had heard about Icky second-or third-hand.

In the meantime, Marilyn had grabbed Seala by the hand and led her over to where Icky and Slinky were playing. By then, Slinky had sat down on the ground to contemplate what he had heard and what he had seen.

"Slinky," Marilyn called, "did you see Icky Growler kiss a bee?"

Now, during the whole of the events of our story so far, Icky had been standing with his back to the street where Seala and Marilyn had passed by.

Slinky sat still and scratched his chin for a moment. Then he scratched his right ear, and then he ran his hand several times in a circle over his close-cropped hair. Marilyn was right: he wasn't the sort of boy to lie. Everyone waited as Slinky put his hand over his mouth and pondered. Finally he pulled it away.

"I don't rightly know for sure," he said.

"Ugggghhhhhh!" Seala uttered a sound of deeply committed disgust.

"You were right there, Slinky! You had to see him!"

Slinky thought for another moment, and he got a brilliant idea: he did try to see through someone else's eyes.

"Did you see him?" he asked Seala. "He had his back turned to you."

"Is that true?" Marilyn asked, a hint of irritation at her friend appearing in her voice. "Did he have his back turned to you: the whole time?"

That put Seala back on her heels, and she had to think about what she saw. "No—well, maybe—no, no, not the whole time! After the bee flew by, he turned around, and his lips were, you know, scrunched up, like in a kiss! The bee flew right up to him and . . ."

"While his back was turned to you . . ." Marilyn said.

"Yes, and it stopped for a minute in front of his face, and I couldn't see the bee anymore because he had his back turned this way, and then I saw his head bob, and then the bee flew up over his head, and then it flew this way and zig-zagged over that way!" Seala pointed to add emphasis to her story.

"A minute?" Marilyn asked. "The bee stood there for a whole minute?"

"Well, no, just for a second or two—but long enough for a kiss!"

"Is that true, Slinky?" Marilyn asked. "Is that what happened?"

Again Slinky covered his mouth for a moment and then gradually peeled it away. "I can't rightly say for sure. 'Bout then I was bending over to pick up the ball."

"But you saw something?" Seala exclaimed. You must have seen something!"

"Maybe," Slinky said. "Maybe."

By then Icky was looking at his friend, but he had no particular expression on his face. Famous for his taciturnity, Icky also had a mop of brown hair that fell down over his forehead sufficiently to make many of his expressions inscrutable, too. Just then he seemed almost to be pondering what had happened, not sure of it himself.

Slinky was also giving careful thought to the whole matter. He didn't want to betray his friend and get it wrong, but then whether Icky had kissed a bee didn't especially affect him one way or another, as long as both parties had consented.

"Icky!" Seala called. "Tell the truth. Did you kiss that bee?"

Finally Icky turned to Seala, who from his point of view was doing nothing but causing trouble. He neither shook his head one way or another nor spoke. He did grimace at Seala, though.

"Oh, Icky, don't you give me that mean look!" Seala warned. "You kissed a bee, and you know you did, and now everybody's going to know about it!"

Slinky rubbed his hand over his head. "Why?" he asked. "Mar'lyn, why does everybody have to know? Why would anyone want to know?"

Slinky was always a sensible fellow, which is why he and Icky were friends.

Seala was getting herself thoroughly wound up. "Because it's so weird, weird, WEIRD!" On the last syllable she fairly screeched.

By that time, Mrs. Farquhar, who lived next to the Growlers, had come outside to investigate the racket, most of which had come from Seala.

"What's going on, you kids! Play nicely, now, or just go your own ways and don't fight." That was how parents faced such situations in those days.

"Mrs. Farquhar! Get Icky to tell the truth! You can do it! Or we'll all go and tell his mother!" Seala spoke as if she felt someone had to defend the bee, whose honor had been smirched by a small boy's unwanted advances.

"The truth about what, Seala? Did he do you some harm?"

"Well, no, not me. But wait till you hear, Mrs. Farquhar, just wait till you heard what he did!"

"I'm waiting. What did he do?"

"Seala says he kissed a bee," Marilyn said, scooping her friend.

"He wha—he kissed who? What did you do, Icky!"

"Not who, what: Icky Growler kissed a bee! I saw it!" Seala called out for all the world to hear.

"She didn't really see it," Slinky explained. "Icky's back was turned, and she thought she saw it."

"You just tell the truth now, Slinky. I think you know more than you're saying!" Seala insisted.

"You kids!" Mrs. Farquhar said in disgust, shaking her head vigorously. "I've always said you have too much time on your hands. School should go all summer, too." She wiped her hands on her apron and stalked right back inside her house.

By that time kids had appeared from all over the neighborhood, and the event had turned from probably nothing into a memorable hullabaloo. Everyone wanted to know exactly what happened, and pretty soon everyone had an opinion whether or not he or she had been anywhere near at the time.

Then out came Farly Farquhar, Mrs. Farquhar's sixteen-year-old son. Because he was sixteen all the kids respected him enormously, and they all went silent immediately as soon as he began to speak.

What's all this about Icky Growler kissing a bee?" he asked, laughing. "Ain't you got anyone better to kiss?"

Icky gave Farly a look akin to the one he'd given Seala. He lived next door to Farly and so, despite Farly's sixteen years, didn't respect him as much as the others did, knowing more about the troubles Farly had gotten into over time— though he never spoke to anyone about them, not even to Slinky or to his other best friend, Little Fotungus.

"He did, he did!" Seala insisted. "I saw him do it! Well, I almost saw it. Anyway, it sure looked like that!" Whatever had happened, Seala had already convinced herself for all time that Icky Growler had indeed kissed a bee, simply by repeating it often enough to herself and to other people.

"Icky," Farly said, "you're one weird little dude."

"That's what I keep saying!" Seala agreed.

"Come on," Marilyn said to Seala, by that time tired of the whole thing. "Let's go play somewhere else. If Icky wants to kiss a bee, what should we care?"

"Because it's weird, weird, WEIRD!"

"You are one loud little girl," Farly commented. "That's pretty weird, too."

At that Seala's face grew nearly as purple as an onion. She was loud, but having someone notice it and tell her so made her deadly embarrassed.

About that time someone noticed that Little Fotungus had strolled up. He was twirling a long piece of grass in one hand and occasionally chewing on the other end of it. A number of the small children called out his name. He also had a reputation for telling the truth, enough so that even Farly, who was much older and taller, asked him, "Little Fotungus, did you see anything?"

Little Fotungus twirled his strand of grass a few times and finally spoke. "Yes."

"I knew it! I knew it!" Seala shouted gleefully.

"Well," Farley asked, "what did you see?"

Again Little Fotungus paused, as if for effect. "I'm not telling."

"What!" Seala screamed. "You have to tell the truth, even if Icky's your friend. You have to!"

"It's Icky's business, not yours. He has the right to say something or not as he pleases." At that Little Fotungus and Icky Growler nodded to each other, and Little Fotungus rambled off.

"WEIRD!" Seala shouted one more time, and she grabbed Marilyn's hand and pulled her along, and pretty soon they were both gone.

Farly shook his head like his mother did and went back inside. Some of the bigger kids teased Icky a little before they left, and some of the little kids hung around the yard for a bit just in case whatever had happened might happen again. They felt like they'd just missed some monumental event that people would remember for years. Icky and Slinky began to play ball again, but nobody said anything more, so eventually all the other kids ambled off, too.

You may think that nothing more came of the story, but not if you knew Seala McGee. She wasn't about to let it rest. That evening she got her older sister Montmorency—yes, I know that's an odd name for a girl, but she was born with a noble look on her face, so her parents thought they needed something special—to go along with that look. Then Seala collected Marilyn Carrolton and her brother Herbie and Josiah Glee, who was a neighbor of the McGees and almost an adult, and together they marched on the Growlers' house and knocked on the front door.

Mrs. Growler, always amiable, answered, smiling. "Well hi there, kids. What can I do for you?" Everyone liked Mrs. Growler—you couldn't help yourself. One look at her round, peach-colored face and little round chin and those enormous brown eyes with all the smile lines around them and her big white smile and you'd find yourself saying, without conscious intervention, I like this woman! She's nice. Icky, on the other hand, had inherited his taciturnity from his father, who was watching a baseball game on TV and didn't come to the door.

Mrs. Growler's welcome put Seala off her game for a moment, and she almost retired from the battle-line as she forgot for an instant why she'd come.

"Pssst. The bee! Ask her what you came to ask." From the back of the group Josiah whispered to Seala. He wasn't even sure he should be there, so he just wanted to get their business done and go home.

"Oh!" Seala said. "Mrs. Growler, why did Icky kiss a bee?"

"Kiss a what?" That had the poor woman puzzled. She'd been away at the market during the afternoon's ruckus.

"A bee! A big one! One of those big, noisy bumbletybees! We saw him do it!"

"You did? All of you did?" Mrs. Growler asked.

"No," Marilyn interjected. "Only Seala actually saw it."

Seala felt betrayed by her friend, but she couldn't object out loud, since Marilyn was telling the truth.

"What exactly did you see, hon? Tell me as clearly as you can," Mrs. Growler said. She thought Seala was pulling some kind of joke, but just in case, she wasn't sure she wanted her son to be the subject of strange gossip.

Seala tried to explain at greater length, but she was only getting more and more excited and confused, so finally Mrs. Growler interrupted. "Well, dear, why don't we just go out back and ask him? Go around the house to the back, and I'll meet you."

Mrs. Growler sent them around presumably so she could go straight back through the house and get to Icky first to find out what if anything had happened. But she didn't reckon on the kids' dashing full speed to get there before she did. She stopped to ask her husband if he knew anything about what was going on, but he just raised his eyebrows and shrugged. He was busy watching the game and had no intention of getting involved in matters better left to kids.

When Mrs. Growler got down the back steps to the yard, a crowd of neighbors, following the visiting kids, had already begun to gather around the fence. In the yard Icky and Slinky and Little Fotungus were playing—actually they were building something out of red bricks they'd collected plus some mud, wood chips, and a few old plant pots.

"What are you up to, boys?" she asked.

Slinky ran his hand over his head a couple times and replied. "We're building an igloo, or trying to figure out how to do it."

Everyone else was too astonished to laugh, but Mrs. Growler chuckled and asked, "In the summer? With bricks?"

"We're using the bricks to stimulate ice blocks," Slinky explained. He'd meant simulate, of course, but everybody knew that, so no one said anything. Slinky looked around very seriously at everyone's faces, and then he said sternly, "We're trying to figure out how they work, and we need to concentrate!"

Nobody said anything for a moment as Icky and Slinky were massaging mud into the chinks between bricks to hold them together, and Little Fotungus was figuring out how to position some broken bricks and strips of wood to assemble a chimney. After a moment the three boys stepped back from their creation, smiling. A few of the neighbors offered light applause for their work. Then Mrs. Growler went up to Icky and kneeled down to look him in the face.

"Icky, Seala says she saw you kiss a bee."

Icky's face reddened, but he said nothing.

"Well, didn't you!" Seala shouted.

"Did you see anything?" Mrs. Growler asked Slinky. She didn't so much want to pry. She just didn't want her son to go around kissing bees: he might, after all, get stung, and she, too, was fond of bees, especially fuzzy bumblebees, and didn't want them to get hurt, either.

"Can't rightly say," Slinky replied. "I was picking up the ball at the time and didn't exactly see anything."

"Come on, Slinky! You were right there at the time!" Seala shouted.

Slinky moved his head slowly from side to side a couple times. "I just don't know for sure."

Mrs. Growler nodded her head in understanding. She valued people who weren't eager to say more than they knew. "And what about you, Little Fotungus?"

"He says he won't tell," Marilyn said. And then, just a little, she glared at her friend. She wished sincerely that they hadn't walked by that particular house at that particular time on that particular lovely summer day. "And I don't blame him," Marilyn added decisively.

"What!" Seala screamed.

"Well," one of the neighbors said, "I can see the little girl's point. We can't just have folk going around kissing bees, can we? It's . . . it's . . ."

"WEIRD!" Seala wouldn't let go of that idea.

"I'd have said not safe," the neighbor responded, "for the boy or the bee."

"And a little bit weird," mumbled another of the neighbors.

"Did you see something, Little Fotungus?" Mrs. Growler asked.

"Yes," Little Fotungus said firmly. He was trying to decide what to say. He was fiercely loyal to his friends, but he wouldn't lie either. He thought about what he had seen, and tried to get it right.

"What happened, Little Fotungus?" everyone asked in unison.

"Did my son kiss a bumblebee?" Mrs. Growler asked.

"No," Little Fotungus said, just as firmly as the last time.

"I'm glad for that," Mrs. Growler said, patting her son on the head.

"He's lying!" Seala screamed. "I know something happened! I know it!"

Little Fotungus felt everyone's eyes on him, and he didn't like having someone accuse him of lying. So he decided simply to tell what he saw.

"Icky didn't kiss the bee," Little Fotungus said. "The bee kissed him."

"The bee kissed him?" Mrs. Growler asked.

"That's the same thing!" Seala insisted. "He kissed the bee, the bee kissed him: it doesn't matter because they both kissed!"

"You may not think that when you get older, Seala," Mrs. Growler explained. "It's not always the same thing, to kiss or be kissed. What did you see, Little Fotungus?"

"I was coming over to visit Icky. He and Slinky were playing catch. I waved to Slinky, and he looked toward me, so the ball dropped, and he bent to pick it up. I heard the bee, a great big bumblebee, fly right over my head. They always fly along this path: I see them and hear them all the time. They always fly right through your yard, right along here. The bee was so loud it was easy to follow, and it went right up to Icky and touched him right on the lip. Then it bobbed up over his head and flew away. That's exactly what happened, near as I could tell."

Even Seala McGee was beginning to feel satisfied with that explanation. She had prepared herself to get angry and throw a real fit, but at least she had got her story partially confirmed.

"See, everyone," she said. "Icky did kiss a bee."

"It's not the same thing," her friend Marilyn explained. "The bee kissed him."

"Maybe a bird will kiss him next time," Josiah said slyly.

"It's all part of nature," Slinky explained, nodding his head. "These things just happen."

"The bee chose Icky," Marilyn said. "It's kind of an honor."

Seala felt ready to let things go at that. She believed herself vindicated, and she also felt better to think that Icky hadn't done anything wrong.

"Be careful, Icky," Mrs. Growler said. "Don't get stung, and try not to hurt the bee if it flies by again.

Icky nodded.

Mrs. Growler went back inside, the crowd dispersed, the other children went home, and Icky, Slinky, and Little Fotungus put the finishing touches on their brick igloo. They looked at it admiringly for a bit, and then went off elsewhere to play. The igloo stood for about two weeks until the boys decided on a new project, how to make an apartment building for birds that would be both appealing to the birds and affordable to build.

Lunch Date

"Friendship is like money, easier made than kept."
—Samuel Butler

Not all stories that begin in Harmon Falls end in Harmon Falls. Not all stories that begin with friendship end with friendship. But, then, not all stories that begin end at all, and some end when they've barely begun.

Romantic stories of childhood or teenage loves persist. Apparently everybody loves Romeo and Juliet. Almost everybody will think back at one time or another and ask, I wonder what would have happened if I'd married that person I had a crush on in grade school or my high school sweetheart or that cutie in my freshman psychology class in college?

Every now and then, someone has actually done that. Sometimes it works out, and sometimes it doesn't. Sometimes you really don't know, because the story hasn't entirely ended yet.

Lindi and Hoag were childhood sweethearts. They were almost together already when we tried to save our favorite park all those years ago in Harmon Falls. They were just too young to make any commitment yet. They went through ups and downs like anyone, but the real problems came later when they got to having more downs than ups. They decided to move up to The City to go to college, and afterwards they got better jobs there than they ever could have got back at home. So they stayed in The City and got married and began to settle down.

I don't know if staying caused more harm than good, or if their lives would have taken pretty much the same course anyway. I don't know if anyone else can learn from their story. Most storytellers don't do didactic literature anymore except in some children's books—we know we don't know more than anyone else does.

***

Hoag left work one grey morning at about five after ten, dashed to the train station, and just caught the 10:17. The trees were almost budding with the first green of March, but a mist of rain hung from the flat, slate sky. A few degrees lower temperature and it would have turned to heavy snowflakes. Plenty of seats on the train at that hour . . .

Hoag settled into a seat two rows behind a woman primly dressed in dark blue with white gloves. She looked like a schoolteacher, but was probably a maid for one of the old-money families along the Boulevard. The train track cut right down the middle of that road, which was lined with fancy Tudor, Georgian Colonial, and Craftsman-style houses, with an occasional French Provincial. A dissipated old man in ragged brown tweed and a beret sat in the very first row in front. He looked like a wino, but was probably a long-tenured French professor from the University, and he took the train to remain frugal and so he wouldn't have to find a parking space. A teenager, probably skipping school, sat two rows behind the professor with his boom box turned low but rapping steady as raindrops.

Trees along the tracks glowed in the mist. Sitting, Hoag felt colder now, a draft over his damp feet, and his hair tussled with a breeze every time the train stopped and the doors popped open. He looked at his reflection in the window, took off his gloves, loosened the heavy, grey muffler that Lindi had given him for his birthday, and combed his hair quickly with his fingers. He wanted to think about the new gaming program that he had been building at work, but try as he would, the game wouldn't come fully back to mind. It floated along outside the train, just beyond his window, fuzzy in the wet air.

The train pulled into downtown terminal at 10:38. Hoag slipped the crowd and brushed out into the street. Lindi was waiting under the concrete overhang of the terminal building by the street along the outside rim of the City Square. In cream slacks and light green sweater with a halfway buttoned tan trenchcoat, she looked a season too early, pale and tired and cold. Her leather purse tugged at her shoulder like a soul-burden, and she hunched her shoulders against the wind. Her glasses fogged with the damp, and her hair lay flat beneath a wool cap. She spotted Hoag, offered an expressionless "hi," and tried to smile, but the corners of her mouth drooped. The lines in her forehead creased a little deeper than usual. The rain turned to slow, heavy snowflakes.

"You look good," she said. "New sweater? It matches the grey in your eyes."

"Thanks," he answered. "Got it with my new credit card. You feeling okay? You look tired."

"Thanks a lot. I'm all right."

They began to walk. Lindi was wearing heels, which she had never done until recently, and she looked a little wobbly yet. They made her just the tiniest bit taller than Hoag, though you wouldn't have noticed unless you'd seen them standing right together more than once.

"Have any trouble getting off work to come?" Hoag asked.

"A little. They always have a tough time getting subs, and they don't like to pay them. El cheapo principal." When they first got out of college, Lindi had done clerical work for a large real estate agency. She'd finished an Honors degree in Math with a Teaching Certification and was much too smart for that kind of job, but teaching jobs were few at the time. The previous fall she'd finally got a job at City West High School at the far end of town from their old apartment.

"Yeah," Hoag said, nodding. "You want my gloves? The air's chilly." Lindi invariably forgot her gloves. When they'd first married, Hoag had always stuffed an extra pair in his coat pocket, but that day he had brought only one.

"No. Let's walk a little faster and I'll warm up, maybe. That's our bus ahead."

"Sure. Sounds good." Regardless of what he said, Hoag's voice sounded empty in his own ears, the thin sounds rising, echoing off the buildings, and disappearing up into the clouds.

The snow faded into rain again, and the rain calmed to intermittent drops, then started again in earnest as they reached the bus stop seconds after the bus pulled away. Lindi hunched back under the awning of a print shop to wait for the next one. She sniffed, and Hoag handed her a kleenex, which she used to swab her glasses instead.

"Want a peppermint? he said. "It can cut the sniffles."

"Okay."

"Where'd you park?"

"Over by the Colony Cinema, not too far. I just feel a little cold coming on."

A few minutes later another bus pulled up with a screech, and Lindi stepped in.

"Watch your step," Hoag said. "You never did feel comfortable in heels," he almost said, and then thought better of it. Hoag followed, hit a wet patch on the flooring, and his leg flew out from under him. Lindi turned quickly and caught him by the arm.

"Good catch," he muttered. She smiled but didn't laugh. They settled into seats and felt each other's warmth against the bone-numbing damp cold of the last days of winter. They sat silently watching downtown, filtered through the rain, as the bus drove by building after building, some with thriving businesses, some operating on the margins, some entirely emptied and even boarded up.

"So how's stuff at school?" Hoag said.

"Not too bad. Sometimes the kids are hard to control. But I have a few bright ones. I like teaching math, because the boys try as hard as the girls. The language teachers have a tougher time: the boys think it's a sissy subject and won't do any of the work. They just disrupt class all the time. I hear the other teachers talk about it in the lounge. Math and science work better for most of us, except with the kids who are already convinced it's too hard for them. I've got three girls who stay late and help me clean up, and they play clarinet, all three." Lindi continued, but for Hoag her voice faded in amidst the sound of the raindrops against the windows.

"Sounds good," Hoag said when he realized Lindi had stopped talking. He found himself falling back on that old conversation filler, and he felt stupid for repeating it.

Then Lindi told Hoag about all the children, what they did, what they said, what their parents did and what they said. Hoag looked past her left ear at the buildings standing sentry just beyond the thick-falling rain. Hoag didn't find the children interesting. He thought he was doing his best to listen.

"Here's our stop," he said.

"Sounds good," Lindi replied.

The Justice Center loomed out of the fog, and they slipped out together into the puddled street, hurried past the contorted sculpture by the front door. Hoag opened the door, and Lindi entered with the push of a gust of wind. She wiped water from both eyes. He handed her another kleenex. Businesspeople strode by inside, all looking just past the tips of their shoes. Their lawyer, dressed in a charcoal suit, red tie, and grey trenchcoat, stood inside, glancing at his watch. They shook off waterlogged shoes and greeted him.

"Hi, Mr. Feinman," Lindi said.

"Morning. We should be able to make it to court on time," the lawyer answered, checking his watch again. "Coffee?"

"No, thanks," both replied.

"I'm not anticipating any trouble here. This should be simple, right?" Hoag wasn't sure whether Stan Feinman were asking a question, making a statement, or issuing a command. He sounded like a lieutenant fresh out of OCS that Hoag had known in the Navy: Hoag had done two years after college and just after he and Lindi were married, but had gotten a discharge for a back injury that didn't want to heal.

"Yes," Hoag said, "it shouldn't be any problem."

"I hate to say so," the lawyer said, "right after you've come in from the rain, but the best way to get there from here is back outside and around the corner."

"Lead on," Lindi said.

The door opened with a suck of wind. A thin ray of sun broke through the clouds. It looked like a tunnel into the sky. The rain eased like a sigh, and people hurried out of doorways into buses, cabs, and adjacent buildings. They passed a news stand and a candy shop and a gyro vender perched under a broad green and white awning. They turned the corner, dodged a wedge-shaped spray of water from a turning Saab, and angled for the door ahead. The clouds closed up, becoming again a flat, slate-grey ceiling. The rain began to pound again in heavy drops that sounded like boots running across the pavement. A gust whirled and dashed up the façade, nearly lifting Lindi's hat with it. They pulled their collars tight, trudged on, and re-entered the building.

They wiped their feet on a huge, brown mat, shook off their coats, and sniffed. The stairwell smelled dank and musty at the bottom, but as they climbed, the air cleared and got almost antiseptic: painted plaster, cold metal, slick concrete. It reminded Hoag of some labyrinthine prison from a James Cagney gangster movie. At the top they opened a heavy door that closed behind them with a loud click. A sterile, checkerboard corridor spread before them. Tall walnut wall panels and the distant click of somber footfalls steady as a ticking clock made the main floor of the building grave, aloof, austere, cold. They took an elevator to the fourth floor, turned down another corridor, and then another, this one lined with tall windows that let in dull light that belied the coming noontime. Hoag and Lindi would quickly have got lost, but the lawyer strode on, steady and serious as Charon crossing his river. He had taken that same walk many times.

"You getting to bed before midnight these days?" Hoag said to Lindi, his whisper echoing through the hall as though he had shouted.

Lindi started to look at him, but instead turned to focus her glance just beyond Hoag's feet. "Closer to two, usually. You know I have to do that to keep up with lesson plans." She paused. "What about you?"

"I'm not going out, if that's what you mean. Some nights I can't seem to concentrate much after ten. Mr. Reilly likes to see us at our desks practically before dawn—you'd think a guy who makes games for a living wouldn't be so up-tight. I haven't been sleeping too well."

"Sorry," she said.

"Thanks. Back hurts, and I never have been a good sleeper anyway."

The lawyer stopped in front of a door that looked to Hoag exactly like all the other doors they had passed. "Wait here a moment," he said, and stepped in noiselessly in his Rockports. Hoag and Lindi waited together under the grey light of the tall windows. Hoag resisted an impulse to clasp Lindi's hand. He thought he noticed her hand move just the smallest bit toward him, but then she slid both hands into her coat pockets.

"How are your parents?" Lindi asked.

"Fine," Hoag answered. "Mother asked about you. How are yours?"

"Fine, too—almost fine. Oh, Dad's always little cranky, and Mom is having hip pain that doesn't seem to want to go away, but they're all right. They didn't ask about you."

"I suppose not."

"They're aging," Lindi continued after a pause. "I hate to hear them yelling at each other, but they do sometimes—a lot of times, actually. Same old stuff: Dad thinks Mom is spending too much money on doctors since she never seems gets any better. They both drink too much." Lindi was almost whispering, and she brushed the back of her hand across her nose. "It's cold in here," she said. "I thought government buildings would be warmer."

They paused, and then both tried to talk at the same time. They laughed nervously, and they paused again. Finally Lindi spoke. "You remember that day we went out on the lake in my brother's boat? It was late September, but grey and cold, like today, almost."

"Yeah, I remember. Didn't he sell that boat?"

"Yes, he had to, but he's thinking about getting another one this summer."

"We had some good times on that boat, fishing, sitting in the sun, playing music and drinking beer."

"What was it, two summers ago, that we stayed for a few days at that cabin right on the lake?"

"Yeah: the citrus-cedary smell of the pine trees in the evening, and the all the stars painted thick on the sky like a box full of dominoes . . . That was a good time. That's the only vacation we ever took."

"That's not my fault."

"I didn't say it was. Both of us are to blame, I suppose. We always spent all our time working, thinking about the future, never taking a break. What is it Eliot wrote? Something like, 'This is the way the world goes: not with a bang, but a whimper.' Remember that from English class?"

Lindi looked almost at Hoag for a minute, didn't say anything, then tried to look outside, and finally turned back to the windows. "This is the way the world ends."

"What?"

"That's the line from Eliot: "This is the way the world ends, not with a bang but a whimper."

They stood there in silence for a few minutes, trying not to feel anything.

"I guess there's nothing else to do now," Hoag said. Lindi didn't answer. "Tell me about your new apartment."

They eased into small talk again until they heard the door opening. The lawyer emerged.

"You two look cozy enough," he said flatly. "I've never handled both sides in a case before. I'm only doing this because Frank referred you, Lindi. Your brother Frank and I have been friends a long time. If you both promise me no hassles once we get started, I'll have you out in five minutes. Come in. Don't want to keep the judge waiting. She doesn't mess around."

They stepped into a squarish, carpeted room with benches that looked like church pews, and they advanced carefully to the sounds of a few muffled coughs and shuffled papers. The lawyer motioned them to sit, then whispered for a moment with the judge. Hoag and Lindi sat together in the second row on the straight wooden bench, trying not to look at each other. Lindi pulled off her hat, and her hair stood up, tousled. She tried to suppress a shiver, and Hoag tucked his muffler more tightly around his throat, then took it off, feeling for the first time the heat of the courtroom. Makes sense that it's warmer than the hallway, he thought.

"It's time," Mr. Feinman said, appearing beside them. Hoag and Lindi slid out and walked toward the judge's bench without looking right or left. They stood together before the bench, the lawyer in the middle, between them. Stan by your man, Hoag thought, trying to think of something funny and wanting to make Lindi laugh.

The lawyer touched his elbow, and Hoag looked up at the judge. Lindi thought she'd never seen a more serious-looking person in her whole life. The judge wore a black robe, and she had half-lensed glasses perched on the end of her long, aristocratic nose. Her brown eyes bore no expression, and her voice hinted no emotion, no predisposition or judgment. Hoag wondered if she disapproved. When she spoke, she did so solemnly, but not gravely. She spoke clearly and with authority, briefly to the lawyer and then to them. Hoag did not hear what she was saying. He was remembering a weekend on the lake, countless movies, coffees, a wedding, high school, trying together to save an old baseball park back in Harmon Falls when they were kids.

The judge turned to Lindi. "Lindi, do you want this divorce?" Hoag felt a spasm in his stomach, and for a moment wished she'd say no. Please, just say no, he thought.

"Yes, your Honor," Lindi replied—no hesitation, no emotion in her voice.

"And do you, Charles, also want this divorce?"

Hoag could only remember two times when someone had called him Charles, at their wedding and on his job interview.

Yes no no no yes I don't know oh God I don't know yes oh yes no: not a fraction of a second passed before Hoag answered, "Yes, your Honor." His voice escaped tonelessly, but without hitch, without waiver. He felt surprised that he had spoken and wondered if it wasn't really his voice.

"Then by the power vested in me, I grant this divorce. Thank you, Mr. Feinman."

The judge nodded and began shuffling papers, perhaps for the next case.

Lindi couldn't believe that it was over so quickly, and Hoag was having a hard time pinning down any particular thought in his head.

They followed the lawyer noiselessly from the courtroom, but as they stepped outside, the sound of their footsteps ran away and echoed through the corridor. Lindi nearly slipped, and Hoag clasped her elbow and held on. They walked back, around, down, down the staircase. Lindi sniffed. Hoag stroked his chin, found a spot that he'd missed shaving. He felt strangely like laughing.

"You okay?" Hoag asked Lindi.

"Yes. You?" Lindi answered.

"Okay. You sound a little hoarse. Like a cough drop?" Hoag said.

"Sure, please," Lindi replied. "Don't forget your muffler. The damp air will give you a cold for sure."

"Oh, yeah, thank you." Hoag had almost dropped his scarf, then fumbled with it trying to tie it around his neck.

They returned through the labyrinth and finally passed outside again, the wind and rain striking at them furiously. Someone carrying an umbrella that had blown inside-out rushed past them, and they too hurried around the corner.

"Let's stop in this coffee shop for a minute," the lawyer said through an opening in his coat collar, "long enough to make sure all the papers are in order." It's right here, almost next door.

They turned in, felt the warm air rush, smelled fresh coffee, day-old pastries, frying potatoes, pastrami, and the sweat of people long nuzzled in their winter coats.

"Want a coffee, Mr. Feinman?" Lindi asked. "I'll buy."

"No, no thank you, but Hoag looks like he could use one." He popped open his briefcase, checked signatures, organized papers, gave them each an envelope.

"Did we pay you enough?" Lindi asked. "It seems like so little for your trouble."

"Quite enough," the lawyer answered. "Very little trouble. You two had everything done to crossing the last t, and the hearing went smoothly—she's a really good judge, and she gets people in and out. I could use a cognac instead of a coffee—wouldn't be a bad idea in this weather. Oooh. Look," he said, watching Hoag help Lindi get her coat off and hang it on a peg, "it's raining again. You know, I can't understand you two. I've never seen a divorcing couple who look like they like each other so much, not even with convenience marriages, where both partners get something. I've done quite a few of those."

Hoag and Lindi stared at the table and then at the cups of black coffee that a waitress placed in front of them.

Finally the lawyer shrugged and closed his briefcase.

"Well, I've got to get back to my office, so you two take care. Good luck, huh?"

"Thank you for all your help," Hoag said. "You've made this as easy as possible."

"You two made it easy," the lawyer replied.

"Bye, and thanks," Lindi said. "We'll recommend you to our friends." The lawyer looked at her. "Well, you know what I mean," she added, "if they need a lawyer for anything." He nodded, pulled his coat collar tight, and left into the rain. Stretched-out raindrops lashed against the windows, making a sound like a crowd cheering.

"Thanks for the coffee," Hoag said.

"Sokay."

They sipped in silence, the coffee warming their throats. "Hey," Hoag said, "I don't have to get back at work for almost an hour. Want to have a bite of lunch?"

Lindi sniffed stale bread and greasy potatoes. "Not here," she said.

"How about Trifles—you know the place? It's nice, just down a block or two."

Lindi paused, didn't look up. "Okay." She almost whispered.

They buttoned up tight, ducked their heads, and went out into the rain. The thick drops clattered like hail, exploded at their feet. After only a short wait, they hopped on a bus: Trifles was actually several blocks away. As Hoag searched his pocket for change, Lindi paid for two fares. Unable to find a seat, they stood in the aisle, dripping. Four blocks later the bus poured them out in front of the little bistro, the name printed in yellow script on a dark green awning. When Hoag pulled open the tight door, mingled voices of the lunchtime crowd rushed at their ears like a heavy moan.

Despite the crowd, a waiter seated them immediately, and they shook off their coats and the rain. They ordered coffee with cream and slumped behind their open menus. When the waiter returned, they ordered salad and a sandwich to share, two cups of clam chowder, and a muffin. Steam rose from the coffee like mist off the lake, and the waiter brought their food almost immediately.

"So what are you doing this evening?" Hoag asked.

Lindi looked up at him, but didn't answer.

"Sorry. Didn't mean anything by asking. Just making small talk."

"Some of the other new teachers are going out for dinner. I'll probably go with them, then back home to grade papers. They're talking about going to a movie on Friday, and maybe to the symphony on Sunday afternoon," Lindi said.

"Sounds good."

"What about you?"

"Oh, I've got a new game program to finish. And I got a couple of new computer games off the network that I'd like to install and try out, to see if I can learn anything from them. No plans for the weekend. I'll go to the Y Saturday morning for a workout and watch basketball Sunday with a couple of guys from work. We'll probably order a pizza."

"Seems like the only thing we ever had in common is food."

Hoag paused. "You really think so? Seven years married, and all those years back home when we were kids, and food's all we have?"

"I don't know," Lindi answered. "You don't like music, and I don't like sports. You don't like to talk, and I don't like computers."

"You know, that's strange for a math teacher. Eventually you're going to have to learn computers. All the schools will be going . . ."

"I know."

Silence.

"I'll be going out of town next week again, to Toronto, then two weeks later to Buffalo for a few days. Jeez, you'd think they send me to Florida every now and then, at least at this time of year," Hoag said.

"Or let you stay home now and then."

The meal came, and they ate without speaking. As customers arrived or departed, the wind and rain blew them in the doorway or enveloped them and pulled them back into the storm.

"You want dessert?" Hoag offered. "Sorry I ate the muffin."

"No, thank you."

"You're the one who always has the dessert."

"Not today, thank you."

Silence again.

"You ever see that girl?" Lindi asked.

"What girl? Oh, that one. No. Well, around work now and then, but not often, not even to say hello. You still seeing Jim?"

Lindi glared. "We should probably finish and get back to work."

"I thought you were off for the afternoon."

"There's always work to do. Maybe I'll go back in. No, I've been reading this book on the psychology of relationships. I was thinking maybe . . ."

Hoag was looking at the door as a tall couple entered, shaking the rain from their long, grey coats. "See that guy, the one who just came in? I think he used to play professional football, maybe ten years ago. He still looks like he could take out a fullback without trying very hard."

"Forget it."

"Forget what?"

"The book."

"What book?"

"Forget it."

They drained their coffee cups and got up to leave. Hoag reached for the bill.

"No," Lindi said.

"It's all right, really. You got coffee earlier, and the bus fare."

"That only cost a couple of dollars."

"Please. I'd like to. It's my turn, and—it may be the last time."

Lindi paused, nodded, noticed the scuff marks on the toes of her shoes now that they were drying. She left the tip while Hoag paid the bill at the front counter, moved slowly to the door, stepped back as another couple blew in, bringing the rain with them. Hoag touched her elbow.

"Should I call a cab to take you back to the parking lot?"

"No."

"You can't walk in this rain," Hoag said.

"I'll take the bus. Or we could share a cab."

"I would, but you're going west, I'm going east."

"Well, I'll just get the bus."

"Sure?"

"Yeah."

"All right."

As they opened the door, the wind rushed in again with a hiss like a deep breath. Lindi's bus appeared immediately from among the steaming cars.

"That's my bus, and if I run I can catch it. The light's red. Thanks for lunch, Hoagy. Bye." She ran into the street, waving at the bus driver, who thrust the doors open for her.

"Lindi!"

She turned, one foot on the bus, one drenched in water from the street.

"Take care. Still friends?"

Lindi waved and bent her head a little to one side, but she said nothing and disappeared into her West-Side bus. Traffic started to move with the light change, and the bus whisked into the stream and faded down the street, kicking out water like a fountain.

Hoag stepped back under the awning and turned from the sprays of water shot up by the passing traffic. He saw himself in the window of the restaurant, right under the name, Trifles. He noticed that his face looked thin, and his hair looked silly, twisted up into a curl on top by the wind. He wondered if it had looked that way since he'd got off the train. At least no one had laughed at him.

Hoag turned again to the street. He was several blocks from a train station, and the rain wasn't letting up. Surely the city would have a flood on its hands if the rain didn't let up. He pulled his collar tight. A bus might not come for ten minutes, and he'd be lucky to flag down a cab in such bad weather. He pulled on his gloves, took a deep breath, and hustled up the street.

Only when he finally stepped into the train, soaked and freezing, did he realize that he'd lost his muffler. Must have been at the bistro, he thought. The doors of the train slammed tight. Hoag watched raindrops bouncing crazily in the streets till the fogging windows blurred them from view. He shivered, missing his scarf, and as he sat, he noticed the raindrops turning once again into large, heavy snowflakes.

His thoughts went back to a park in Harmon Falls, under the summer lights, when he and Lindi had, hesitantly, almost feverishly, let their hands touch for the first time. He tried to take a deep breath, and it caught in his throat. I wonder what I'll find in those new games, he thought, trying to fill his head when his heart felt empty. The train rattled and blew along the track to the east side of town.

He remembered an older relative, an aunt, telling him once, "It's harder to lose a best friend than to lose a lover." What if it's both at once? Hoag wondered.

About the saddest story you can tell is when the love between people dies, romance or friendship or both. Maybe sadder yet is when it doesn't die, but they just let it drift away.

Breakfast with Andrea

"Friendship consists in forgetting what one gives and remembering what one receives."
—Alexandre Dumas

"I hope I didn't keep you waiting too long? Good. Oh, call me Andrea, dear. You've been out of school for how long? No need for the old formalities."

"That will take me some getting used to, Professor—Andrea. But ten years," Lana said, "that's why I'm back, to write a story for my local newspaper on attending a ten-year college reunion." She'd brought a fresh pen and a small, new, empty notebook to take notes, but she set them down, hoping for some time just to talk first.

"Yes, that's right" Andrea said. "My, how the time flies. It's always the tenth year for someone, or the twentieth or even the thirtieth. Not many classes come back for Homecoming or reunions or anything after that. Fewer each year: everyone has children, grandchildren, job commitments, too much travel already. Some come by in the summer if they're driving through. Not many of the students stay around here: the town doesn't have much without the College. But I'm so flattered that you'd think of me and call and want to visit. What can I tell you about? Things don't change much here."

"Well, for one thing, tell me what you're working on now. You always had such interesting projects beyond teaching the courses we all took. Everybody talked about the classes we took with Dr. Andrea Valens. Are you working on a new book project?"

"I just finished one last spring, and I'm giving myself a little break before moving on to something new. I've made some notes over the summer, but I'm still in the reading and conceptualizing stage for something new. I'm not sure how many more books I have in me."

"What can I get you for breakfast, ladies?" The server had sauntered up, waited a moment for a break in the conversation, and, suspecting none was forthcoming, interrupted gently.

"Oh, my regular, please, dear," Dr. Valens said. "You know just how I like it."

"Yes, ma'am. And you, ma'am?"

The server turned politely to Lana, who wasn't at all accustomed to having someone call her "ma'am." She looked over at her favorite professor, who read the look on her face, smiled, and nodded with understanding. Lana realized that when she'd graduated from Maldon College, their server would probably have been about nine years old.

"Oh, I hadn't even thought about it. We used to come here, the students anyway, for french toast or pancakes or waffles or muffins. They were always loaded with fresh fruit in those days."

She looked over at the professor, who mouthed "omelet."

"Oh, okay," Lana said. "I'll try an omelet, two egg"—she ran her eye down the menu—the Veggie and Herb." The professor nodded again, her eyes wide.

"Yes, ma'am," the server said. "That's my personal favorite. Fresh herbs came in just this morning."

When the server had gone back to the kitchen, the professor leaned toward Lana. "The mixes and baked goods aren't quite what they used to be. The cook uses mostly canned or frozen fruit rather than fresh—I hope that's not the new owner's idea of how to save money. Funny: I come here now mostly with alumnae or when we have job candidates in to interview—which isn't often these days, given all the cutbacks. The alums all remember the Café and Cream. Some of the interviewees will turn up their noses or give it tsk tsk. I think the place is still charming in its way. So did you marry that boy from—Harmon Falls, was it?—the baseball player? I see a ring on your finger." She smiled slyly, not entirely approvingly.

"Yes, I did."

"Any children?"

"Yes, we have a little daughter. She's great."

"I'm sure of it. Sometimes I think of a young woman from your class—she had such an unusual name, Alouette. You knew her, right? She had so much academic promise, but she got pregnant in her sophomore year. She took two years off, tried to come back, then four more years and tried again, but she never finished. I've always wondered what happened to her. What's your daughter's name?"

"We named her after . . ."

"Hello, Professor! It's so good to see you!"

Two other women, both older than Lana, had sidled up to the table. They ignored Lana, having eyes only for the woman who was doubtless their favorite professor, too.

"Oh, ladies, how good of you to stop to say hi. Are you here for the class reunion?"

"Yes!" one of them said. "Hard to believe twenty years have gone by already."

"Well, you both look just the same as when you were in school. Of course I remember you! And it's easy, because you haven't aged a day."

They smiled, perhaps believing that they hadn't.

"I still remember the first time I read your book "The Sharpest Edge: Journalism in the Third World," one of them said. "To this day that book has affected me more than any other I've ever read. I took up social work because of your class."

"And I teach journalism at the local high school," the second woman said. "I tried writing, but never got very far. Published two novels: neither did very well, so I gave it up." The two friends and their professor chuckled.

"My dear, you shouldn't give up unless you don't enjoy the writing. You can never tell: the next book may be the one to break through!"

"You're so inspiring. You always were," the first woman said. She put a hand out toward the professor's shoulder, but pulled back short of touching.

"So what's your latest? Somebody told me you have a new one out. I can't wait to get it!"

"Oh, I think the College bookstore has copies if you'd like, but academic books are so expensive lately, so don't feel obligated."

"What's it about?" the second woman asked.

"When We Tried to Tell the Truth," Lana said: the title of the book.

"You haven't read it already, dear, have you? That's marvelous that you even know about it," the professor glowed at Lana.

"It's about the diminishing of the Fairness Doctrine and the Hatch Act during the Reagan years," Lana said. The other two women had been ignoring her and continued to do so. "I picked up a copy at the bookstore yesterday. Just had time to thumb through a little before bed last night. Pretty powerful stuff."

"Well, we have to go now, Professor. Sorry to hurry off, but once we'd seen you, we couldn't leave without saying hello. Take good care of yourself. We both miss you! Bye-bye!"

The professor waved, wished the two women well, and turned to smile at Lana.

"This sort of thing must happen to you pretty often," Lana said. "Seemed like nearly everyone waved to you when you came in."

"Oh, not so often, but it happens more here than anywhere else because the place has been here for so long and has always been a College hang-out. You know, that is so very kind of you to have bought the book. But we were talking about something else. Let me think—oh, your daughter: do tell me about her."

"Oh, yeah: we named her after . . ."

"Oh, no, look who's coming over."

"Someone you know?"

"Yes: brand new Department Chair. Ugh. Not a bad fellow all in all, but overeager. Loves meetings." She mouthed the last word, the man having gotten close enough to hear.

"Hi, Andi. Sorry to interrupt." He turned his head part way toward Lana without actually looking at her, offering only a small nod. "Look, we lost our new hire just before the contract-signing. Yes, I know he said he was in, but he called me yesterday evening to tell me he took a job at an R1: an offer he couldn't refuse, just like The Godfather. So we're going to need to meet first of the week to figure out what to do with classes and how to beg to restart the search. I'll bet we've lost all the other decent candidates by now. Starting from scratch again won't be easy, but I think we'll have to."

The professor listened patiently, then sighed. "Right. I can't meet on Monday: I have an interview, and I need to prepare for this one. Tuesday all right? Maybe a lunch meeting so everybody at least gets something out of it. I'll call the old timers—maybe they'll take it better from me—if you call the junior faculty. May be hard to find some of them: either off to vacation or on research trips. But we can try, and you're right: the sooner we get going, the better chance we have to find someone. Oh: call Liz first thing Monday morning to see if she has anything left from the pile of apps. She normally keeps a batch top to bottom for a couple of months at least—though we may be too late."

"Thanks, Andi: you're the best. Miss . . ." Again the man almost looked at Lana before he turned and serpentined his way over to his table, where a younger woman waited for him looking annoyed.

"Andi?" Lana asked. "Your colleagues call you Andi?"

"Oh, the younger ones do. Back in the day we all called one another "Professor Smith" and "Professor Jones": all very formal. I think people full of self-doubt just liked to hear themselves called Professor to get an ego boost, and they were even willing to call others by title just to hear it applied to them, too. Do you remember old Professor Humboldt? He was from Europe, Switzerland—born in Austria—he wouldn't call anyone who didn't have full rank and at least thirty years of experience Professor. He said in Europe it's a special title of distinction, so we shouldn't use it blithely. He called everyone Doctor—at least everyone who had a PhD—instead. But he reserved Professor for the few. Most everyone's loosened up a bit since those days. The old folks call me Andrea. Only the younger ones say Andi." She shivered a little. "Even my parents and my sisters never called me that. I should say something, I suppose, but we're often pretty stuffy already, so maybe I should just let it go." She laughed—it sounded to Lana a little forced.

"Is that what being a professor—I mean the everyday stuff, like classes and meeting students and department meetings and coffee in the Faculty Lounge and all that stuff—is really like? I thought you could spend your time as you like, talking about books and ideas."

"Funny you'd ask that. It's the idea I'm mulling for my next book. In my mind I'm calling it "The Real Professor": sort of an exposé of what the day-to-day life is really like. I don't know if anyone would read it, but I can tell you it's much different than other people—students especially—imagine. But the last book is more interesting, I think." She outlined some of the chapter ideas from the book Lana had bought, describing the research she'd needed to do to write it.

The server delivered their food, smiled, accepted their thanks with a nod, and hurried off to take another order. Lana felt overwhelmed by the smell of the omelet, full of delightful herby, savory, creamy eggs, and she dug in without a word or a verbal thought, concentrating on the sensations.

"You eat with admirable gusto, my dear."

"Mmm hmm," Lana mumbled, feeling no obligation to change her focus right away.

The professor decided not to interrupt, instead looked around at the other diners, now and then waving at someone, as she took her time with a plate of Garden Benedict with Seasonal Fruit—fresh fruit, not canned.

When Lana looked up from her food, she noticed Andrea people-watching, so she looked around a little herself. In a back-of-room corner table she saw two girls of about undergraduate age. They were holding hands across their table, leaning forward, looking into each other's eyes and appearing to have a *tête-a-tête*. One stood up just a little and kissed the other on the cheek. The second girl blushed, and they both smiled. Lana remembered how at a high-school graduation party Cardolyn Cadogan had come up behind her and given her a hug. Cardolyn had drawn her head around and kissed Lana on the check and whispered in her ear, lingering for a couple extra seconds. "I really love you, you know," Cardolyn had said. "I always have." Cardolyn gave her another squeeze and then moved away. They had been friends—not the closest of friends, but friends—since not long after a group of children, Lana's friends, had saved their beloved park from some businessmen led by Cardolyn's father who wanted to turn the land into a used-car lot. After the cheek-kissing incident the two had remained friends, though Lana, confused about what it meant, had allowed the friendship to cool from what it had been in their younger years. Was that the right thing to do? Was it unfair of her? She shook off the memory and returned to her breakfast.

When Lana had nearly finished, she said, "So tell me about the ideas for the next book, for "The Real Professor." Could you write that so you won't get in trouble?" She took a long draught of cold iced tea.

"Probably, if I take a little care to keep it under control. I wonder, though, if I could sell it, either to a publisher or to readers."

"Come on: you must have no trouble finding publishers by now."

"Mmm, you'd be surprised. If you keep doing the same sort of thing, and it keeps selling, you can keep an old publisher or find a new one. But if you move into something different, they can get uneasy. They want to sell books. I don't think even academic novels sell all that well outside of Academe. If somebody from a big university wrote a true tell-all, that might draw some readers, but also some lawsuits. Schools don't like their reputations sullied or even questioned."

"You have tenure, right?"

"Of course, but what most people don't know is that your school can revoke it for conduct they consider inappropriate or damaging to the institution or profession. And of course my experience comes mostly from right here, little Maldon College, where not much happens. The occasional steamy affair, some intradepartmental squabbling, a bad tenure or promotion decision, the teacher students like but who drinks too much gets caught dancing naked in the Quad fountain—yes, that really happened once, and yes, they dismissed him to great uproar, especially from the fraternities and sororities, who mostly considered it standard behavior. But I'm thinking not so much about the spicey episodes as about what teaching and research and living the life are like for most of us."

"I'm listening."

The Professor spoke for another ten minutes about some possible directions for chapters and episodes.

"Most of us thought it must be pretty cool, that the faculty always hang out together talking about amazing things that we couldn't understand," Lana said.

"Excuse me, Professor Valens," the server came to collect the plates and offer drink refills. "You have a call on the restaurant phone. Do you want to take it, or should I have them call you at work or at home? I think it's someone from the newspaper downtown. You know, the big City paper."

"Imagine someone thinking to call me here. I must have become too predictable. I guess if they think it's important enough to call me at breakfast, I should give them the leeway and answer them. Excuse me for a moment, dear."

The professor went over to the front desk, where the proprietor, who didn't look particularly happy about taking a customer's call, handed her the phone. Lana thought the woman said "Don't stay on too long. We get calls for reservations." The professor stayed on long enough that the proprietor had time to do some work and come back to stare at her guest, which she did without saying anything more. Finally Andrea handed the phone back to her with what looked like an effusive apology, but the proprietor just nodded and waved her off as if to say "no problem" when that wasn't exactly what the expression on her face was saying. The two women talked for a moment longer as some other patrons collected at the cash register to pay their bills.

On her way back to the table Andrea stopped twice to respond to diners who greeted her.

Lana was beginning to wish she'd brough along something to read.

The server brought Lana an iced-tea refill, and she listened absent-mindedly to two College girls telling their mother about how bad the professors were in the courses where they'd gotten Bs.

When Andrea got back to their table, she didn't return to her seat.

"I'm so sorry, dear, but that was the interviewer from the newspaper. She's needing to cancel for tomorrow and wants to do the interview today. Only time she has for the next week, she said, and, as we know, journalists don't always get Sundays off."

"Right."

"I need a little prep time for her questions, so I'll have to hurry to the office. I'm so sorry to run off after you took so much trouble to visit. Would have loved to hear your thoughts on the book—maybe next time you visit! Don't worry about the breakfast bill. I covered the tip, too, and they'll bring you as many free refills of tea as you'd like. It's still a cute place, isn't it, just to sit and think and people-watch? Well, have a good day and a safe trip home."

The professor gave Lana a little wave and a quick smile and would have hurried out the door except for two groups waiting for a table who stopped her to say hello.

"Thanks for breakfast!" Lana called out as the professor retreated.

Lana sipped her tea and picked up the menu to read it again for something to do. The thought struck her that she should check to make sure the professor had covered the bill and then leave so she could free up a table for those waiting in the lobby. But a voice interrupted her half-shaped thoughts.

"So you got "Andread," did you? Happens to lots of us. Lana, right? Andrea's here, she's there, she's off, and we wonder what happened."

The voice came from a woman of middle age with a friendly grin, on the short side, with smooth, wrinkle-free skin and hair greying around the edges but brushed back long and neatly from her face. She wore shorts and a comfortable-looking black top that looked to have paint stains near the right wrist and elbow.

"You don't remember me, do you?"

Lana didn't, but that made her feel bad, so she kept looking, and finally her memory cleared.

"Josephine—I mean Professor Holiday, right? You look almost the same."

"Ha, you called me 'Josephine' back then, so no need for the 'Professor' stuff now. Most of us in art use first names even with undergraduate students. Pretty standard for art folks to be casual."

"I was just about to leave, or I'd ask you to sit down. Lots of people waiting for tables—the old place is still popular, and that's nice to see," Lana said.

"Sure. Thoughtful of you. But I have a table. You can bring your tea and sit with me, if you'd like. I was just having breakfast with a colleague, but he had to leave early, so I'd be glad for some company."

"Well, sure—thank you!"

Josephine pointed to a table, and they both sat down. "Been about ten years, right?"

"Yes, ten since I graduated. Do you remember everyone from all your classes? I only took one course from you. And I was a terrible artist."

"Ha, no, not everyone, and I don't remember that you were terrible. I recall that you had talent—that's why I remember you—but you were focused on other things at the time. You were in English, right?—no, journalism and something else."

"Yes, journalism and psychology. Practical, right?"

They both laughed.

"Who ever knows what will turn out to be practical?" Josephine said.

"I actually worked pretty hard in your class, though. Got an AB."

"Oh, no, you're not a Grade Grudger, are you, still angry about not getting an A?"

"Of course not. Well, not much. Not anymore, anyway."

"What I remember is that you turned in a great course journal and a bunch of thoughtful paintings, but you didn't do all the assignments, or you didn't do much on some of them. Am I mistaken?"

"That's right. I really wanted to take a painting course, but they told me I had to do the pre-req first. So I spent time on the fun assignments and hurried through the others. Sorry."

"Hey, I did the same thing when I took that course twenty-five years ago. I got a B if I remember right. The guy who taught it was a sculptor, more of a materials guy. He would have given me a C if he could have, but even he had to admit I learned all the principles and my paintings were pretty cool. But let's not talk about grades: grades are stupid. How about you tell me what you've been up to while I finish my omelet."

"You got the Veggie and Herb—that's what I had. It's really good."

"Mmm hmm."

So Lana gave Josephine the story of her last ten years, pausing occasionally for questions about specifics. "It's not an important life, but it's mine, and I like it pretty well," Lana concluded.

"Of course it's important, because it's yours and because you like it and you've lived it mindfully and with your heart. You don't have to be a Senator or a CEO or a famous author/professor or a brilliant starving artist to live an important life."

"You're not a starving artist, are you?"

"Me? Ha, no. We're the lowest paid of all faculty—everybody knows that—but I sell a painting now and then, so all in all I'm doing all right."

"I remember some really cool paintings you showed in the College gallery: you had several of them, some of fantastic draperies painted on wood and others with images of wooden objects painted on draperies!"

"Oh, yeah, one of the English faculty said they reminded him of Georgia O'Keeffe."

"They weren't anything like Georgia O'Keeffe. Even I knew that."

"For a lot of men, she's the only female artist they know, so every woman painter reminds them of her. It's funny who gets famous and who doesn't. Everybody knows Leonardo, and maybe some people would recognize Piero della Francesca, but hardly anyone, at least in the US would know, say, Luca Signorelli, and they should: he changed everything. Anyway, those were fun paintings to make, kind of silly and frivolous at times but with layers for anyone interested in looking more deeply."

"I thought the painting, the actual painting, was awesome."

"Thanks for remembering them. You should have told me then. I didn't get much commentary on those paintings and always wondered if anybody liked them."

"I didn't think I knew enough to comment on them to a real painter. I'd have felt silly. But I sure liked them. Do you still make those?"

"No, that was several series ago. Very different sort of stuff now. I don't want to make just the same old Josephines, though I'd probably sell more if I did."

"Would you mind telling me about them, the paintings you're doing now?"

"You sure you want to hear about that?"

"Absolutely sure. Mind if I take some notes?" Lana got her book and pen.

"Well, I guess not. What do you want to know?"

"Whatever you think is important to know. Whatever you'd like to tell."

"About what?"

"About your work, what you do, how and why you do it, and about you."

"Me? Ha ha ha ha! I'm no Andrea Valens, you know. Nobody famous, just a hard-working artist and art professor. Not that I grudge Andrea her success: she works really hard, you know?"

"You think of yourself as an artist first or a professor first?"

"Now that's an interesting question. Let me think about that for a minute."

"Any interesting travels?"

"I've been to Europe. Studied in France for a semester in undergrad. Went to Peru once. I was born in Canada. Back to the first question: artist first, teacher second. Does that trouble you, since you were a student here?"

"Not at all. But why do you say so?"

"To teach you have to know something, and to know you have to practice. Beware of the self-proclaimed guru types: first comes goo; then comes rue."

Lana laughed out loud. "Okay, I think I understand. How do you think about art work, about what to paint and how to paint it?"

"Hmm . . . You read, you take some notes, you try things, you study other artists, you make mistakes and then improvements, you take long walks in the woods and hope to God for inspiration." Josephine explained, with Lana's questions interspersed. Finally she said, "Hey, you talk like someone who knows something about painting. Have you kept up with your work at all?"

"Oh, that? Only a little. My husband says he likes them, but my little girl just laughs at them."

"Aw, you have a little girl. Tell me about her."

She did, but then feared she was talking too much about herself and her family, so she changed the topic.

"How do you look at the value of education, especially an art degree in times like these when everybody's talking about practicality and making a living?"

"You may have heard this before, but College serves two purposes: it helps you figure out how to live a happy life and how to live a good life, whatever you determine them both to be. If you've done that, you got your education. With an education, you learn how to live a life and then make a living."

"I do remember hearing that. Professor Valens, Andrea, told us that in class. Did she tell you that, too? Did you take a class from her when you were in school?"

Josephine smiled. "I told you that in class."

"You did? But I remember it from . . . Let me think for a minute. Yes! That's right! You told us that. I remember now. Wow. I remember that she told us something about grades, too, like what you said earlier. Something like, "Think about the work, not the grade, and the grade will take care of itself.""

Josephine smiled.

"That was you, too?"

"On the first day of every class, when I hand out the syllabus, I always say that. It comes from Thomas Merton, sort of: 'Do not depend on the hope of results . . .'"

"'But on the truth of the work itself.' You gave us that."

"I just relayed it from Merton."

"I'm remembering so much now that I'd forgotten. You also said something about how we shouldn't get so caught up in all the self-actualization stuff that was so popular then. Better to let go of the self . . ."

"And be alive in the moment. Yup. The more you focus on yourself, the less you see of everybody else and everything else. If you think only about you, then everything becomes about you, even when it really isn't."

"The joy comes in doing the work and sharing it with others . . ."

"Not in obsessing over how wonderful you are for doing it."

"Wow. I can't believe I really got all that from you!"

"Ha! Why not?"

"Sorry: I didn't mean it that way. I mean: why did I think it came from Andrea when it came from you?"

"It didn't really come from me. It's all common sense, and lots of teachers—the ones not obsessed with themselves—will tell you the same things. You can feel it to be true if you pay attention. Enjoy the process, and you enjoy life; if you think about yourself all the time, you never live. You associate what we talked about with Andrea because she was your major professor, your image of what a professor should be. You took one course from me, a general education course, which I hope was more fun than drudge, while you were thinking about all the wonderful things she was teaching you that you've used all these years. You know, here's another thing: it doesn't matter who taught you those things or, more accurately, from whom you learned them. What matters is that you learned them, that they've stayed with you and, I hope, helped you when you needed them."

"Wow. Wow. I need to take a few more quick notes. Do you mind?"

"Not at all."

A few minutes later Lana said, "I think I've had a little too much iced tea. I feel kind of shaky."

"Oh," Josephine said, "gotcha. I really bent your ear today considering that you didn't come to talk with me. Time for me to get going anyway."

"Can you wait just a minute for me, please?"

"Sure."

Lana got to the restroom and splashed her face repeatedly with cold water. When she came out, Josephine was waiting in the lobby to say goodbye. She had a backpack slung over one shoulder.

"I feel embarrassed," Lana said.

"Why?"

"All this time I've owed you so much, and I didn't even know it."

"You don't owe me anything, and you never did. You owe to yourself and your family and friends that you've become a fine woman. I so enjoyed talking with you. If you come back for another reunion, look me up if you feel like it. Or bring some paintings to show me."

"Can I maybe see your studio sometime?"

"Well, sure—why not? Take good care, okay?"

"You, too. Josephine, do you mind if I write up my notes and use them for an article for my local newspaper?"

"Why would you want to?"

"All of a sudden they mean an awful lot to me."

"Well, sure, help yourself, but maybe change my name so the FBI doesn't come after me. Wouldn't want to be arrested for subverting students' memories of their professors."

"What I didn't know is that it was you I should have interviewed all along. Thank you! Bye."

Lana watched, her feelings jumbled, but her thoughts clearing as Josephine walked over to a lamppost beside the parking lot and unlocked a bicycle that was leaning there. She took a helmet from her backpack and strapped it on, got on the bike and pedaled west down the road.

Lana thought of a title for her newspaper article: "The College Professor You Didn't Remember, But Should." "I wonder if she could have been a friend?" She said it out loud without realizing she'd spoken.

Friends with Chocolate

"There is nothing better than a friend, unless it is a friend with chocolate."
—Linda Grayson

"Daphne's Confectionesse": that's what she called her new shop.

As soon as it opened, everyone went there, since nothing new had come to Harmon Falls in years. In recent years the town had seen businesses, families, and investments of all sorts begin, grow, fail, and leave, but recently no one had shown the courage or good heart to open up something so roundly interesting, different—and delicious.

Years ago we used to have an ice cream shop, the lunch counter at Woolworth's, a family-owned dog-and-burger shop, and a pizza shop right in the middle of town. The south end of town had pizza, a Dairy Queen, a famous-named burger joint, and even a franchise of a family-style restaurant, a real sit-down place with distinct menu sections for breakfast, lunch, and dinner. The grocery store had a deli counter for a while, back in the sixties and seventies. Scattered through town you could find what we used to call "corner stores," little shops, normally at intersections, that sold bread, milk, vegetables, candy bars and baseball cards, and sundries. The north end of town had, for a time, a drive-in along the main road out of town. All that seems like a long time ago.

The downtown, if you want to call it that, had never grown very big, even when the town had reached its greatest population and level of prosperity, back when the mines and mills were working three shifts. But it stayed busy even if it was small. We had about three streets with three blocks each of stores and businesses and offices. But over the years nearly all of the original stores and even storefronts had gone. Some new businesses had replaced them temporarily until they had gone, too. At one time we had a movie theater and two furniture stores, a hardware store, a sporting-goods store, two clothing shops, three newsstands, a public library, and all the assorted bars, barber shops and hair salons, law offices, even a cobbler who made shoes to order, and such, men's and women's clubs, and you could find four banks in a span of four blocks. We had active churches on nearly every corner, almost any denomination you could ask for. Most of the old stores have now passed nearly beyond memory. There's a McDonald's where a gritty state highway cuts through town.

So you can understand the excitement when Daph-with-the-Laugh, a childhood friend, returned from The City after many years as a chef and restauranteur to open her little chocolate shop back in old Harmon Falls. She bought the building that had once been the ice-cream shop and remodeled it with contemporary tables, soft lights, a few shelves of gift-products, a coffee-and-tea bar, some fancy ice-cream flavors, and a large counter for service and filled with all sorts of samples of chocolates and chocolate-related confections.

Daph scheduled a Grand Opening on a Friday evening in early June.

She opened the doors early enough that parents could bring their children, and she stayed open long enough that lovers could bring their dates.

None of us could have expected such a thing. None of us could have dared to hope for it.

Just as Daph opened the door, Samula told me later, the bells of the Catholic church a block north had begun chiming joyfully—not for Daph's store, but for a wedding that had taken place that afternoon—not many of those in town anymore.

The best part of that evening was that people actually came for the opening, people from Harmon Falls and nearly all the other local towns, and even a reporter from the nearest newspaper.

Daph had opened her door at five, but Lana and I couldn't get there until nearly nine.

The place was still nearly packed. Heads and eyes had rolled back, tongues were licking lips, and sounds of scrumptiousness echoed in every corner of the dining room. We saw cups of hot chocolates and café mochas and spicy chai and cappuccinos, iced coffees and chocolate milkshakes and frappuccinos, dark chocolates and white chocolates and milk chocolates and turtles, nut clusters and mint mochas and butter creams and truffles, dipped fruits and shortbreads and florentines and milanos, fondues and nutellas and brownies and blondies, crispy clusters and brittles and s'mores and pirouettes with icing, a bundt cake and a pound cake and a three-layer chocolate cake—and four empty tins that had once held chocolate silk pies.

As we walked in, Flip the Cat was just about to take a bite from the last piece of a chocolate pie. He stopped with the fork poised before his lips as he recognized us.

"I can't do it," he said. "I've already had two pieces. You guys have got to taste this. Here sit down by—you remember my wife, Alma—and I'll pull up two more chairs. I'd tell you about it, but you won't believe me. Here are two forks: forgive me if I watch you while you eat, but this is just too good."

After hurried hugs from Alma we both took a bite of the Confectionesse special chocolate pie.

"Ooooooooh," Lana moaned.

I couldn't have said it better, but, then, I couldn't utter a sound: in seconds I had reached the height of chocolate ecstasy.

Before we realized it, Daph was standing behind us with a hand on Lana's shoulder and one on mine.

"Well," she said, "what do you think? Do you like it?"

"No," Lana said.

"No!"

"Like doesn't begin to get it," Lana said. It's amazing, it's joy on a fork, it's edible art, it's Oscar-winning food enlightenment, it's miraculous!"

Daph smiled. "Good to see you, too." Off she went to continue circulating among her customers.

"She's not even charging people," Flip said, nibbling on the edges of Alma's pie. She just put tip jars around the store and asked people to pay whatever they want to help the store get going.

"Unbelievable," Lana said, taking another bite. "I mean the tip-jar thing, too, but this pie: I can't believe you were willing to give it up. And the very last piece, too!"

"I value my friends more than my palate," Flip said with a wink.

Daph picked up a plate of dark-chocolate cordials from the bar and offered them around.

Before long all our old friends from childhood, from the days of saving the baseball park and getting through school and learning what friendship means and leaving to find work had gathered around, and I felt like I had fallen from a vat of perfect chocolate into another full of caramel nostalgia.

"This ice-cream bar is amazing," Shoemaker said, "dark chocolate with something like Rice Krispies sprinkles, but something else, toffee, maybe, between the chocolate and the ice cream."

"This is the best hot chocolate I've ever had," Jenver said. "It's so creamy, and it has something else, hazelnut, and just a hint of something else, like Bailey's Irish Cream. It's amazing."

"And these pretzels with bitter chocolate and sea salt," her husband Jeff said.

"And these tiny sandwiches with sweet pumpernickel bread and peanut butter and Nutella," Hoag said.

"Anybody else try this three-chocolate layer cake?" asked Les: he's Flip's older brother, and though he didn't hang out with us when we were kids, and he hardly ever ate sweets, he was getting very glad that he'd joined in for the opening of Daphne's store. "I've never, ever had anything this good. I'm going to have to lift weights for two extra hours tomorrow and run five miles to make up for eating all this."

"I feel like I'm in Italy," Jenver said, sipping a large cappuccino, "and don't tell me I'm not, 'cause I won't believe you. And don't try to feed me anything else, 'cause I won't need to eat for two more days. Too bad Lindi couldn't make it. She's such a coffee fan."

Later, when Daph had officially closed the shop and turned off most of the lights, the old gang sat together around a couple of tables under a single spotlight.

Greco hauled out the cooler that he'd hidden behind some large containers in the kitchen and pulled from it two bottles of Pol Roger Brut Réserve Champagne.

He had picked up a good deal of knowledge about wines in his travels, and everyone applauded. Flip exhumed champagne flutes from deep in what looked like a book bag, and everyone applauded again.

"I wasn't expecting that," Daph laughed, "but I have one more surprise, too: something I was saving in case something special happened."

She went back behind the counter and gently extracted one last box, which she opened with a flourish: dark chocolate, dark cherry truffles with just a drizzle of vanilla icing.

"Just the complement for champagne," she said, and everyone cheered, and no one waited to dig in.

"This is amazing," Joli said. "I mean, the truffle and the champagne together. It's like, it's just like . . ."

"I know what it's like," her husband said, smiling, and everyone laughed.

I know of few pleasanter sounds than laughter among very old friends when they're all laughing with one another, not at someone else.

"This really is a cool little place," Leon said. "But I don't know about this funky little town. So this is where you all grew up?"

"If we grew up at all," Shoemaker answered to a general murmur of agreement.

"You know," Greco said, as the munching and slurping and sipping and cooing had finally calmed down, "this is a great event—I mean a great event." Everyone nodded and mmm-hmmmed. "But we shouldn't stop here. Think of what Daph's shop can do for the old town. I mean, this place fell into depression, what, fifty years ago, maybe even before that? Think about that dying old baseball park we tried to save. And after a while, even the bikers stopped going to the Dutch Oven, and it finally closed—not that that's such a bad thing in itself. But the town's slid down and down and down since then, and who has done anything to pick it up? Here's what I'm saying"—he was slurring his words just a bit—"why should we stop here? Can't we think of other things to bring the place back to life? Maybe not to what it was when the Harmons were still here, but to the best of what it had when we grew up."

"Pizza shop's still here," Pizza said, and everyone laughed. "And it always will be, until somebody drops an atom bomb on it."

"The mills won't ever come back," Samula said, "or the old foundry: all that work went overseas years ago, decades ago. The politicians always say they'll bring back the old jobs, but they never will. The mines have closed. Some guys want them back, but nobody liked working in them when they were open, and people died in there. The place needs something else, something new. Maybe new factories that build something people don't build somewhere else. Then there'd be jobs for anybody. Maybe people would start to move back."

"I had a dream once," Lana said, "that developers had got an idea and rebuilt the whole valley as retro-Victorian towns. It was a great dream: a lot of the big old houses here are Victorian—they just need refurbishing. And someone brought back the old riverboats, and there were specialty restaurants in the different neighborhoods, and shops, and little theaters for plays, and somebody built a new cinema right where we had the old one so new movies could come in, and they had special showings of old movies from the thirties and forties of Dickens and Jane Austen stories. Somebody rebuilt the old marina, and boats would bring people in from other towns to eat and see shows. The old town became a new old-town, and it was great."

"Great dream," Greco said, "but I don't know how you'd get anyone to invest in it in real life. Places like Harmon Falls never went for the tourist crowd. Even the big cities have a hard time attracting enough capital for ventures like that."

"But it would be great, so much fun, something really different," Lenny said, patting his sister on the shoulder. "And sometime in the summer, not the same time as the Strawberry Festival, and not when it's too hot, we could have an antique car rally. People could come from all over to show their custom cars and see what others would bring."

"You'd need a hotel or two for that," Shoemaker said, "or a whole bunch of B&Bs."

"Too bad somebody can't bring back the glass industry," Connie said. "It helped put this place on the map a long time ago."

"Hard to bring back old industries," Flip said. "No artisans around anymore, and the market goes more for antiques than new stuff. Isn't that right, Greco?"

"Yeh, I think so. We need to think of something new."

"We still have the shells of all those old factory buildings. What about a factory to make really simple, everyday things that are easy to design and that everybody needs, things like spatulas and back scratchers and scrubbies and hairbrushes?" Connie asked, bringing some nods of agreement. "We'd pay the workers more than they do in poor countries, but we'd save on shipping."

"Or factories to design and make electronics," Samula said, "like a new Silicon Valley."

"Or we could grow specialty plants and vegetables," Connie added.

"Mar-i-ju-an-aaa," Pizza said.

"People still wouldn't go for that around here," Jenver said. "Remember how good the water used to be when we were kids and it all came from artesian wells? Not anymore, or we could have bottled that and sold it."

"No catfish around anymore," Lenny said, "or we could have a catfish-fishing tournament or festival or something."

"Or maybe a cat festival," Shoemaker suggested, "like the big dog shows on TV. I know they have those in the big cities, but maybe if we would do cats instead, or rabbits, we could start it small to see if people would come, and then we'd build it up. But then we'd need those hotels or B&Bs, wouldn't we?"

"We need something for the wintertime, too," Flip said. "Other than the stuff the churches do at Christmastime, it's pretty boring between Christmas season and spring compared to what bigger towns can do. Maybe a jazz festival in January, or, better yet, in February. I could get some bands to come down from The City."

"And a street art show in the fall, before the weather gets cold—but not on a football weekend!" Joli said. "They have those in The City pretty often, downtown and in the suburbs."

"If you think of companies like mine," Hoag said, "we're in The City, but we don't have to be. We design games, and you don't have to live in a big place to do that, just a nice one, where the designers might want to live. If we could clean up this place, it has plenty of natural beauty. Across the river, just beyond where the hills open up, they used to have an airport. If we had even a small airport, people from anywhere could get here more easily."

"Those are the sorts of ideas we need," Greco said, "a whole bunch of them until we think through what people might be willing and able to do. Investment money doesn't come easily or quickly, but sometimes, once you get some, you can get more."

"And think about how it all will have started with Daphne's sweetshop," Flip mused.

"Daphne's Confectionesse," Alma added. "Who could ask for a better start?"

"Who could ask for a better opening night?" Daph said.

Somebody knocked on the front window: it was a police officer, old Mr. Provezis's son, who followed his dad into the family profession. He waved, and Daph went to the door, spoke with him, and came right back.

"He was just checking to make sure everything's all right. I gave him a couple chocolates," she said.

"Will," Lana said, "you haven't said a word all evening."

"He's thinking about baseball," Flip said.

"He's thinking about chocolates," Jenver said.

"It's the champagne," Samula said: "his head's full of it, and now he can't think of anything at all."

"Oh, he's thinking, all right," Joli said. "He was always thinking, even when he wouldn't admit it. Maybe the champagne just addled those thoughts a little."

Lana put her arm around my shoulder and kissed me on the cheek. "What are you thinking about, Hon?"

I looked around at Daphne's splendid new chocolate shop and at people who had been my friends for forty years.

"I'm thinking about you, Lana, and about all of you, and about Daph's shop, and my head is so full of memories I can't figure out what to do with them all. I'm thinking about Harmon Falls and about all the little towns so much like it spread all over the place. I'm thinking about all the times in my life that I wanted to be anywhere but here. And right now I'm thinking that I don't want to be anywhere else but right here with my friends."

"I'll drink to that," Pizza said.

"Too bad," Daph replied, "we're out of champagne."

"Maybe somebody can open a wine shop so that never happens again," Greco said.

"Thanks for coming in tonight, everybody," Daph said. "I couldn't be happier than to see you all again and to have you here to support my shop. I don't know if we could bring our old town back to life or if anyone can. But this I can tell you truly: nothing I know is sweeter than having friends. Thank you all very much." She still had the old laugh. "And all those great ideas! Maybe tonight is the start of something big."

EDWARD S. LOUIS lives and works in Wisconsin
with his wife, Kristy, and his cat, Bingley.
His hobbies include jogging, daily practice of tai chi chuan,
and Mediterranean cooking.

By the same author:
The Monster Specialist (2014)
Odysseus on the Rhine (2005)
White Shoes (2017)
The Streets of Harmon Falls (2016)
Between Such Distant Shores (2020)
The Quantum Detectives (2021)

Co-authored, along with artist Kristy Deetz:
The Singular Adventures of Rabbit and Kitty Boy (2019)
Holidays Unfolding: The Continuing Adventures of Rabbit and Kitty Boy
(2021) Both available from Elm Grove Publishing

www.ingramcontent.com/pod-product-compliance
Ingram Content Group UK Ltd.
Pitfield, Milton Keynes, MK11 3LW, UK
UKHW040619250125
454058UK00011B/63/J